SUSAN FARRIS

High Horse

SWEET STORIES WITH SOUTHERN SASS

Contents

Also by Susan E. Farris

Fiction

The Gravedigger's Guild

Midnight Bluff Romance Series:
Nuts About You
Taken For Granted
Piece Of Cake
High Horse

Poetry

Heartwork: Poetry for Growth
Flooding the Delta: A Journey Through Things Found &
Forgotten

Dedication

For my dad, who was my first inspiration to write.

Companion Short Story

Want to see more of Vada and Son's story?

Read the free sequel short story "Camp Sleepaway" and see how this hardworking cowgirl and empathetic pastor build a life together!

Claim your free copy of "Camp Sleepaway" today by heading to https://susanfarris.me/free-reads/

Chapter 1

⚜

Vada swirled the slowly melting ice of what had been her gin and tonic as she leaned on the bar at Southern Comfort. Around her, the few happy hour regulars chatted over the clack of pool balls. Just a couple of years ago, she'd scoffed at the worn-down people who haunted this bar at odd hours. Didn't they have anything better to do than drink their lives away?

Now, she was one of them.

Lester nodded at her glass as he wiped down the already meticulous bar. "Need another?"

"Not tonight." She sipped at the ice water, savoring the last bite of gin as it swirled over her tongue. "Gotta pick the kiddo up and head home." She patted a bill down onto the polished mahogany.

With a nod, Lester walked over to the register to cash her out. A few minutes later, Vada sat in her truck in front of Al's with Mahalia next to her. It had taken longer than usual to coax Mahalia into leaving Carmel's house. Vada hated using

1

threats and commands to get her young cousin to do as she said. But sometimes, she was tired and just wanted to shake the teenager into less bratty behavior.

Vada paused as she turned the truck off to study her phone as a text from Willow glowed on the screen. A fire at the Nettles' meant a meal train needed to be put together, and Willow was asking her to head it up.

She squinted at the too-bright screen. She'd have ignored it if it had been anyone other than Willow. Well, she'd answer for Cress too. And Mayor Patty. Ok, so her number was probably #1 on the speed dials of half the folks in town.

The thought used to invigorate her, give her purpose. Now, all she felt was one more weight settling onto her shoulders. She closed her eyes and sighed. At least she was at the right place to get the ball rolling on the meal train. She glanced up at the brilliant front of Al's diner.

Looking down at herself, she grimaced. Mud from the stable splashed up her boots and jeans, and her faded plaid shirt was ringed with sweat. Pretty standard attire for Southern Comfort, but she hadn't exactly planned to do anything more than dash in and out at Al's. But—necessity and all.

"Be back in a sec," she said as she swung the door open. Her cousin, Mahalia, barely nodded at her, she was so absorbed in her phone. Probably texting Carmel. Teenagers. Vada rolled her eyes, left the A/C running, and jogged inside.

Their dinner order sat in the to-go window, ready for her. Vada grabbed the bags then turned, looking for Mira. She spotted her taking Pastor Riser's order in the back of the restaurant.

Great. Now she had to walk her smelly self all the way back there, where the hottest man in town could get an eyeful of her in all her slovenly glory. Rolling her shoulders back, she headed for Mira. In for a penny, in for a pound.

"Mira! Could I borrow you for a sec?" Her voice wavered between cheerful and insistent.

"Of course, honey!" Mira smiled, teeth practically glowing. Vada had to get the name of the brightening strips she used. "Hold on one sec, doll." She patted Pastor Riser's table as she turned to Vada.

Vada sucked in a breath as Pastor Riser looked her up and down, then picked up his coke with a smirk that on any other man, Vada would have described as "smoldering." He leaned forward onto his elbows, the sleeves of his crisp button-down rolled up past his muscular forearms, and blatantly listened as she explained the situation to Mira.

Heat flooding her chest, she tried to focus on Mira. Despite her attempt to ignore him, she caught Pastor Riser's eye just as she said to a nodding Mira, "Help me get the word out?"

Mira patted her arm, smiling knowingly as she glanced from her to Pastor Riser. "Sure thing, honey. You leave it to me." Vada wilted in relief. Having Mira onboard meant she didn't have to call people one by one. The older lady trotted off to another table, leaving Vada standing awkwardly next to Pastor Riser.

Who was still staring at her. With a tight smile, she turned to scoot away. But just as she swung around, Pastor Riser moved to set his drink down on the edge of the table… right in the way of her to-go bags.

Coke spewed everywhere, splattering not only the table, the booth, and the wall, but drenching Pastor Riser's clean, white shirt. With a gasp, Vada dove for the napkin dispenser.

"Oh, my God. I am so sorry!" She threw a wad of napkins

onto a puddle that was making a beeline across the table toward his lap. Two more handfuls stopped the worst of the sticky beverage from hitting the floor. Without thinking, she pressed another napkin to his sopping shirt, the material clinging to his muscular chest.

At a low chuckle, Vada froze, her hand on his pec. Tingles shot up her arm. Horrified, she looked into his crinkled eyes, closer than she'd ever seen them, as he took the napkins from her invading hands. She froze, mesmerized by the gold flecks in his dark irises.

"I think I can take it from here." His fingers brushed softly against hers as he plucked the disintegrating paper away from her. His lips worked up and down against an amused smile as she slowly eased away.

Coming out of her stupor, Vada looked around at the aftermath of her klutziness. "I am so sorry," she repeated. "Your shirt! It's…"

"It's nothing that a little laundry spray can't take out." He dabbed at it, even as the shirt was clearly a lost cause.

"Still. You're soaked and your evening…" Vada waved her hands, the bags rustling on her arm.

He flicked her words away. "My evenings haven't seen this much excitement since seminary." She tilted her head, confused. With a shrug, all he offered was, "Pranks."

Mira bustled over with a damp towel and began busily wiping down the table. "Here. I've got that, Mira." Vada took the towel from her. "You've got better things to do than clean up my messes." Mira shook her head with a smile and headed back to the kitchen.

As Vada wiped down the table and wall, Pastor Riser continued to dab at his shirt. "Sorry, again."

"As I said, there's no need. Things happen." He looked up at her. "That's why we all pitch in." He sniffed. "Speaking of which, I heard what you told Mira."

"I noticed," she replied drily. His eavesdropping had been hard to miss.

He grinned at her, unrepentant. "If you like, I would be happy to make an announcement about the meal train on Sunday."

"Really?" She blinked at him, surprised. Midnight Bluff Baptist released a prayer list once a week that was little more than everyone's current ailments; it was entirely new for the pastor to announce community needs from the pulpit.

But Paster Riser was already nodding at her. "What is the church for, if not helping our neighbors?"

"That would be amazing. Thank you." She fidgeted, shocked by his helpful attitude... even after she'd baptized him with soda.

"My pleasure."

She twisted the towel between her hands. "Ok. I'm going to go now before I create another catastrophe. Thank you again." As she slipped out the door, she cast one last glance over her shoulder. Pastor Riser waved at her, a broad smile on his stupidly handsome face.

Why did all the best men have to be out of her league? Because no matter how sexy she found him, she didn't have a snowball's chance in hell of a pastor dating someone like her.

Back in the truck, Vada plunked the bags in Mahalia's lap, her spirit already lifting at their fragrant smell. Her cousin squawked as she shoved her face through the fluttering white plastic.

"Do you have to smother me?" Mahalia batted the tops of

5

the bags down.

Vada handed her the USB cord with a grin. "Get us some tunes going!"

"Some tunes? What, are we in the seventies?"

With a snort, Vada shoved her shoulder. "You know what I mean. Put some music on!" She turned up the volume as Mahalia grinned and selected a fizzy pop song. Rolling down the windows, they laughed and bounced with the beat, the wind whipping around them.

A content smile worked its way onto Vada's face as she watched Mahalia wave her arms and clap her hands, head bobbing. It had been too long since she'd seen her young cousin this carefree, and it was doing her soul a world of good.

Being there for the ones she loved was all that mattered. No matter how much a certain, sexy pastor might steal into her thoughts.

* * *

As he watched Vada hustle out the door, Son Riser relaxed into his usual booth with a sigh and mopped at his sticky shirt. Slowly, his heartbeat returned to normal as he dabbed at the spot where her hands had been just seconds before.

Now that the commotion was over, everyone turned back to what they had been doing: talking and eating. Regulars buzzed from table to table, their humming voices a welcome relief from the stiflingly quiet parsonage Son had come here to escape.

He gazed around the homey interior, content to be surrounded by familiar faces. The sun was just beginning to set, casting long arms of amber light across the black-and-white tiles of the floor. Mira buzzed from table to table, refilling drinks and smiling her wide smile. A couple of tables away, Lou Ellen, his secretary, giggled and smiled with Missy Pipkin and Janie Kelly. Thomas and Floyd, Missy and Janie's husbands, stood talking with Bo McBride toward the front of the diner. And Son sat alone in the back.

Maybe he should have asked Vada to join him. The thought popped into his head like a cuckoo clock, and he frowned. Yes, Vada was an attractive woman, and she certainly filled out a pair of jeans well. But he only saw her in passing on Sunday mornings. He scrubbed harder at his shirt. No beautiful woman would be interested in a small-town pastor.

Just as he gave up on his shirt, the booth squeaked, and Bo dropped into the seat across from him. "Got yourself a little excitement this evening."

"You could say that again." Son dabbed at his shirt one more time then laid down the napkin. It was a lost cause. "Although I think Vada was more embarrassed by it than I was."

Bo nodded, a gleam in his eye. "She's a good girl. I didn't know y'all knew each other."

"We don't. Not really." He shook his head. "I think that's the most I've ever talked to her."

They paused as Mira came over, wiped down the table one more time, then turned to Son. "Your usual?"

Son nodded, and she bustled off to the kitchen to retrieve his meatloaf with potatoes and green beans. Bo leaned forward onto his elbows. "I've known Vada before she came outta the womb. Her sister too." He added with a smile. "Real nice young lady from a great family."

Bo was up to something. "What are you getting at?" Son

asked.

"Just… if you ever find that parsonage too big to be knocking around in by yourself, I'd be happy to say a word on your behalf."

"To Vada?" Son clarified.

With a pleased smile, Bo nodded. "Help you get things moving."

Son shook his head with a grin. "I'm good." As enticing as a date with Vada sounded, he didn't want anyone playing matchmaker on his behalf. "I don't really believe in dating parishioners."

"That's about all the options you have out here."

He couldn't argue with that. As he waffled in silence for what to say, Bo chuckled and stood to leave. "No worries, pastor. I'll leave you to your own devices." He tapped a knuckle against the tabletop. "But if you reconsider, let me know."

"Will do!" Son waved as the older man strode away. A flicker of uncertainty crackled in his chest. What Bo had said was true. There weren't a lot of dating options around Midnight Bluff. And he wasn't exactly going out of his way to find someone. Maybe he should take Bo up on his offer.

Then again, he'd been just fine on his own up to this point. He'd let God handle his love life.

Chapter 2

⚬⚬⚬

F og lay on the ground in a thin, curling mist. Vada opened the gate to the pasture, breathing in the cool morning air deeply as she waited, listening for the clopping of hooves on the lane behind her.

Any minute now, a galloping wall of horses would come over the hill and into the wide-open pasture, their home for the day. She inhaled again, closing her eyes as the scent of grass and mud tickled her nose and birdsong drifted from the trees. It was always so peaceful out here, just before the day truly broke.

A trickle of sound caught her ear, and she hopped up on the fence post, watching as a rush of horses came trotting down the lane in a rippling wave. Some threw their heads back in wide-eyed excitement, rushing forward to the green pasture with its sprinkling of cool shade trees. Others trotted along at a more sedate pace, as if meditating on the peaceful world around them. Each one filled Vada's heart with a beat of joy.

As the last horse entered the gate, she swung it shut behind them, securing it carefully. No escapees on her watch. Especially since only a handful of these were her horses. The rest were boarders.

She strolled back up the lane toward the barn and the corral beside it, a quick burst of energy firing through her at the task ahead. Today she was doing rope work with a colt who was rather dodgy, and the challenge thrilled her.

As she entered the corral, the colt eyed her, unsure of what was happening. She picked up the thin coil of rope and strolled up to him, staying in his field of view. He nickered but let her rub behind his ear and down his neck with her free hand. Slowly, she brought the coil of rope up and touched him on the flank. He shied away, and she repeated the process until she could touch him several times with the rope before he would shy away.

Her training style was slow and methodical. It had to be because of the hours she kept, but it worked. As she let the colt out into the pasture with the other horses, she leaned on the fence, admiring their shiny coats and powerful necks. A rare sense of contentment filled her.

A crunch sounded behind her as her dad walked up and wrapped an arm around her shoulder. "Stalls are clean."

"Thank you." She stared out over the pasture. Guilt twinged in her stomach, shattering her peaceful moment. He and Mom should be enjoying their retirement in the mountains. Not stuck here helping her keep her struggling equestrian school afloat. Some days, she thought it would be better for everyone if she just shut the place down.

"I saw you working with Jackie's colt. Looking real good." He leaned on the fence next to her.

"He's got a long way to go. And I need to get him saddle

broke by the end of the summer." She twisted a finger in her hair, thinking through the monumental list of things to do in that time. And all of it had to be accomplished in a couple of hours every morning and evening.

"You know, Mahalia might enjoy working with the horses." Vada eyed her dad as he spoke. They'd argued over this before. "She's always following you around."

Vada imagined Mahalia, bouncing with eagerness, around the jumpy colt or a skittish mare. The thought of a flying hoof made her cringe. "She's too young to be training horses."

Her dad sucked on his teeth. "You and Eve started working with horses when you were younger than her." He touched her shoulder. "And Mahalia is a fast learner."

Alarm flooded through Vada. Eve had always been the better horsewoman and teacher. How was she supposed to run this place, and keep her cousin safe, without her sister's level head? Willing an escape from the conversation, Vada looked at her watch, relieved to see how late in the morning it already was.

"My shift is about to start." She straightened. "I just don't think Mahalia is ready."

"We'll talk about it more when you get home tonight," her dad tossed out as she turned. Vada could hear his sigh as she walked away. But she knew she was right; Mahalia wasn't Eve. And Vada couldn't bear to put her in any sort of danger.

* * *

Son squinted at the cramped writing scrawled across the yellowed pages. Tentatively, he tapped the name into the spreadsheet on his computer. He peered closer at the name on the page. Was that a "J" or a lopsided "S?" With a snort, he typed a question mark next to the name.

The next entry listed Sacia and Waymond Wilson, Vada's parents. He stared at the name, remembering her anxious face last night as she tried to dry him off. How his breath had caught at her touch. He shook his head, banishing the image.

Updating the member logs from the church merger was proving far more tedious and difficult than he'd expected. No wonder he kept flitting off into daydreams.

As he set the old ledger down and rubbed at his eyes, he wondered if half of these people were still in the state or even alive. If they were, they certainly weren't coming to church. And now Son had a very long list of questions for Lou Ellen which would inevitably end with him spending hours being assaulted with the genealogy and blood feuds of half the county.

A knock at the door drew his attention. The youth pastor stood, silhouetted by a flickering halogen bulb in the hall, shifting nervously from foot to foot and with a binder in his hand. "Can I talk to you for a second?" Son didn't particularly care for the youth pastor. He was too tall, gangly, and quiet for his liking. But his teaching was proficient, and the kids seemed to like him, so Son let things be. And right now, he welcomed any break from... he glanced at the ledgers and shuddered.

"Of course. Have a seat." He waved at the leather chairs arranged in front of his desk. The young man sat, the leather squeaking beneath him. He shifted, the chair squeaking as he wriggled around.

Son waited for him to settle, hands clasped in front of him.

Finally, red-faced, the younger man sat up on the edge of the chair and pulled a sheet of paper from the binder. He handed

12

it to Son.

"What's this?" Son scanned the sheet, his brain stuttering to a halt even as his eyes took in the words.

"I've been offered an assistant pastor position in Ruleville, and I've accepted. This is my resignation." He tried to slide back in the chair with a strident squeak.

"I can see that, but… why an assistant pastor?" Son looked at him, confused.

The young man reddened further. "I… have my Doctor of Divinity. I frequently guest preach. And I've got the experience." What started as a stutter turned into indignation.

He had the experience from Midnight Bluff Baptist Church, the place he was about to abandon. Son kept his mouth shut as he inhaled, letting the stab of anger flow away. The young man was a pastor in his own standing; he had every right to pursue other positions.

"I'm sorry." He cleared his throat. "I misspoke. This is a big step and congratulations are in order. You've done well." He set the paper down and laced his fingers, trying to school his bucking emotions. "I'm just surprised. When you took this job, you indicated you wanted to make serving youth your focus."

"At the time, that was true." The youth pastor nodded as he leaned forward. "But I always meant to grow and…" His eyes slid away.

Son sighed silently. "You can be frank with me."

"Forgive me. But I haven't received the mentorship with you as I was with Pastor Daniel. I feel that it's time for me to move on."

Son swallowed at the mention of his predecessor. Pastor Daniel had been beloved by everyone, and he'd often felt that he'd not adequately filled the hole he left. "I wish I had known," he murmured. The younger pastor had been so quiet around him, so withdrawn, that he'd assumed his advice wasn't wanted. Maybe because he hadn't offered a sign of friendship, the younger man hadn't felt comfortable approaching him.

He rubbed a hand over his mouth. What was done was done. Now, all he could do was ensure that his own reaction to the situation was grace-filled.

"Well, this certainly is a big bit of news." He stood and offered his hand, forcing a smile. "Congratulations. I'm sure you'll do well in Ruleville."

With a grin back at him, the youth pastor shook his hand. He held up the binder. "Here are the lesson plans that I've completed for summer camp, should you need them."

Son thanked him and the younger man left, power walking out of his office as if the squeaky chair would chase him. Slumping down, Son covered his eyes.

He hadn't even thought about summer camp. How in the world was he supposed to find a new youth pastor in time for that?

Flipping through the binder, he gaped at the sparse notes. A handful of verses and a few bullet points marked each page. The activities section stared up at him, a big blank space. Nothing had been done. This was the church's big summer outreach. Families from the surrounding counties even enrolled their teens in the camp; it was one of the prime ways they grew membership. It couldn't fail.

With a groan, Son punched a number on his office phone. "Lou Ellen, can you bring me any materials we have from the last couple of years of youth camps?"

Her reply echoed over the line, oddly garbled. As he hung up, he fought the constricting panic in his chest, forcing himself to breathe. Summer was still a month away. He had time to find someone, right?

* * *

A tap on Vada's shoulder made her jerk awake. Crap. She'd dozed off at the front desk.

She clutched her thermos of coffee to her chest and gazed up apologetically at Lewis, her boss at the Midnight Bluff Co-Op. Getting up at four a.m. every morning was really wearing on her.

"I know no customers are in right now," he crossed his arms as he looked at her, "But there has to be a better use of your time, young lady." Lewis was the only one who could get away with calling her "young lady" anymore and he used the phrase freely.

She scrunched her forehead, faking consideration. "Nope. Everything's all good." Even as she said the words, she stood from her stool and stretched. She knew as well as Lewis that there was always something to be done around the Co-Op, from stocking the shelves to cleaning the unfortunate employee bathroom.

He handed her a broom. "The garden section is looking a little rough."

She took the broom and yawned as she trudged toward the door. By now, she had hoped to hire someone to help at the equestrian school. Or to at least go full-time herself in her own business. Instead, as much as she loved Lewis, she was stuck taking the early shift at the Co-Op to make ends meet.

And keep her health insurance. Good ole U.S. of A.

Lewis stepped in front of her before she could take another step. "How are things going?" He peered at her, his eyes kind under his bushy gray brows. She knew what he meant, and she did not want to admit how much she was struggling.

"Well enough. Got a couple more boarders for the summer with people traveling. And had a sign-up for riding lessons." She smiled at him.

And, of course, he called her on her bull hockey. "That's a lot to handle."

"My parents lend a hand, and Cress comes out to help now and then." Although that help had been less and less frequent lately with the little one at home. Not that Vada blamed her, but she missed seeing her friend.

Lewis patted her shoulder. "Things will pick up. You just got to keep trying. Remember, the offer still stands to put a poster up in the window."

"Thanks, Lewis. But I'm running some Facebook ads." Ads that she'd turned off weeks ago because they were costing her a lot and earning her nothing.

He shook his head as he shoved his hands in his back pockets and stepped aside. "Well, I hope things pick up soon. You're a hard worker. Best one I've ever had. I just don't want to see you get so bogged down in the work that you end up a lonely ole coot like me."

With a laugh, she picked up the broom. "I can assure you, my marital status is very much in God's hands."

Her mind skipped to the memory of Pastor Riser's warm fingers brushing against her skin. She huffed. God hadn't answered her prayers in a very long time. There was no way he'd start now.

Chapter 2

* * *

Son scribbled out a brief comment below the bullet points on the third lesson. He had been working furiously to flesh out the sparse notes with substantial lessons. Even if they got a new youth pastor in time, he would need to provide him with all the materials for the camp upfront. He couldn't expect the pastor to have eight weeks of lesson plans ready to go.

He glanced at the clock. It had been over an hour. Where was Lou Ellen with those other materials?

Needing a glass of water and to stretch his legs, Son headed down the hall to the church's small kitchen. As he rounded the corner into the room, he spotted Lou Ellen at the sink, hands wrapped around her stomach, crying silently, chest heaving. Next to her, the coffee pot sputtered, dribbling out a pungent stream of disgusting bean water into the carafe.

He tried to backpedal and tripped over a frayed edge of the carpet. Lou Ellen looked up, her eyes red and furious.

"This! This is all your fault!" She pointed a finger at him.

He'd blown his silent retreat. "What's my fault?" Stepping into the kitchen, he pulled a glass from a cupboard.

"Dereck leaving!" She slapped the counter. "The one friend I have in this crypt of a workplace. And we were… I thought… But you ran him off!" She smoothed a shaking hand through her hair.

"Whoa!" That was a lot to take in. "I didn't run him off." Son set his glass down and reached for the fridge and its Brita pitcher. Although now that he thought about it, he hadn't exactly encouraged him to stay. Or even asked him to stay. He winced. "Ok, I didn't exactly help things."

"Help things?" Lou Ellen laughed bitterly and crossed her

arms, her bubblegum pink nails tapping against her elbows. In the silence, Son could hear the cuckoo clock above the door ticking.

Son bit the inside of his lip. Obviously, Lou Ellen and Dereck had been close. Closer than Son had suspected. And if that were the case, she was justifiably upset about him leaving, but this reaction. It was beyond what was called for. Something else was eating at her. His dad's advice rang in his ears: listen beneath the words.

"What do you mean, your one friend?" he turned to her. He couldn't do anything about... whatever... they had been. But maybe he could solve the other problem. She looked up at him and sniffed. Her mascara was smudged under her eyes in wet little rings.

"If you hadn't noticed, I spend all my time here or helping my dad at the courthouse. I don't exactly have a raging social life."

He leaned against the counter and grabbed a paper towel, handing it to her. From the phone calls he heard echoing down the hall, he would have thought she partied every weekend. "What about Missy and Janie?"

She waved one hand as she blotted at her makeup with the other. "They've got families of their own. I hardly see them anymore. The rest of my friends have their own lives and problems."

"Aren't friends supposed to help each other with their problems?" He took a sip of his water.

The look she gave him was venomous. "Says the man who eats out alone every night."

She had him there. He bobbed his head. Reaching for the coffee pot, he pulled down a mug from the cabinet, filled it, and handed it to her.

Gingerly, she took the mug and looked up at him suspiciously. "No lecture on the evils of caffeine dependence?"

He shook his head and smiled. "Sometimes, you just need a pick-me-up. Innocent enough." She side-eyed him as she sipped her coffee.

"Look, Lou Ellen, I'm sorry for…" He waved a hand. "All this. I've been clueless," he told her, sincerity ringing in his words, and she grimaced. "About a lot of things. It's my first time being a lead pastor, and I'm learning. Still, being there for my co-laborers in Christ—that should have been a no-brainer. And I take full responsibility for that."

She rolled her shoulders. After a moment, she murmured. "What's done is done." She sighed. "No need to hold on to it."

Son looked at her, realizing for the first time how foolish he'd been. Lou Ellen might worry over her hair and nails. But she'd also grown up in this community. She knew everything about everyone. And she cared, a lot, if her outburst today indicated anything.

"Lou Ellen, would you help me?" She looked up at him but pressed her lips together. He continued, "Our children are our heart." He thought of the empty play set behind his house and how he hoped to see it overrun one day with smiling faces. "And I don't want to let them down as I've let you down."

Her face softened, and she swiped at her eyes one more time with the paper towel. "You've got a lot to learn, mister." She smiled at him. "But I think we can manage." She picked up her mug. "I'll go pull those files, see what I can find."

"And I've got a job to post with the Southern Baptist Convention." He paused in the doorway. "And thank you, Lou Ellen. I hope in time you can look at me as a friend."

"You would be so lucky!"

He laughed as he headed back to his office. He was going to need a friend if he was going to get through this summer.

Chapter 3

S unday dawned bright, clear, and hot. Vada pulled a sundress over her head and hopped in the car with her family, already dreading the morning ahead in the stuffy church.

As they settled into their pew, whispers rustled around them with the swishing of fans and flapping of hats. The decades-old air conditioner had finally given out just in time for the warming weather. Vada plucked at the front of her dress as Willow slid into the pew next to her with a grin, her boyfriend Ruffin on duty at the fire station.

With the final opening hymn, Pastor Riser stood and walked to the pulpit. Vada squinted; Ellie had told her just the day before about the youth pastor absconding. Pastor Riser looked tired, with bags beneath his eyes and his face unusually dim. Despite the crisp suit and shined shoes, he leaned on the pulpit as he looked out over the congregation and began his sermon, the news clearly weighing on him. Her heart pinched at his worn-down appearance.

Willow leaned toward Vada. "Pastor looks a bit beat."

Vada glanced at her. "With good reason."

In the pew in front of them, Lou Ellen glanced over her shoulder at their whispers. Vada waved her away. Lou Ellen was always poking her nose where it didn't belong.

Willow whispered, "And what reason would that be?"

"I heard from Ellie when she came out to see me yesterday that the youth pastor quit unexpectedly. Got his hands full now."

Vada stared at the back of Lou Ellen's head, knowing exactly where Ellie had gotten the news; she'd admitted to it yesterday. Her gut knotted and churned. While she didn't envy Ellie and Lou Ellen their friendship, it did sting that she could no longer talk to her former best friend.

She glanced back at Pastor Riser, who braced his hands on the pulpit as he continued preaching. A small flicker of worry for him wavered in her chest. Being a pastor came with so much responsibility as it was. The youth group would exponentially increase his load.

The only reasonable solution she could see was for the church to cancel the summer camp.

Settling back in the pew, she tried to concentrate on the sermon even as her eyes flickered from Pastor Riser to Mahalia. Her cousin had been so looking forward to youth camp and her first full summer spent here with her friends. Vada's parents—and many others in Midnight Bluff—had been counting on the activities to keep their kids out of trouble for a couple of days a week.

Despite the situation, Vada smiled to herself at the memory. Her days at youth camp had been filled with shenanigans and pranks that would have stood her parents' hair on end had they known. Most of it at Eve's urging.

Still, if summer camp were canceled, she should consider her dad's suggestion to teach Mahalia how to work with horses...

Pastor Riser asked them to bow their heads in prayer, and Vada frowned as she realized she'd spent most of the sermon lost in her own thoughts.

"Amen." Vada raised her eyes and startled at finding Pastor Riser looking at her before he glanced away. "I have a few brief announcements to make."

The congregation shifted and grumbled, ready to get out of the stifling sanctuary. "Have patience, brothers and sisters. I won't hold you long."

He cleared his throat. "As you may have guessed, we need a new A/C unit. So, starting today, we're beginning a fundraising campaign. If you would like to give any offerings above your usual tithes for this endeavor, simply mark it on your giving envelope."

Around the room, heads nodded as wives poked husbands and ladies dove into purses. With a small smile, Vada whispered to Willow, "I don't think this campaign will take long."

Willow shook her head, lips pressed together in a suppressed grin.

"And now, the announcement some of you are already aware of. Our youth pastor, Dereck, has accepted a position as assistant pastor in Ruleville..."

Murmurs skittered around the room, passing from neighbor to neighbor with alarmed glances. "...which is a wonderful step for him. I hope you'll join me in congratulations." Pastor Riser clapped his hands, and everyone followed suit reluctantly, as Dereck waved sheepishly from the front pew.

"However, that leaves us with a position to fill. We've already posted a job opening with the SBC, and I have made a few calls as well."

Next to Vada, Mahalia grumbled, "There goes the summer." She flipped her braids over her shoulder and huffed. The congregation seemed to agree, muttering as they rose to sing the Doxology together and receive the benediction.

"There's no way he'll find someone in time for camp." Willow glanced toward the front of the room where Pastor Riser was already surrounded by a group of irate parents.

As they scooched down the aisle, Vada threw over her shoulder, half-laughing, "If I were him, I'd book a bunch of activities with the local business owners." Out of the corner of her eye, she noticed Lou Ellen watching them, clearly eavesdropping. Let her eavesdrop; it wouldn't make any difference. Pastor Riser had much better people to advise him than Vada or Lou Ellen. Still, she couldn't help adding, "It would keep the kids busy, and he'd get to know his parishioners all at one go."

Plus, the summers were slow for most businesses in Midnight Bluff, they'd probably welcome the diversion—and the extra cash.

Willow agreed. "That's a great idea! I could totally host a group in the bakery."

Vada nodded as she thought about what having the entire youth group out to her equestrian school could do for her business. She shook her head; that was only a dream. With a finger wave to Willow, Vada wrapped an arm around Mahalia and slid down the aisle.

* * *

Son rubbed his hands over his face, blinking away the glare from his computer screen. Of the few applications they had received for the youth pastor position, none of them were acceptable—lacking degrees or the amount of experience he'd like to see. And none of the leads he'd been slipped by other pastors had been interested in a backwater like Midnight Bluff.

What had happened to pastors who were more dedicated to serving the Lord than pursuing a high-paying job?

He swept aside a stack of applications and stared at the phone on the corner of his desk. His dad would know what to do, always knew what to do. But Son didn't want to call him and admit that he was floundering.

Still, their kids deserved a good leader. He reached for the phone.

Lou Ellen bounced into his office and stood in front of his desk, tapping her brightly painted nails on the shiny surface.

"Just come on in," he groused, as he set the phone back on the cradle.

Without preamble, she asked, "Have you found someone yet?"

He stared at her. "You know I haven't."

She folded her arms behind her back and shook out her hair. "You've still got a couple of weeks. You should go with Vada's idea before it's too late." He tried to protest that Vada's idea was too wild, too much, but she kept talking. "I know for a fact that she has availability at her equestrian school this summer. I bet a lot of the other businesses do as well."

With a grin, she sauntered toward the door. As she vanished down the hall, she tossed over her shoulder, "Consider it."

The nerve of that woman. If he'd known he was getting a nagging busybody when he offered to be friends with her... He

25

sighed. He would still have offered because she needed a friend. They both did.

And she was right. It was looking more and more like he'd need a Plan B for their youth group after all. He wasn't all that fond of Vada's plan—it entailed a lot more coordination than he was prepared to do—but he had to admit that it had plenty of merits.

Maybe he should give it a try. Besides, how hard could it be for him to run a youth group for the summer?

The stack of member rolls teetered on the edge of his desk, and he sighed. Sitting back in his chair, he chuckled darkly at the thought of adding anything more to his pile. He still needed to meet with the deacons about a new maintenance plan. Leora wanted to meet with him about some sort of capital fundraiser for "outstanding repairs." And to top it off, he had to find a new youth pastor. How was he supposed to get it all done?

Delegation. His dad was always on him to delegate more. "A pastor can't—and shouldn't—do it all."

He ran through a mental list of people who might take on such an enormous task as the summer youth camp. It was depressingly short.

But Vada had suggested this plan, and Vada always seemed to make things happen. Son bobbed his head as he thought. The people of Midnight Bluff clearly trusted her when something needed to get done. And she was one of the business owners who would naturally be interested in this sort of arrangement.

Flipping open the church directory, he scanned down the page for Vada's number. Hitting "call," he held his breath as he listened to the line ring.

"Hello?" Vada sounded breathless, the whoosh of wind

crackling over the line. Wherever she was, it was outside. The image made him smile.

"Vada." Her name rolled sweetly off his tongue, like a drip of honey across one of Al's biscuits.

"Yes. Who is this?"

Son sucked in his breath. Of course, she wouldn't be expecting him to call. He gave her his name. "Could you meet with me? Today, possibly?" He cleared his throat. "I have a… business proposition… for you."

Vada paused, the silence crackling over the line. He tightened his grip on the phone. "Ok. Meet me in an hour at Loveless."

Tension melted off Son's shoulders as he hung up. The first step was done. Now he just needed to get ready for a meeting. In an hour. He was going to need help.

"Lou Ellen!" he hollered as he jogged down the hall.

Chapter 4

V ada stared into her coffee. "Tell me again why I'm doing this."

"Because you're a good person. And, secretly, you love helping others." Willow spun her hands in the air. "Saint Vada."

"Saint Nothing." Vada shook her head, laughing. "He wants something. I just don't know what yet."

"So skeptical." Willow whacked her with a tea towel. "Maybe he woke up from his lonely bachelorhood and is now madly in love with you. Business is just an excuse to see you."

Vada doubled over laughing. "Sure. And cows fart rainbows."

"Don't be gross."

Vada sobered and clasped her hands around her coffee. "I'm serious, though. I have no idea what 'business proposition' he could have. I've already told the deacons a half dozen times I don't have donkeys to rent out for biblical scenes. And Pastor Riser doesn't exactly strike me as the horse-loving type."

Although he'd look amazing in jeans atop a horse, riding down a trail just at daybreak.

"Maybe he needs something besides horseback riding lessons." Willow stacked up a few baking trays with a clatter, jerking Vada out of her reverie, and turned toward the back curtain.

"What else can I do?" Vada clenched the mug. Eve had always been the mastermind behind their plans. What did she offer by herself?

With a shrug, Willow disappeared into the back. The clatter of metal and whoosh of running water filtered out to Vada. She took a deep breath and sipped at her coffee, her second cup of the afternoon.

There was not enough caffeine in the world to ease the ache in her muscles or the fatigue just behind her eyes. She closed her eyes and inhaled, letting the calm of the bakery wash over her.

The bells on the front door jingled, shattering her momentary peace. Pastor Riser strode in, smiling. He stretched out a hand. "Thank you for meeting with me on such short notice, Vada."

Her eyes swept from his tan leather loafers to his blindingly bright smile. He wore jeans and an army green Henley, the sleeves rolled up to reveal muscular forearms. Despite her misgivings about this meeting, Vada had to admit the man had style.

As she shook his hand, Lou Ellen trailed in the door behind him, a notepad tucked under her arm. Interesting. Vada returned his smile, hoping to set the meeting off on a friendly note. "Not a problem at all, Pastor Riser. Happy to help if I can."

"Son."

"Huh?" She looked at him, confused. Lou Ellen looked between the two of them, a bemused expression on her face.

"Call me Son. Pastor Riser always makes me think of my father." He spoke with a smile, but his eyes squinted, tightening. Some hidden family drama, no doubt.

She skimmed past this tidbit to set him at ease. "A pastor's kid. So, preaching runs in the family." He nodded, and she gestured to her table, inviting them to sit. Son pulled her chair out for her then Lou Ellen. The man had not only looks but manners, too. She made a mental note as he sat back in his chair and slung one leg casually across the other.

Willow bustled out, taking their orders. Vada got her coffee topped off and a blueberry muffin; Lou Ellen asked for a glass of sweet tea and a cupcake; and Son ordered water and a croissant.

Vada looked at his rather plain order. "I wasn't expecting two of you."

Son gestured to Lou Ellen. "I asked Lou Ellen to take notes so we could concentrate on talking."

With a snicker, Lou Ellen muttered, "To act as a chaperone, you mean." Son shot her an irritated look and shook his head slightly. Vada's stomach fluttered as he glanced back at her, his eyes softening.

She pressed a hand to her mouth, trying not to smile as Son shot her an apologetic look. It was good to see Lou Ellen was up to her old tricks. And that the matchmaking gossips in this town hadn't changed.

Despite her discomfort with Lou Ellen, it was probably a good thing she was here. Vada could hardly expect the single, attractive pastor to meet alone with a single lady of "marriageable" age without starting a passel of rumors.

"Don't worry about it. Totally understand." She waved a hand. "What can I do for you? You said something on the phone about a business proposition."

Son nodded. "You know about our youth pastor?" He looked at her, his dark eyes sweeping over her face.

She blinked at the odd question; he had looked straight at her the day he made the announcement. Besides, Midnight Bluff was so small everyone knew about it by now, whether or not they had been in church on Sunday. "Of course. My cousin is in the youth group."

He blinked, tilting his head. "Mahalia?"

"Yes." She folded her hands, politely waiting for him to continue.

"Then you know of the difficult situation we're in with the youth camp, starting in a couple of weeks."

"Of course. I've been making alternative plans for Mahalia…"

He raised a hand. "I'd like you to coordinate the activities for our summer camp." His chest rose as he inhaled sharply like the request was painful.

She paused, words clogging in her throat. "I'm sorry… what did you say?" Son reached toward her, then drew back his hand as she coughed to clear her voice.

"I'd like you to coordinate…" he repeated.

"I got that." She raised a hand. "Why me?"

He shifted in his seat, casting a look at Lou Ellen. "Because you know all the business owners in Midnight Bluff." Vada glanced at Lou Ellen, who looked back at her with an enigmatic expression. "Don't you?"

"Of course. The Loveless Bakery and Uncle Ray's Bait shop,

off the top of my head, would be perfect."

A smile flitted across his face, lighting him up from within. Sweet Jesus, if he smiled at her like that all the time, she'd be in real trouble. "Your selflessness does you credit. But I want something to be in this for you as well."

Vada shook her head. "Just being practical. I'm sure you've already been informed…" She glanced at Lou Ellen again. "… What I can do. And there are eight weeks of activities to plan."

He leaned forward. "True. With two days each week, that's sixteen activities we'll need. I was thinking they could spend one session a week at your equestrian school—if you're available."

Lou Ellen's lips were definitely curving up now. From behind the counter, Willow snorted. This man knew dang well that she was available. But Vada didn't want to give away all her power in this negotiation. "I'll have to check, but I might be able to work something out." Lou Ellen's eyes sparkled as Vada spoke.

"If you could." He sat forward and broke off a piece of his croissant.

"Are there any other details I need to know?" She picked at her muffin.

He frowned and nodded. "We end each camp with an overnight trip to one of the State Parks." Vada nodded; she remembered from her youth group days. "And I could use some help with a couple of extra volunteers to help things go smoothly."

"Is that all?" It was a lot to come up with in just two weeks, and he sat there nonchalantly shredding his croissant.

Ignoring her ironic tone, he nodded. "Yes. I'll be leading the lessons, so no need to worry over that."

She raised her eyebrows. "I didn't realize you'd be involved." The thought of spending more time with him made her pause, anticipation and dread warring in her stomach.

His eyes traveled up to meet hers. "I don't see another option right now. Our kids are too important to let this go." His eyes bore into hers, holding her gaze and warming her through.

After a moment, she nodded, breaking his stare. "You said *extra* volunteers…" She let her voice drift, hoping he would catch her meaning. While she would be crazy to let this opportunity go, she couldn't live without a paycheck.

"Oh! The church will pay you." He clasped his hands. "I couldn't find a website for your equestrian school to look at your rates, but we have a discretionary budget for the camp. I want to be fair—for all your time and expertise."

She smiled and shook her head. Expertise. He was asking her to make a bunch of phone calls, but she wouldn't enlighten him. "I have another job I can't just abandon—"

"If you're unable to change your schedule to make this work, no hard feelings." He sipped at his water. "But Lewis is a deacon. I'm certain he'll work with you so you can serve."

He paused, leaning forward. Gently, he took her hand, his palms warm on her skin. "Vada, I know this is a lot to ask. But please, if you can, help me. It would mean more to me than you know."

Lou Ellen's pen, which had been going constantly this whole time, paused as she studied them. Vada swallowed and glanced at Willow. She bobbed her head in encouragement. While Vada looked into Son's eyes, so deep and entrancing, Mahalia's disappointment a few weeks ago came back to her.

Even if she had to drop a couple of shifts at the Co-Op, she'd do anything to make sure her cousin had one good summer.

And this would be a way to spend more time with her, as her dad had suggested.

"Ok." She murmured the word, already wondering what she was getting herself into. Lou Ellen and Willow beamed at her.

Son squeezed her hand with that boyish grin, sending tingles up her arm. "Thank you! We're going to be a great team."

She wasn't so sure about the team part, but as she looked into Son's glimmering eyes, she couldn't help smiling back.

* * *

"Yes!" Mahalia launched herself at Vada, encircling her waist in a strangling hug. "This is going to be so sick. Together!" She bumped Vada's hip with hers, then danced around the room.

Vada laughed and joined her, spinning her around. It was so good to see a smile on Mahalia's face. Her parents beamed at them from the kitchen. Outside, cicadas droned in the humid evening air, a peaceful backdrop to their celebration.

"Wait! Does this make me an assistant counselor?" Mahalia paused her dancing.

"Not quite." Vada stuck her tongue out at her. "But you can help me."

"Sweet!" Mahalia bopped around the room again, then dashed for the hall. "I've got to tell Carmel. She's gonna freak. With you in charge, this is going to be the best summer ever."

Shaking her head, Vada watched her go. She walked over to her parents and asked, "Should I be concerned that a teenager is this excited to hang out with her family all summer?"

"Look at it as a blessing." Her mom poured a glass of sweet tea and handed it to her. "With everything that's happened with her mother, being shuffled around as she's been, it's a wonder she wants to be around family at all."

Vada wobbled her head in agreement as she sipped at her tea.

"So, did you have anyone in mind to help you, volunteer-wise?" Her mother opened the refrigerator and placed the jug of sweet tea back in.

"I was thinking Bo McBride." At her mother's skeptical look, Vada explained. "He's practically retired now. And everyone loves him, even the kids. They'd listen to him."

"Ahh. Wise."

"And Leora might help with a couple of the inside activities. I can't see her at the barn, but baking lessons with Willow? For the rest of it, I was thinking I'd ask people as needed. Some activities are going to need more... corralling... than others." Vada smiled.

Her mother shot her a knowing look. "True. Sounds like you have a plan."

"I hope so." Vada thought of the lists she'd already begun making of places, times, supplies, and helpers. It would be a lot to pull together in just two weeks.

"You've got this, honey." Her mother hugged her, kissing her cheek. "I'm so proud to see you finally working on your business. Only good things can come from this."

As her mother left the room, heading to bed, Vada mulled over her words, bitterness clouding her fizzling triumph. Good things. How could anything truly good come from Eve missing out on this?

Chapter 5

The next morning, Vada cracked open the door of the Co-Op and peeked inside five minutes before her shift was due to start. She scanned the empty aisles. A light glowed in the back office, beckoning through the dim interior.

Good, it looked like Lewis was the only one there. She didn't want her co-worker, Dewayne Strange, lurking about while she talked to him. Why in the world Dewayne hung around the Co-Op on his off days was beyond Vada.

As the bells jingled with the closing of the door behind her, Lewis popped his head out of the back office. "Ah, Vada! We got a new shipment of fertilizer in. Need you to add it to the inventory."

"No problem." Vada picked up a scanner from the front desk, walked over to the office door, and hovered at the entrance. Lewis looked up at her, surprised.

"Something on your mind?" He took his hand off the computer mouse and turned to face her.

Vada stepped in and fiddled with the scanner. "I've got a favor to ask."

A knowing smile stretched across Lewis' face. "It wouldn't have anything to do with that meeting you had yesterday with Pastor Riser, would it?"

Surprise rippled through Vada. It always shocked her how fast word spread in Midnight Bluff despite living here all her life. Hiding her dismay, she nodded. "Son asked me to lead the activities for youth camp this summer. And he wants one day a week out at my school."

Lewis whistled. "That's quite the windfall for you. What do you need from me?"

"To shift my schedule?" Vada shoved her hands in her pockets. "I could still do the early morning shifts, but it would be tight and…"

"You don't want to be running late all the time." Lewis waved a hand and pulled out a clipboard. "You know Dewayne has been pestering me for years for more morning shifts. He'll be delighted to grab any he can get."

"As long as he knows it's temporary!" Vada thought possessively of her prime morning slot. Right now, the Co-Op was her one steady gig, and it worked perfectly with her schedule at the barn. Dread curled behind her breastbone at the idea of losing her job.

Lewis laughed, his rumbly voice filling the tiny space. "Of course." He flipped some pages. "That will leave you working doubles on your other days. Unless you want to drop a couple of shifts altogether this summer?"

Vada tilted her head, thinking. It would be wise to stay as present as she could at the Co-Op. But the thought of working doubles all summer with her already full schedule made her toes curl with fatigue.

Lewis took one look at her face and nodded. "We'll just drop you from your Tuesday and Thursday shifts and you can keep your others. I'll add you to the top of the call-out list on Saturdays. Chances are, I'll have a couple folks wanting to take off for vacations and whatnot, and you can pick up some extra hours if you need them."

Relief washed over Vada. This conversation had gone so much better than she'd imagined. For three years, she'd worked her butt off to keep Lewis happy. It was nice to see him return the favor. "Thank you, Lewis. I can't tell you how…"

He waved her off. "No need. Been waiting for you to take the next step with your business." With a smile, he nodded. "Good to see you finally coming into your own."

"Lewis…" She didn't want him to think she was abandoning him just because of one job.

He shook his head. "Nope. Don't you 'Lewis' me." He stood up and stretched. "You may be my best employee, but I've been here for decades. I know how it goes." With a pat on her shoulder, he added, "Growth is a good thing, Vada. Don't shy away from it on my account."

He slipped out the door. "Get on that inventory, will you?"

With a smile, Vada picked up the scanner and headed to the loading dock. That conversation had gone better than she could have imagined.

* * *

Son poked at his sunny-side-up eggs, watching the golden yolks pool on the plate. "I don't know, Dr. Washburn. I'm still not sure if asking Vada to lead youth camp was the right call."

Dr. Clay Washburn slurped his coffee then set it down. "And why is that?" Behind them, Al clattered pans in the kitchen while Mira bustled about the hostess stand.

Swallowing, Son admitted, "I've seen too many churches torn apart by whispers of the pastor having an affair. And with Vada's other responsibilities, I'm not sure how dedicated she will be to the kids."

Clay cut off a bite of pancakes and eyed him. "Let's take this one piece at a time. You're not married so…"

"I know! But appearances are ninety percent of the reputation game. And you have to admit, reputation matters, especially in a small town like this. I can't have it look like I'm singling out one woman to… to court." He winced at the word.

Frowning, Clay set down his fork. "You're overthinking this. Asking Vada to be a camp leader isn't 'courting' her. Nor…" He held up a finger as Son tried to protest. "…Does it look like it to any sensible person."

"It's the insensible ones I'm worried about," Son muttered.

"And they're not worth worrying about, in my experience." Dr. Washburn shook his head. "As for her dedication, I can assure you she gives 100% to everything she takes on. Any other rebuttals? Might as well get them out of the way."

"I just don't…" Son flapped his hand, struggling to articulate what was bothering him. "…Know her that well. It's hard to put my trust in someone I've never worked with before."

Clay snorted and shook his head as he picked up his fork. "Get to know her then! While Vada has her flaws, she is one of the most caring and trustworthy people in Midnight Bluff. I think she'll surprise you."

Son scooped up a bite of his egg. Trustworthy. He

considered the word. Clay was a level-headed man with a keen sense of character. His opinion stood for something. Which meant his opinion of Vada carried weight. "Perhaps," Son conceded, as Clay sliced off another bite of pancake. "Perhaps she's just what I need after all."

* * *

"Hey, O.C., can you put Ray on?" Vada smoothed a curry comb over the bay mare, Flick, in front of her. This was the last activity she needed to book to fill out the schedule. If she could get Ray to finally agree...

His voice crackled over the line. "Howdy."

"Ray. It's Vada again." She heard him grunt. "I want you to reconsider the fishing trip with the youth group. We'll buy all the bait and tackle we need from you! And..." she hastened to add, "...We'll rent out your kayaks for the day too."

She heard Ray spit into a cup. "I still don't know about wrangling a group of teenagers on the water all day. I didn't exactly open a bait shop to be a tour guide."

"I know. And this isn't a regular thing, I promise. Just one trip is all I'm asking." She crossed her fingers and leaned her head against Flick's side as she added her final bit of goading. "Imagine if you could get a couple kids hooked on fishing. Customers for life."

"Still not sure the hassle's worth it, sugar."

Vada sighed, defeated. The man was just too stubborn for her. She'd have to regroup. "It's ok, Ray. Maybe I can get Herb to do a second building project with them."

"Herb is working with you?" Ray's voice perked up, suddenly interested.

An idea sparked in her. She'd forgotten Herb and Ray had a low-key rivalry going; they each claimed to own the most popular business in Midnight Bluff. She'd never told them the Co-Op had them both easily beat. "Yep. He was eager to get some customers in for the slow summer months."

Muttering echoed over the line as Ray chewed on that thought. "What day do you need me for?" he finally asked. Vada did a little jig, then stopped as Flick looked askance at her. No need to spook the horses with her flailing.

Vada gave him the date and listened as he laid out his rules for the trip. "And absolutely no one takes their vest off! I'll yank everyone off the water and make them hike back."

"Of course, Ray. We'll follow your rules to a T." She hung up, stepped out of the stall, and threw her arms up with a whoop.

From the next stall, her mom looked at her with a grin and shook her head. "Looks like the summer is shaping up for you."

Vada bobbed her head, face cracking with her grin. "About time too!"

* * *

Son leaned on the pulpit in the dimly lit sanctuary. He glanced at the dark wood pews and the red carpet stretching down the center aisle, feeling guilty for his fatigue. He'd spent most of the week cramming in notes for his lessons with the youth group, and now he was too exhausted to practice his sermon for tomorrow.

He stared down at his handwritten notes in his portfolio, willing the letters to make some sense. But try as he might, his brain refused to make heads or tails of them. He knew vaguely they were about Jesus' atonement on the cross, but recalling the details was beyond him right now.

With a sigh, he shut the leather portfolio and slumped into the front pew, trying to collect himself. He just needed a minute to rest and then he would get back to practicing.

He jerked upright as his phone rang. How long had he been out? The numbers on the screen glowed nine p.m., much later than he'd expected. With a groan, he straightened slightly from his slump and hit "Answer."

"Hey, Dad."

"Was beginning to wonder if you were going to pick up."

Son rubbed at his face. "Just a long night. How are you?" Over the line, Son heard the rustle of pages and imagined his father shuffling his own sermon notes back into an orderly stack.

"I'm fine. Say, that camp of yours starts Tuesday, doesn't it?"

"Yep." Son slumped down further into the pew, sighing as he contemplated trying to reach a bunch of unruly teenagers. Despite all his degrees and preparation, when he thought about connecting with an entire group, he felt woefully inadequate. He hadn't exactly been a normal teenager himself. How was he supposed to connect with them?

"God's got you." His dad's voice was steady. The reassurance warmed Son.

"God's gonna have to have me because I don't know if I have myself." Son stretched and leaned his head back against the pew.

A chuckle answered him. "You're still learning. It's going to be uncomfortable."

Uncomfortable was mild compared to what Son was feeling. His skin prickled with foreboding at the thought of the youth group. Still, he was not about to admit that to his father, the pastor who always had everything together. "I know, Dad. It will be fine."

"Ok." Silence hung between them for a moment. "Well, I know you have a big day on Tuesday. Anything else I can pray about for you?"

"Just…" Son pinched the bridge of his nose. "…That everything will go well. And that my co-leader pulls through." His mind flashed to Vada's warm eyes as she leaned in, listening at the bakery. "A lot is banking on Vada."

"All right." His father began praying, and Son closed his eyes, letting his dad's raspy voice echo through him. "Our Father, thank you for letting us come before you. Thank you for your love for us and your work to redeem this fallen world. May we be your instruments in that work."

Son sank further into the pew as his father continued, letting his soothing voice wash over him. "Please be with my son as he begins a new ministry, and may Your blessing be on all he does. May the kids he ministers to be filled with Your presence and love as they come to know You. And may Your hand of blessing be on Vada, guiding her and giving her wisdom in this venture. Amen."

Son echoed, "Amen." He sniffed. "Thanks, Dad."

"I am so proud of you. And I know your mom would be too."

"That's all I want," Son said as he stared out the darkened windows of the sanctuary. "To make you proud." He hung up and stood, rolling the kinks out of his back. It was time to get some shut-eye. This week signaled a tremendous change in his life, and he had a feeling he would need all the energy he could get.

Chapter 6

Vada rubbed her hands anxiously along her arms, trying to brush away the goosebumps that had arisen despite the June heat. More nervous energy than a pot of coffee bubbled in her stomach.

Beside her, Mahalia bounced on the balls of her feet as they watched the church van roll up before the barn. Her mother squeezed her shoulder encouragingly as the van came to a stop, a light cloud of dust rising around it.

Lou Ellen jumped from the passenger seat and slid open the side door as Son slowly tucked the keys in his pocket while surveying the barn behind Vada. Her heart sped up as she took in his crisp, white T-shirt and dark jeans hugging his muscular thighs.

She froze as she watched him take in the farm. She'd power washed the barn last week so that the paint shone, but no amount of water could make the old façade look new. Son's eyes shifted and his mouth tightened as he looked up at the gigantic structure, and Vada wondered if it was disapproval he felt or the same apprehension that rumbled in her gut.

Teenagers poured from the van in a riot of colorful clothes and babbling voices. Carmel and Preston ran over to Mahalia, greeting her with high-fives.

Vada wished for some of their energy for herself. Years of rising before dawn had left her feeling drained and sluggish. She watched enviously as the kids milled around the yard, looking at the horses in the paddock and ogling the dark interior of the barn.

Lou Ellen trotted over to her and handed her a clipboard. "Good luck!" Her eyes sparkled as she retreated to lean against the van while Vada glanced down at the names scrawled illegibly across the sheet.

Her eyes flitted to the barn as trepidation rippled through her. As she looked at the barn, she steadied herself, wiping her palms on her jeans. This was her and Eve's dream. She wouldn't back out now because her nerves got the best of her.

Sucking in a deep breath, Vada decided there wasn't anything for it except to dive in feet first. "All right, everyone, gather 'round!" She tucked the clipboard under her arm and clapped her hands.

With a shuffle, the kids formed a staggered semi-circle around her, Mahalia elbowing her friends to stand at the front. Vada smiled at her. "How many of you have been around horses before?" Only a couple of hands rose despite a lot of these kids being farmer's children. Good, for most of the group, this would be a completely new experience.

She'd start with safety rules. "First rule, don't enter a stall, corral, or pasture without me or one of the other leaders with you." She waved a hand at her mom, dad, and Bo McBride, who sat on a hay bale in the shade. "Second—"

Son cleared his throat, interrupting her. "Why don't we call roll first?" He nodded at the clipboard pressed beneath her elbow.

"Didn't y'all do that at drop-off?" She stared at him, wondering just how chaotic things had been at the church that they hadn't taken roll yet.

Shaking his head, Son replied, "Yes. But we must do it before and after every stop." He shrugged. "Safety first."

"If you say so," she said as exasperation pinged her between the shoulders. Snickers floated softly through the group. *Whoops.* Getting ahold of her runaway mouth would be a necessity with these teens. Couldn't be teaching them it was ok to sass the preacher.

She held up the clipboard and squinted at the messy scrawl. Son glanced nervously at the kids. As she hastily called the words out, names blurring together, her eyes flicked to him, standing beside but a few steps away from the group. He rubbed at his brow in the bright light of the yard.

"All right, we're going to split you into two groups—" Just as she began motioning kids forward to get the day's activities started, Son raised his voice. He smiled at her apologetically, his bright teeth gleaming in the sun.

"Let's take a few minutes to think about our Lord." The kids shot looks at each other at the antiquated phrasing. With a sigh, Vada took a couple of steps back from the group so Son could take the lead. Whatever he was up to, it would be helpful if he filled her in on it.

Mahalia turned to Vada and rolled her eyes. Trying to suppress a smile, Vada dutifully pointed to Son, urging her to pay attention.

With surprise, she listened as Son launched into a mini-sermon. In the wavering heat, Son spoke in his flowery Sunday language about submitting and allowing the self to be led by bridles like horses. Around her, the kids shuffled, exchanging baffled glances. Vada understood where he was going with the overwrought metaphor, but one glance at the kids told her it wasn't landing. Finally, Son finished with a long prayer.

Vada stared at him, anticipating another interruption. He stared back, his eyes widening. She waited, unwilling to be interrupted again. Finally, he prompted her, "Why don't we get started now?" Chuckles echoed around Vada.

"All right." She turned to the kids, realizing her mind hadn't held onto a single name. "You there, Curly." She pointed at a tall girl with long ringlets. "To the right." She gestured at a boy wearing a band T-shirt. "MTV to the left." Laughter echoed around her at the colorful nicknames as she sorted the kids.

"All right, Curly, would you lead your group to leather crafts?" she pointed at her parents, who smiled and waved at the kids. "Y'all will go with Sacia and Waymond." Her parents' first names sounded foreign on her lips.

"MTV's group, you're with Bo and me." Bo stood from his hay bale and shuffled into the barn, a smaller group forming around him. Lou Ellen and Son blinked back at her, and she realized she hadn't thought about where to put them. "Lou Ellen, why don't you go with my mom and dad? Pastor, you can come with me."

"Works for me!" Lou Ellen trotted after the group headed to the pergola, where her parents had set up a craft station.

Son trailed several feet behind her as she stepped into the cool barn. Two horses stood at makeshift hitching posts, swishing their tails. They placidly surveyed the mob of kids hanging a few paces away with muffled giggles and shuffling.

"All right, today, we're learning how to mount and dismount a horse, with and without help, and what the various bits of tack are." Bo waved at them from next to a table loaded with tack. Grumbling met her ears, and she surveyed the group, eyes narrowed. "Being an expert rider isn't just about riding through fields at sunset, like some old Western."

She walked over to one of the old mares and stroked her neck. "It's about knowing your horse's temperament and needs—what they'll do willingly and what they need coaxing to do and what you should never-ever ask them to do. It's about taking care of them properly, from their hooves to their blankets." She looked around at a sea of curious eyes. "And you can't do that unless you master the basics."

"So, who wants to ride a horse?" A few kids looked at her nervously, but everyone raised their hands. "All right, then let's start."

She gestured for Mahalia and Son to join her. "We're going to start with the easiest way to mount a horse: with a mounting block." Mahalia stepped up onto the block, fitted her foot into the stirrup, grasped the pommel, and easily swung herself up onto the mare's back. She sat proudly on the horse, a grin on her face.

Vada smiled. Mahalia had been watching her more closely than she had suspected. "Very good." With Mahalia helping her demonstrate, she showed the group of kids how to dismount onto the block. Going to the next horse, she spotted Mahalia as she mounted without the help of the block. The kids murmured in admiration as she sat atop the massive horse.

"If you need help to get up or down, let me or Pastor Riser know. Horses are surprisingly large up close, and it can be a bit to get used to." She arranged the kids at rotating stations, starting at the tack table with Bo and ending with her at the horse without a mounting block.

She glanced at Son, who stood by the mounting block, tentatively patting his horse's flank. The horse shifted, and he shied away from the mare, flinching. If he couldn't get over his fear, he would not be much help in later lessons.

As she grunted, helping one klutzy kid scramble up the horse like he was climbing a mountain, she watched Mahalia at the tack table, naming off pieces of equipment with confidence. Eve would have been proud to see how well their cousin was doing.

The day would have been perfect if only her sister could have been here to see it.

* * *

Son slumped onto a picnic table at lunchtime, stomach growling. Large oak trees soared overhead, forming a shady grove to the side of the Wilsons' house. A gentle breeze stirred the trees with soft rustlings and whooshes. He surveyed the kids rambling around him, a weight settling onto his shoulders.

While the kids had immediately warmed to Vada's brusque instructions, the rolled eyes and muttering each time he spoke weren't lost on him. He just wasn't sure what he was saying during his lessons that were so… odious… to them.

A couple of tables over, Vada and Lou Ellen moved back and forth, handing the kids sandwiches and cokes. Belatedly, he realized he should be over there helping them.

As he walked up, Vada glanced at him, her lips curving into

a dazzling smile. She handed him a sandwich without asking. "Actually," he set the wrapped little parcel back down on the stack, "I came over to help."

Lou Ellen murmured, "Thank God! Because I really need to pee." She shoved a couple of cokes into his hands and high-tailed it to the house. Vada laughed as she watched Lou Ellen power walk away, sweeping strands of windblown hair out of her face.

Son stared after Lou Ellen, feeling weirdly exposed without his ally, as he stood next to Vada. "She always just says what's on her mind, doesn't she?"

"It is her best and worst trait." Vada handed a sandwich to a kid with an unfortunate set of braces, who grinned at her, flashing colorful bands. The same kid sobered when Son handed him a coke.

As the kid walked away, Son muttered, "You'd think I had leprosy or something."

Vada laughed, her voice floating up into the leaves about them. "You have the next worst thing." He looked at her curiously. She explained, "They have deemed you 'lame.'"

"Lame?" he repeated.

She nodded. "As in uncool, hopelessly bougie, and just..." She smiled at him, softening her voice. "...A little out of touch with the modern teen."

He groaned. "I know everything about these kids. I memorized their enrollment forms to make sure I knew them all!" Pointing, he continued, "That kid over there? Allergic to peanuts. That one? Her favorite color is periwinkle." He dropped his hand, feeling defeated. "How do you do it? Make them like you?"

She studied him as she weighed a sandwich in her hand.

"Well, for starters, I'm not making them do anything."

He shook his head, bewildered. "But they're obeying you."

She smiled and ducked her head, hair falling around her shoulders. "No. They're doing what they choose to do." Her lips curled up as she handed him a popsicle. "Think on it a bit. And why don't you eat something? Low blood sugar always makes everything feel... dire."

He stared at the popsicle, a sad, frozen excuse of sugar and flavored water. But her words drew attention to his empty stomach and his shaking hands. Maybe he did need some sugar.

Wordlessly, he ripped open the popsicle and sucked on the cold, sweet treat. Almost immediately, his head cleared. And with the rush of cold against his tongue, Vada's words took on new meaning for him.

"You're asking them!" He glanced at her and found her grinning at him.

"Yep. As I said, they're doing what they choose to do. I just make their options clear." She waved at the group milling beneath the trees. "It boils down to participate or be left out. And no kid wants to be left out."

Sucking at the popsicle, he considered. "You must have a lot of experience with kids."

Shaking her head, curls bouncing, she laughed. "I've picked up a thing or two from Mahalia. But mostly, I remember how it was to be a teen. The hopeless awkwardness of it. How intense everything felt all the time."

She smiled, eyes clouding with memories. "So many times, our parents and teachers and coaches carted us from one carefully selected activity to another like we were already locked into one life path. I wouldn't have admitted it then, but being given a choice by an adult—would have made them the coolest person in the world to me."

Shuffled around. Directionless. Son would never have described Vada as directionless. She seemed so in charge of it all as she spoke. "We're not doing them any favors by not allowing them to practice decision-making while they're still protected."

With a jerk, she pulled herself back, glancing nervously at him. "Here." Her smile was tight as she shoved a sandwich into his hands. "Why don't you take a break while we have a chance? Got a long afternoon ahead of us. We've got the rowdy group next."

"Ah, what I've been dreading all day," he quipped.

Vada grinned at him, "Me too."

"Glad to know I'm not the only one terrified by teenagers," he threw over his shoulder as he strolled away. A rewarding laugh floated back to him.

As he settled at the table beside Vada's parents, he couldn't help glancing at Vada as she continued to hand out food.

Give them a choice. It was such a strange notion, raised as he had been to follow adult instructions like the Law. But, yes, choice was the better path. As he watched the kids float around her like butterflies in a field, peace washed over him as a breeze blew through the grove.

* * *

That evening, Son sat in his quiet office at the church, looking at his lesson plans. He stared at the scrawl of notes on each page, wondering why he had thought such elaborate lessons were necessary. The kids were obviously not paying attention.

An image of Vada, showing the proper way to walk and move around a horse, floated to him. She'd had no plan beyond the activities and keeping the kids safe, yet they had flocked to her, drawn to her easygoing persona.

With a click of his pen, he decided to change tactics. He reached for a fresh notepad. It was time to throw out his idea of what church camp should look like and develop one that let the kids lead the way.

As he stared at the blank page in front of him, he smiled to himself, imagining what he would have wanted to learn as a teenager. The words came to him, and he began to write.

Chapter 7

Vada approached the colt slowly, a heavy saddle blanket draped over her arm. This same blanket had hung on the fence for her last few sessions with the colt, and now that the colt had stopped snorting and rolling his eyes every time he spotted it, the time had come to introduce a little weight on his back.

The colt eyed her but didn't shy away as she approached. Slowly, she touched the blanket to his side. He snorted but stayed still. Carefully, she began swinging the blanket against his back, flanks, and legs. Touch was the best way to get a horse used to a new object, and teaching a horse to trust her even when strange things were happening was essential. The colt eyed her and shifted his feet, leaning away.

She stopped, letting him come back to a more natural stance, then began again. By the end of today's session, she wanted to lay the blanket over his back.

A clanging echoed behind her, and the colt bolted, causing her to drop the blanket. Spinning, Vada spotted Mahalia clambering through the corral's rails. Irritation snapped through Vada.

She bent and picked up the blanket, shaking the dust from it. "Mahalia, what have I told you about coming into the corral while I'm working?" She eyed the colt as he skittered back and forth on the other side of the corral.

Mahalia halted by the fence, studying the colt. "But you said I did well yesterday. I thought…"

Vada cut in. "You did do well. That doesn't mean you're ready to train unbroken horses."

"But I want to learn." Mahalia's eyes were large, dark, and pleading. With long, quick steps, Mahalia walked toward the colt. He snorted, ears going back.

"Mahalia!" The colt bolted toward Vada. She let him pass by her as he champed at the bit in his mouth. "Mahalia, stop. You don't know what you're doing."

Mahalia strode toward her, a determined light in her eye. The colt reared and brayed. If she came any closer, they could both get seriously hurt.

Vada held up a hand, scowling. "Dagnabbit, stop! Can't you see you're making things worse?" Vada hissed the words, and they flew from her lips with a sting.

Flinching, Mahalia halted, uncertainty finally flashing across her face. "Why can't I help?"

"Because you don't know what you're doing. And that's dangerous." Vada shook with anger and alarm. She had to keep Mahalia from coming closer. She was already in too much danger as it was, and she couldn't bear to lose another family member.

Behind her, the colt trotted back and forth anxiously, all her hard work from that morning undone. He jerked and tossed his head in panic. "Just go, please."

"You don't care about me. You only care about your stupid horses!" The words ripped from Mahalia. She spun on her heel and stalked from the corral.

Vada watched her go, stunned. If Eve had been here, she would have left the colt where he was and gone running after her. She turned back to the colt, eyes stinging, and picked up a coil of rope. Well, she wasn't her sister; Mahalia could sulk all she wanted. Vada concentrated on the colt while rolling the rope between her fingers.

As she made soothing noises in her throat, reaching out with her voice to the wound-up creature, guilt snaked around Vada's shoulders. The colt quieted, shaking his head, sunlight glimmering on his mane.

Vada could calm a horse without words, but with her cousin, she was hopelessly inept. Slowly, she touched him with the rope, patting him with it as they practiced. After a few minutes, the colt stopped snorting and rolling his eyes. The eyes were always the tell with a horse—when they were calm, if they felt nervous, when they'd absolutely had enough.

She rolled her shoulders as she replayed the incident in her head. With a wince, she remembered the hurt in Mahalia's eyes. Maybe she had been too harsh with her. And there was some truth to her treating horses with more care. After all, horses didn't understand what you were saying, just what you meant. Maybe the same went for teenagers.

Her glance trailed toward the house, where Mahalia had disappeared. Tonight, she would find Mahalia and apologize. But she would give her some space for her feelings until then.

* * *

"Pastor, could I speak with you?"

Son glanced up at the lady standing in his door. Pale red hair streamed down her shoulders as she clasped her hands, fidgeting. He dimly recognized her as Preston's mother from the camp drop-off yesterday.

"Mrs. Langford, of course. Have a seat." He set his sermon notes aside, unsure how long this meeting would be. But his dad had always said that being a pastor was less about perfect sermons and more about connecting with your flock. He studied Mrs. Langford as she shifted in the squeaky leather chair in front of him. She opened and closed her thin lips a few times, looking like a catfish out of water.

"What can I do for you?" he prompted as the silence drug on.

"I was hoping… Well… With Preston's dad gone so much for work…" She snapped her mouth shut and shook her head, then began again. "I was hoping you could mentor Preston a little more yourself?" She twisted her hands. "He's been acting out a bit, getting into mischief, and I'm not sure what to do. He won't really listen to me anymore." She smiled weakly.

Son tilted his head, listening. Regret ached through him for their situation. "Unfortunately, we're not really set up this summer to do one-on-one sessions. Being short-handed and all."

Mrs. Langford drooped in the chair. "I understand." She stood hastily, blinking. "I was just hoping he could get some of the… guidance… he's not getting at home." Taking a step toward the door, she sniffed loudly, cheeks reddening. "Thank you for your time."

Son sighed, misgiving already filling him. "Mrs. Langford, wait." She turned back to him, eyes swimming. "I'll do my best to spend some time with him this summer. I'm not sure how much that will be. But I'll try."

She blinked. "Thank you." With an odd little curtsy, she slipped from the room. Lou Ellen peered after her as stepped into the door.

"Well, that was odd." She set a stack of folders on his desk, more entries in the member rolls from years past.

"Did she really curtsy at me?" Son shook his head.

"You do inspire a certain... formality." Lou Ellen leaned against his desk.

He grimaced, discomfort squirming in his chest. "That was a little much."

She gestured at him as he sat at his dark wood desk in a button-up shirt and tie. "Can you blame her? You hold court in here like it's a throne room." She sniffed. "I'm impressed she came in at all."

He picked up his fountain pen. "Now you're just messing with me."

Lou Ellen smiled, her eyes glittering. "A little. But it would do everyone some good if you loosened up."

"Hmmm. Maybe." He shook his head. "I'm still not sure why she came to me, though."

Lou Ellen pushed away from his desk, frowning, as she headed for the door. "Let me tell you one thing that stuck with me from when Dereck was here." Son looked at her as she paused in the doorway. "You're ministering to the parents as much as you are the youth. And like the kids, often they just need someone to listen and see what is causing their worries."

* * *

Twilight was just creeping over the pasture when Vada finally came in from the barn. Regret had stayed stubbornly coiled in her stomach all day after her encounter with Mahalia. As she took her boots off in the kitchen, her mom shot her a reproachful look with a firm nod toward the back porch. Vada held up her hands. "I know, I know. I'm going."

She swung open the backdoor and stepped out. Mahalia sat on the porch swing, pushing herself back and forth with her toes as she stared at her phone.

Vada inhaled and walked over. "May I join you?"

"It's a free country." Mahalia didn't look up, but she halted her swinging.

Vada settled in beside her. "I wanted to apologize. And explain."

Mahalia rolled her eyes and finally looked up. "You don't want me around. What is there to apologize for?" She muttered, "I know when to take a hint."

Vada's heart throbbed as she looked at her young cousin, so often stranded by herself for days as a child. Left alone and unwanted. Her eyes filled as she thought of the dark, filthy apartment they'd pulled her from when they found out about her aunt's latest bender.

"I always want you around."

"Yeah right." Anger and hurt lit up Mahalia's eyes. "No one ever wants me around."

Vada bit back her retort about Carmel and Preston, and how she was forever dropping Mahalia off at their houses. She wasn't here to fight.

"I do! It was just this morning… You scared me."

Mahalia snorted as she tapped at her phone screen. "Didn't look like it."

"I was. I was scared that you were going to get hurt."

Lowering her phone, Mahalia stared at her, eyes narrowing and assessing. "You were mad."

"I was mad too," Vada admitted. "That you had ignored my rule. But under the mad, I was also scared. A panicking horse is unpredictable. You never know if they're going to run, kick, or bite to protect themselves."

"Ok. That still doesn't explain why you snapped at me." She glared at Vada. "You never want me around when you're working with the horses."

Suddenly, Vada knew what she needed to say. And surprisingly, she meant it. "I'm sorry about that." She nodded her head as Mahalia looked skeptically at her. "Really, I am. I was too harsh." She bit the inside of her cheek. "But I've been thinking that it's time I teach you to ride for real." Mahalia took in a sharp breath, her cheeks dimpling with questions. Vada raised a finger. "But you must listen to me and do things my way. I'm serious about horses being dangerous. I've gotten kicked at more times than I like to admit because I rushed something."

Mahalia's face lit up. "I promise!" she gushed. "I'll do everything you say."

It looked like Mahalia had forgiven Vada. She sank back against the swing. "All right. Set your alarm for four A.M."

"What?" Mahalia stared at her wide-eyed.

"I'm serious. If you're going to learn to ride, you do it my way. And my way starts at four A.M." Vada laughed as Mahalia groaned. The kid was getting more than she'd bargained for.

Chapter 8

The river sparkled before Vada in the early morning sunlight, lacy clouds of mist still rising from the water. The soft calls of herons and turtles echoed over the gurgle of the river, creating an achingly beautiful melody. Vada thrummed with excitement for today's fishing trip as she headed for the public restroom beside the boat launch. A day on the water sounded like heaven.

Especially after the early mornings trying to teach Mahalia how to ride. By the third day, her recalcitrant cousin had refused to roll out of bed. She'd begged Vada to teach her later in the afternoon, but with her work schedule at the Co-Op, Vada had no other options. Their ensuing spat had left the entire house silent and tense.

Vada eyed the rippling water, breathing in the cool, damp air in deep lungfuls.

Ray nodded at her from where he stood talking to Son, his face set in a sour wrinkle. As she shut the bathroom door, she hoped Ray would be nice to the kids. She wanted them to enjoy this excursion, not think of it as an exercise in torture.

The air in the single-stalled restroom had already grown stuffy, only a tiny window up at the eaves providing even a breath of air in the gloom.

Vada hurried to complete her business and get back to the group. Sitting on the toilet, she heard a soft pop and felt… something goopy… drip down her leg. Trying not to panic, she glanced down and peered closer at the mess. With a groan, she realized some prankster had wedged a twisted ketchup pack beneath the seat. Not as bad as it could have been, but her khaki shorts had an impossible stain on them.

Wiping away the mess as best she could, Vada turned to the sink and scrubbed at her shorts with a damp paper towel. She chunked the towel in the trashcan and stalked out of the restroom, frustrated by the stubborn splotch.

Lou Ellen's eyebrows shot up at the sight of her. Vada ground out, "Stupid prank." Lou Ellen wisely went back to her clipboard. Several yards away, a group of boys, Preston among them, snickered. Preston shot her a guilty look but turned back to his friends, while beside him, Mahalia giggled, and Carmel gaped at her in horror.

Son glanced her way, then paused, staring. Vada sighed. She had hoped he was one of the clueless guys and wouldn't notice her clothes. But it appeared she was wrong.

Trotting over, Son pulled his long-sleeved fishing shirt off and handed it to her, his Adam's apple bobbing. "Looks like you need this."

He stood in front of her in only a white, ribbed tank top, the muscles in his arms and shoulders highlighted in the sunshine. She gulped, trying not to stare. Holy biceps, Batman!

The girls stirred beside her, and Lou Ellen shot them a

disapproving look as they tittered. The boys stared at him in obvious envy.

Vada shook herself from her stupor and grunted out a chuckle as she glanced at the boys. She turned back to Son, forcing her eyes up to his, from his chest. "Hey! I make ketchup look good." She raised her arms in mock triumph, heat flaring through her cheeks. Had she just tried to flirt with the pastor... in front of the kids?

She swallowed her embarrassment as echoes of "ooh, burn" floated around them. One boy slapped Preston's shoulder. She narrowed her eyes at him, and he looked away. Beside her, Son muttered something that sounded suspiciously like, "You always look good."

She whipped back toward him, but he had already turned away to address the group. "We will talk about this." Preston shuffled and nodded hastily as Son pinned him with a stern look.

Vada laughed at his outrage, sweet as it was. "Why don't we get started? It's too beautiful a day to let a little prank spoil it." Son frowned at her but nodded his agreement. She bobbed her head at Ray, and he stepped forward to give the safety speech.

* * *

Son marveled at how nonchalant Vada was acting about the prank. If someone had ruined his clothes, he was sure he would have gone off in a fit of temper. Not exactly becoming a pastor, but it was the truth.

He shook himself. If Vada could be so easy-going about it, he could too.

As Ray finished his spiel on safety, Son stepped forward. "All right, everyone. Gather 'round!"

Reluctantly, the kids shuffled forward, elbowing each other and rolling their eyes. Son inhaled through his nose. "I have just a quick word today, and then we'll hit the river."

He pulled his phone out of his pocket and opened his notes app. "Let the heavens rejoice, let the earth be glad; let the sea resound, and all that is in it. Let the fields be jubilant, and everything in them; let all the trees of the forest sing for joy."

Finishing the Psalm, Son looked up. Around him, the kids had stilled. Vada watched him with one silky eyebrow arched and a bemused smile on her lips. "All of creation teaches us about God's wisdom and power." He swept his arm toward the river. "So, as we're on the water today, let's take a few minutes to pause and revel in God's joy at giving us such a glorious world to live in."

The kids stared at him, and he realized he needed something to end on. "I'm not going to keep us any longer. Think over this verse while we're out fishing today." He hefted his fishing pole, bought just this morning from Ray. "Now let's go!"

With a cheer, the kids headed to the water, happily jostling over their favorite kayaks. Vada patted him on the shoulder, her hand warm through his shirt. "Looks like you're learning." Her smile was kind as she headed for the water, and Son stared after her.

"She's something else," Lou Ellen quipped, smirking up at him.

"That she is." He grabbed his life jacket and headed toward a kayak. "Come on. Don't want to let the kids beat us onto the river."

Chapter 8

***

Vada watched from the corner of her eye as Son struggled to buckle up his life jacket. "Here." She reached over and untwisted a couple of buckles then cinched the straps with efficient tugs. "Now you won't come out of it."

"Thank you." He bent and tried to strap his fishing pole to the kayak, nearly shoving the boat into the river without him.

Vada snorted. "Not much of an outdoorsman, are you?"

He grinned up at her. "What gave it away?"

She snagged his kayak before the river current could catch it. "Just had a feeling." She looked back at her kayak and realized it was a two-seater. "Why don't you come with me? That way, if you tip over, you have someone to drag you back up."

"That sounds like a magnificent idea." He abandoned his kayak, Lou Ellen grabbing it with an eye roll as it tried to drift off again.

Vada laughed. "This should be interesting." After checking that Lou Ellen was settled in her kayak—she was an excellent paddler, she assured Vada—she turned her attention to helping Son get in their two-seater. Without tipping it.

She giggled as she held the boat steady while Son awkwardly straddled it and then plunked down into his seat. Double checking that their cooler and fishing rods were bungee corded on nice and tight, she lightly hopped into her spot.

"All right, this is how you hold a paddle." Son looked over his shoulder at her and clutched his paddle awkwardly. She shoved them off, and he gripped the gunwale, mouth tightening. "And this is how you use it." She pushed one end, then the other of her paddle into the water, propelling them smoothly into the river.

"Now you try." She watched as Son tentatively dipped his paddle into the water. "That's right. Make your strokes even." She encouraged him as they slipped further from the shore.

Dipping her paddle in, she matched her movements to his, steering them until they were parallel to the riverbank. Amused, she watched as Son slowly found the rhythm of paddling.

He glanced over his shoulder at her with a triumphant grin. "This isn't so bad."

"One of my favorite things to do." She smiled back at him as she navigated them around a submerged tree. Around them, the kids chattered, splashing each other and pointing out sights along the bank.

"Look, an alligator!" Son pointed to a large gator sunning himself on a nearby sandbar. His face crinkled adorably with excitement. "It's not going to come after us, will it?"

Vada laughed. "Probably not—we're too big and there's too many of us. We're safe in the kayaks either way."

They enjoyed a few companionable minutes in silence as Son looked around excitedly. "How do you know how to do all this?" he asked.

"Water sports were my favorite activity when I was at church camp." She couldn't help smiling at the memory. "I went every summer and I'd spend hours on the lake with my sister." Eve had sat in the bow of their canoe, content to let Vada have her way with paddling. She smiled at the memory.

"What was your favorite thing to do with your youth group?" she asked.

He made a face at her question, a small frown of embarrassment. "I didn't really... participate."

She looked at him in surprise. "Really? But you're a

preacher's kid."

He shifted in his seat, gently rocking the kayak. "My dad liked to keep me close. After my mom died. So, I didn't really hang out with the other kids in my group. Or do things like go to camp."

Her heart clenched for him, having spent his teenage years grieving and isolated. "Did you ever get to go to a sleepover?"

He laughed. "One time. But when my dad found out it was co-ed, he came and got me."

Vada winced at the humiliation. Being picked up early from a sleepover as a teen was a great way to become a social pariah. "Sounds awful."

"He meant well." Son shrugged. "He was never mean about any of it. Just a little intense."

His dad sounded a little controlling to Vada, but it also explained a lot of Son's stilted behavior. She considered the back of his head, with his close-cropped hair and sharp edges. She splashed him slightly with her paddle, and he spun to look at her. Holding out her hand, she grinned at him. "Hi! Welcome to camp. I'm Vada and I'll be your counselor over the summer!"

With a chuckle, he shook her hand, his voice rumbling over the water. "Are you going to show me the ropes?"

Her skin tingled at the suggestiveness of his question as he sputtered in embarrassment. "I'll introduce you to all the camp traditions I know." She tried to hide her smirk.

"Sounds like a plan!" He turned back to the river, a huge grin plastered over his face. Her heart sped up as she looked at him. She'd never expected to make friends with the pastor. This summer was going to be exciting after all.

Son scrambled across the sandbar, feet slipping on the small rocks that pebbled the area. Around him, kids splashed and shouted in the shallow elbow of the river, their voices echoing off the banks gleefully.

Ray sat in a camping chair in the middle of the sandbar, observing the frolicking kids. If Son wasn't mistaken, a smile ghosted across his lips before he caught Son looking at him. Occasionally, teens would slosh up onto the sandbar and dig into the coolers he had set out with Vada. For acting all grown up, he'd noticed that the teens happily wolfed down the Capri Sun pouches and peanut butter and jelly sandwiches. Son settled onto a smooth bit of sand and dangled his feet out into the cool river.

Spotting Preston, he waved the boy over to sit beside him. They had a couple of things to talk about. With a sideways glance at his friends, Preston jogged over and plopped down.

"Wassup, Pastor?" Preston stuck his feet out into the water.

Son was suddenly at a loss for words. How was he supposed to relate to a teenager when he'd barely been one himself? Swallowing hard, he went for honesty.

"Your mom dropped by my office the other day." Preston shifted away from him, his face horrified. Son held up a hand. "She's worried about you with your dad away so much. I told her I would do my best to be here for you, but I get it might not be cool to hang out with the preacher."

Preston shot a nervous look at his friends, who milled about in the shallows close by. He shook his long bangs over his face. "Nope."

"Look, I can't force you to spend time with me or listen to

me. But I wanted you to know, well, I get it. My dad wasn't… available… when I was your age. It's tough." He patted his shoulder. "And if you ever want to talk to someone—someone who won't judge—I'm here." He took a deep breath. "If I can offer you one bit of unasked advice: Don't take out how you're feeling on the parent that is there for you."

"But she's always on my case!" Preston burst out.

"I know. But she's only doing it out of love. Because she wants you to be all right." Son blinked as he thought of his own mom, sitting on the edge of his bed after a long day, speaking to him in her gentle voice. He softened his tone. "Being a teenager sucks. She's trying to figure out how to be a good Mom as much as you're trying to figure yourself out."

"Dad always knows…" Preston trailed off, looking over the river. Son's heart pinched at the look on his face.

"I'm not your dad, and I ain't trying to be. But if you let me, I'd be honored to be your friend." Preston looked him over skeptically. "Honest!" Son held up his fingers in the Scout's honor sign.

Bobbing his head, Preston stood. "Cool." As he turned to trot away, Son cleared his throat.

"Oh, and Preston?"

Preston looked back curiously.

"Keep an eye out for stray ketchup packets, will you?" Son quirked an eyebrow at him good-naturedly.

With a laugh, Preston bobbed his head and rejoined his friends. Son leaned back on his elbows as he watched over them. He wasn't sure if he'd made any impression on the boy. But at least Preston hadn't blown up or run away. And that was a start.

Vada looked over at the kids, laughing and jostling each other as they gathered beside the van. After a long day on the water, several bore bright red noses and cheeks, despite their efforts to make sure everyone reapplied sunscreen. Still, the teens smiled and joked with each other, happiness pervading the air.

All except for Mahalia. She sullenly came to stand by Vada, avoiding her gaze. It looked like Vada was deep in the hole with her this time. And she wasn't sure what to do about it. As she'd tried to make Mahalia understand the other night, her offer to teach her had been genuine. But her schedule left only early mornings available.

If Mahalia didn't want to get out of bed for that, then it was on her. Just as Vada's thoughts spiraled, Son called the group together, giving her a reprieve from her glowering.

She'd seen how he'd spoken with Preston at the sandbar and marveled when the teen didn't openly sass him. Preston was a good kid, but he'd recently hit a rough patch. She just hoped he wouldn't go too wild, for his own sake.

Son pulled the van keys from a zipper pocket in his shorts and called everyone together. He wore the same exultant expression as the teens. "All right, let's pray, and then we'll head home." Vada watched the kids shift, glancing at each other. "Anyone have a prayer request? Or thought from the day?"

After a long second of silence, Preston slowly raised his hand. "For my dad. That he'd be safe while he's traveling for work. And that he'll come home soon."

Mahalia shot an odd look at Vada and raised her hand.

"My... mom. That she'll be... ok." Vada reached over and squeezed her hand sympathetically. Mahalia shot her a look but let her hold on to her hand.

Vada did not know where her aunt was or what state she was in, and her heart skipped with worry. So many times they'd pulled her aunt from ratty apartments and abandoned houses, urging her to go to rehab. Each time, they'd failed to convince her. Not knowing anything about her mom had to be that much harder for Mahalia.

After a few seconds, Mahalia squeezed her hand back and then dropped it as she continued to stare straight ahead. With a sigh, Vada looked at the sky. Why did God make teenagers so difficult?

"Of course." Son interrupted her thoughts as he nodded at Preston and Mahalia. Tentatively, a few other kids raised their hands. Vada smiled as she watched them open up about everything from ailing family members to their worries over team tryouts at the end of summer.

Being here and seeing these kids grow made Vada hum with gratitude at the unexpected blessing. She glanced at Son as he instructed them to bow their heads. He winked at her, his face open and happy. As she closed her eyes, she offered her own silent thanks to God for this summer—and a certain handsome pastor.

Chapter 9

❧

S unshine, bright and hot, filtered through the tall sanctuary windows. A tepid stream of air blew from the vents, thanks to a congregant who had temporarily patched the air conditioner. Son dabbed at his brow before striding toward the pulpit. No matter how cool it was in the church, he always seemed to sweat through his shirt while preaching.

As he shuffled his notes, an unusual nervousness zipped through him at his lack of practice this past week. The youth group was taking more time than he thought it would.

He glanced out over the congregation and gripped the sides of the pulpit, calming his nerves. His eyes fell on Vada, seated between her parents and Willow a couple of rows back from the front. Her cheeks crinkled in a luminous smile as she returned his gaze. Reluctantly, he looked back at his notes as his heart sped up.

He cleared his throat. "Let us go before our Father in prayer." He opened the sermon with a request to watch over them and bless their work, and by the time he intoned "Amen," he felt completely at peace, as he often did when communing with God. He smiled out at his brothers and sisters and preached.

At the end of the worship, Son strode to the entrance of the church, where he stood shaking hands and visiting. As he said goodbye to Bo and Clay, out of the corner of his eye, he spotted Mrs. Langford headed his way. Several other mothers had visited his office this past week with "instructions" and complaints—an occurrence Lou Ellen assured him was just part of camp—but Mrs. Langford's unusual request had stood out.

His stomach growled in protest at what was sure to be a lengthy conversation. "Lou Ellen!" He grabbed her elbow as she passed him in the queue and drew her to stand next to him. He turned to her as if deep in conversation. She looked up at him, bemusement on her face.

In his peripheral vision, he watched Mrs. Langford hover, looking anxiously in his direction. Lou Ellen peaked at them over his shoulder. "I take it you don't really need anything from me?"

"Just a reprieve from the Mom Patrol." He swiped his handkerchief across his forehead.

Lou Ellen looked over his shoulder again. "You're in the clear." She smiled up at him.

He groaned in relief. "Thank you." With a chuckle, she slipped away. Before Lou Ellen had fully disappeared into the crowd, a light tap fell on his shoulder.

Traitor. He contemplated hiding the coffee pot from Lou Ellen as payback as he turned to face Mrs. Langford with a smile.

"Pastor, I hope you don't mind…" she stuttered. "I wanted

to say…" She huffed a breath and spit out, "What I mean is, thank you for speaking with Preston. He's listened to me a lot more this week. Whatever you said… it had an impact."

Son softened. He'd had no idea if his words had made any impression on the young man. He shot a quick thank you heavenward as he patted Mrs. Langford's shoulder. "Happy to help."

She twisted her hands together. "Would you mind…" With a flutter, she waved toward a gaggle of teens in the sanctuary's corner. Preston stood in the middle, laughing and holding court with his friends.

Son nodded, catching her meaning. "I'll keep an eye out for him. Don't you worry."

"Thank you!" With another odd little bob, she turned and pushed through the crowd. With a chuckle, Son slipped out the front door. He wished he could solve all problems with a simple conversation. But he put that thought aside as he hustled down the sidewalk to the tune of his growling stomach.

The meatloaf at Al's was calling to him.

* * *

Vada stood beside her parents in the parking lot, talking with the Nettles. Despite the loss of their barn, they were in remarkably good spirits.

"I can't tell you how much we've appreciated the meals everyone has brought us." Isabel, Hiram's wife, peered at Vada with a smile. "Almost like they're on a schedule."

"Almost." Vada grinned at her. She was happy to see her neighbors doing well.

Chapter 9

Mahalia ran up to them. "Can I go with Preston and Carmel to Cleveland for lunch?" She stared pleadingly at Waymond and Sacia.

"I don't see why not. Just keep your phone on you." Vada's mom nodded her approval. Mahalia darted off before she'd finished speaking.

"Her phone is the last thing we have to worry about." Vada chuckled as she watched her go. "She practically lives in that thing."

"Teenagers," Hiram agreed with a snort.

Since their fight, Mahalia had been distant with Vada, not speaking much and doing her best to not be in the same room. The avoidance worried her, and she'd voiced her concerns to her parents after dinner one night.

As she stared after her cousin, Vada couldn't help but feel that worry well up in her again. Her mom bumped her shoulder. "She'll be fine. Girl's gotta have some freedom."

"That's not what I'm worried about." She turned back to the group. "She's just seemed... off... the last few days."

"Who knows? Teenagers have so many ups and downs, it's impossible to keep track of them." Her dad shrugged. "You and your sister had your fair share of them."

"The important thing is to give her space and be available when she needs us," her mom added. They said goodbye to the Nettles and began walking slowly toward Al's for lunch.

"What if she thinks she doesn't need us?" Vada asked, worrying at her lip.

"She needs us." Her dad patted her back. "And we keep an eye on her. If anything major seems wrong, we'll be right there to intervene." He swung the door to Al's open and ushered them in.

Son glanced up from his menu as the bells on the door jingled. Vada's parents waved at him while Vada smiled. Lou Ellen's words about being such a loner hovered over his head, a heavy cloud. With a glance at his near-empty water glass, he decided he could use some company. He waved the Wilsons over with a smile.

"Care to join me?" He tried to sound nonchalant. The Wilsons glanced curiously at each other and at the packed restaurant. Then with a shrug, Waymond slid into the booth across from him.

"Thank you for having us."

His wife slid in beside him, leaving Vada to share Son's bench. He scooted over and patted the seat beside him. Sudden moisture coated his palms.

"What brings y'all to Al's today?" He tried to make conversation but found the words catching awkwardly in his throat.

Vada and Sacia exchanged a bemused look. "Lunch." Vada grinned at him as she picked up his menu.

He cleared his voice. "Of course. I just rarely see you in here on Sundays."

Sacia laughed. "We usually like to eat as a family on Sundays. But with all the extra work this week, well, I'll confess I did not make it to the grocery store in time for the weekend." She added, "But we wouldn't want to miss out on such a wonderful opportunity for Vada."

Beside him, he felt Vada shift on the bench. "Do you have enough room?" he asked.

She looked up at him, startled. "Plenty."

"I'm sorry I've upset your routine," he said, turning back to

Sacia.

Sacia peered at him, a smile playing about her lips. Vada looked so much like her mother that it astonished him. The same full lips and dark eyes, the high cheekbones, the twinkle in her eye. Mrs. Wilson was lovely, and Son could imagine Vada aging in the same soft way.

"It's good to shake things up now and then." She glanced at Vada, who shook her head with a laugh. "It keeps us moving and growing."

"The only thing that's growing right now is my hunger." With a glance at Son, Vada asked, "What are you getting?"

He chuckled. "My usual."

"What? Don't want to shake it up a bit?" Vada plunked her finger on the menu. "I'm getting the special of the day—the fried catfish." She smiled at him. "Treat myself a little."

His mouth watered at the thought of perfectly flaky catfish. He so rarely indulged in fried foods. "That sounds like a plan to me."

"Vada's been telling us all about your excursions together. Must be a lot to keep up with, with that many kids." Waymond leaned forward onto his elbows.

"Son's a natural. You should have seen him the other day with Preston—after the ketchup incident." Vada gestured with her hand to imaginary shorts. "Looked like y'all were having a good conversation." She glanced at Son, lips curved up. Warmth shot through his veins at her glance. He hadn't realized she'd been watching him.

"He's a good kid. Just needs a little sense talked to him now and then." Son swallowed as she nodded, her face lighting up in a smile as he held her gaze.

"Don't all teenagers?" Waymond chuckled and patted Vada's

arm. "This one certainly gave us a run for our money. With her sister, of course."

"Hey! I wasn't the ringleader," Vada protested, laughing.

"Oh, we knew that." Sacia waved a hand. "But where one of you went, the other one followed. That's why we always gave you both consequences."

Son laughed as Vada rolled her eyes. She was such a take-charge kind of lady. He could see how she would have been a strong-willed teen. He wished he had been around to know her then as he studied the side of her face, animated with laughter as she chatted with Sacia and Waymond.

As Mira bustled over to take their orders, he tried to ignore the way they looked back and forth between them. He was just having lunch with his co-worker. And her parents. He turned to scan the menu, stomach flipping. How had he not noticed the variety in here before?

As he stole one more glance at Vada over the top of the menu, he turned the conversation to Waymond's favorite foods, enjoying their bright company.

Chapter 10

⁓✦⁓

"The Fruit of the Spirit's not a coconut!" Son sang along with the teens in the van as they bumped over the gravel driveway leading to the Wilson's barn. The rowdy noises that accompanied each verse made him laugh with the kids as they imitated bananas, cherries, and various other fruits. If it would make learning about the Bible this fun for them, he'd put every verse into a song if he had to.

As they rounded a curve in the drive, the cheerful red barn rose into view, glowing in the morning light. Son's heart lifted as well. He had tossed and turned all night after running into Vada at Al's, the memory of her teasing smile haunting his fitful dreams.

They pulled up to the barn, and, as the kids spilled out of the van, Son looked around surreptitiously. He couldn't see Vada, but Cress and a glowing Ellie, hands sitting proudly atop her belly, came out of the barn with broad smiles on their faces. The kids crowded around them, chattering while Lou Ellen struggled to take roll behind them as they milled about.

Vada came out of the barn with a wave, Mahalia trailing behind her. With a rush, the teens surrounded her, peppering her with questions about the day's activities.

Son strolled over as nonchalantly as possible, and she touched his elbow in greeting while answering the kids. A pins and needles sensation shot up his arm and down his back, causing him to shiver despite the heat.

"All right, everybody! Remember your groups from last time? Good, group up!" Vada called the kids together immediately following Son's prayer. The first group trailed Ellie and Lou Ellen toward the barn for some "hands-on learning" with stable management.

Son trailed Vada and Cress towards a line of horses tied to the fence of a nearby corral. The ladies had already saddled all the horses, and Cress began going down the row double-checking straps and halters.

"Today, we're going to go on a trail ride!" Most of the kids cheered, but a few hung back, looking at the tall horses nervously. Son watched admiringly as Vada swung herself easily up onto a chestnut horse. In a few sentences, she told the kids how to sit as well as hold the reins, then walked her horse back and forth, showing them how to guide their mounts. "This trail is very easy, but if you hit a bumpy part, hold on to the pommel and squeeze with your knees. The reins won't help you hang on, and if you jerk on them, you will annoy your horse."

"These horses are familiar with the trail and should follow the guide." Vada patted the shoulder of her horse. "But if you need help, get the attention of me or Cress." Vada swung down from her horse and led him over to the fence, loosely wrapping the reins around it.

80

"Ok, pick your horse and get up by yourself if you can." The kids scrambled forward, bickering over who got which horse. Cress separated them with a stern point, and much calmer, they dispersed. Some scrambled up into the saddle while a few others made a couple of hopping tries before giving up.

Vada turned to Son. "You too, Pastor." She winked at him as she pointed at a horse farther down the line.

"I'm going with you?" Surprise rippled through him. He knew nothing about riding and would be more helpless on the back of the horse than the kids.

"It's your camp experience too!" She grinned and grabbed his shoulder and gently pushed him forward. "This is Clover. Your ride."

The horse she pointed him toward was even larger up close. With a snort, the horse turned her head and studied Son calmly with her mahogany-colored eyes. "Nice horse." Son patted his flank nervously. "We're ok."

He gripped the pommel, slipped his foot into the stirrup as he'd seen the first day, and heaved himself up. Out of breath from the climb, he panted from his spot atop the saddle. Clover shifted underneath him, and he clutched the pommel, trying not to whimper from terror. People did this for fun?

Around him, kids talked and laughed, calling out to each other. Cress and Vada worked down the row, adjusting stirrups and untying reins. When Vada got to him, she smiled up at him. "You've got it!"

He muttered, "Sure doesn't feel like it."

"That's just because your stirrups are too long." She fiddled with something on his saddle then slid his foot into a stirrup with a pat. "Now, the other side." As she finished, he had to admit that he felt much more stable now. "Now you can ride this ole girl as long as you want to." Vada froze, hand still on his foot, and bit her lip.

Son chuckled softly. Her huge, dark eyes glanced up at him, wide at his laughter. He shrugged. "A pastor can have a sense of humor."

"You're the first I've met."

He held her gaze. "You should get out more."

"I'll take that into consideration." Her eyebrows arched as she stepped back, releasing his foot. His ankle was suddenly cold despite the summer heat as she walked away.

A few seconds later, Vada's whistle drew everyone's attention to where she sat on her horse. "All right, gently turn your horse's head toward me and give them a light tap with your heels." She clicked her tongue at her horse and turned him to a faint opening in the trees several yards away. With a lurch, Son's horse turned and followed Vada, falling into line several horses back from her.

His heart skipped as she disappeared into the trees, his horse following a few seconds later. Ducking his head under the low branches, Son sucked in a breath as they emerged onto a well-worn trail, majestic trees arching overhead.

Beneath him, Clover plodded along at a sedate pace, calmly following the tail of the horse in front of her. Before and behind him, he heard the kids exclaim as they looked around at the shady forest. As birds chirped around them and leaves rustled in the wind, the serenity of the trees washed over Son. Now he understood why some people were so crazy about riding.

The only thing that could make this better was if he were riding closer to Vada, so they could laugh and joke as they did on the river. He studied the distance between them. Mahalia,

Preston, and Carmel talked to each other from the tops of their mounts, their laughter echoing back to him.

Carmel's horse, just behind Vada, lifted its tail. A smelly pile of poop hit the ground, clods rolling everywhere. "Oh, man! Gross!" Mahalia and Preston pressed hands over their noses and made gagging sounds.

"Hey! Be polite." Son admonished them with a grin. They turned around and stared at him, disbelief on their faces. "After all, that's the flies' dinner and you don't want to insult them."

For a second, he stared at their blank faces, fearing his joke had fallen flat. Then Vada's laugh rang out, and the kids doubled over their pommels, giggling. With a smile, he patted Clover and drank in the beautiful day, fully content.

"All right, everybody!" Vada called out. "We're about to cross a small stream. Hold tight to your horses and let them work their own way across."

Son could just see the burbling water that lay ahead through the trees. Nervousness flittered through his stomach, but he gripped the reins and sat up straighter. If the kids could do this, he could too. Carmel and Mahalia crossed with no problem, water dripping from the ends of their horses' tails. With a sigh, Son realized the stream wasn't deep. However, Preston's horse stopped and bent its nose to the rippling surface.

"Ummm…" Preston called out. "Vada, what should I do?"

Son's horse stepped into the water, skin quivering and flinching at the cold. Slowly, Clover worked her way forward until she was even with Preston's mount. Suddenly, the world heaved, and Son felt weightless as he pitched over his horse's shoulder, feet flying above him.

Miraculously, he landed butt first in the stream, unscathed.

Clover stood nearby, placidly sniffing the water around her hooves. The only thing that was hurt was his dignity. And his butt. It ached from smacking into the silty bottom of the streambed.

A splashing resounded nearby, and Vada trotted up to him, eyes squinched in concern. "You a'ight?" Her voice was light, but as she glanced at the kids and horses lined up on the bank, he realized she was doing her best to keep everyone calm. Murmurs ran through the group as Cress trotted up to investigate all the commotion.

Son heaved himself to his feet, water streaming from his back. "Fit as a fiddle," he replied to Vada. Since when did he talk like a cowboy?

Vada reached over and snagged Clover's reins, which drug in the water. "Good, good." She offered the reins to him. "We're about a mile up the trail and have four more to go." She pointed at his soaked clothes. "Can't say either way would be comfortable."

The kids watched them intently. "I'll hike back." The thought of damp clothes rubbing him... places... atop the saddle made him wince.

"Just stay on the trail and you'll head straight to the barn. Ask my dad for a change of clothes. Y'all are about the same size." She wrapped Clover's reins around her pommel. "And watch out for roots. Tripping is a real hazard on this trail."

He nodded and began sloshing his way out of the stream. The kids stayed quiet as he passed them with a nod. Their sober faces nagged at him. Something was off. As he passed Cress, she offered him a mock salute, trying to hide her smile. *That* was more of what he expected.

With one last look behind at the kids, still staring after him, he shrugged and headed into the trees, picking up the bridle path. If he made good time, he'd be back to the house in fifteen, twenty minutes tops.

* * *

Hiking back had not been a good choice. Son's armpits and undercarriage stung where the damp clothes rubbed back and forth across his skin. Thanks to the Mississippi summer humidity that kept his clothes soaking wet the entire way back, he was pretty sure he had blisters in unmentionable places.

As he emerged from the trees into the sunlight, he spotted the barn and the house beyond it with relief. Limping along, he beelined to the barn. Inside, voices rang out, teasing each other. Waymond spotted him immediately as he entered the cool shade of the building.

"Looks like you had a bit of an incident." Waymond pulled his hat off and scratched at his salt and pepper hair as he studied Son's bedraggled state.

Son tried his best not to glare. "You could say that." He wiped at some sweat beading on his upper lip. "Wouldn't happen to have some clothes you could loan me?"

Waymond waved for him to follow, and gritting his teeth against the burn, Son obeyed, trying to not walk bow-legged.

As soon as they were out of earshot of the kids, Waymond turned to him with a glimmer in his eye. "Can't imagine you're real comfortable, soaked like that."

Son winced. "My... bits are screaming at me."

Waymond chuckled. "Don't worry. I think we got some chafe powder somewhere."

"Oh, thank God." Son hurried after him. The clothes

Waymond offered him were a basic white t-shirt and some basketball shorts, but they were clean and dry and that was all that mattered to Son. As he stepped out of the bathroom, he looked around the Wilson's house curiously. He hadn't paid any attention to the two-story farmhouse on the way in, but he perused the portraits on the wall on his way down the stairs.

He paused at a picture of a teenage Vada, braids tumbling around her shoulders. Next to her in the photo was another teenage girl with the same wide grin. He stared, fascinated by the happiness glowing in their eyes, their arms wrapped around one another. Whenever she was still, Vada's eyes took on a melancholy gleam that was nothing like the happy child he saw here.

A cough made him look up. Sacia smiled and climbed the stairs, stopping beside him. She looked at the photo fondly. "My two girls." She touched the edge of the frame. "They were inseparable."

"Vada told me about her." He cleared his throat. "She looks lovely. I'm sorry I never got to meet her." Too many Delta towns suffered their adult children moving away and never coming back. But to lose a child to something as senseless as cancer had to sting even more. A sudden fierceness filled him as he thought of Midnight Bluff Baptist's youth group, bubbling with vitality and joy. He would do anything to protect that peace.

Sacia shook her head, mouth turning down into a frown. "Eve was lovely inside and out. Sometimes, I think she was too lovely to stay on earth and that's why God sent the cancer." She shook her head. "Other days, I wonder if there is a God."

He touched her shoulder, compassion pouring through him.

"I am so sorry. No parent should ever lose a child."

Wiping at her eyes, Sacia sniffed, then smiled at him. "I'm all right. I'm sure my sentiments are nothing new." She sighed. "As much pain as it brings me, my daughter's suffering is over. It's Vada I worry about." She swallowed. "After Eve died, Vada... lost her bearings."

Son nodded his head for her to continue. She waved a hand toward the barn. "Eve and Vada had big plans to run an equestrian school together. But with Eve gone, Vada has floundered. She's a wonderful teacher, but she doesn't take on any students unless we force her to. She mostly boards and trains local farmers' horses." She swiped at her nose. "I haven't seen her this lit up about something in a long time."

Sacia touched his elbow. "Thank you for giving me my little girl back."

Son swallowed against the knot in his throat. "It's not me. I didn't know..."

She waved away his denial. "Whether or not you knew, the effect is the same. And I'm grateful."

Something nagged at Son. He looked outside, considering the bustling kids. Vada was more than capable. The problem wasn't anything external holding her back, but an inner hindrance. When they'd met, she'd seemed so doubtful that he needed *her* skills. "Maybe she's afraid to take a chance. That if she fails, she's failing not just herself or you. But her sister too."

Sacia paused. "That could be." Tapping her fingers on the banister, she pursed her lips. "Her father and I have spent so much time just trying to be there for her that perhaps we've forgotten to encourage her to really live. She has so much more in her than this... holding pattern." A line formed between her brows.

Son's heart pinched. The Wilsons had been through an impossibly painful loss yet were still so dedicated to each other. "Maybe she just needs to know that no matter what, everything will be ok."

Sacia nodded, her eyes thoughtful. They turned toward the front door together. She glanced over her shoulder at him as they descended the stairs. "You won't tell her? What I said?"

"A pastor always keeps confidences." Son smiled at her as they stepped out into the afternoon light.

* * *

As their group emerged from the trail behind the barn, Vada took a deep breath in through her nose, letting her pent-up anxiety flow out of her. They'd made it with no other mishaps.

Cress galloped up to her as the kids made appreciative noises. "Look at her go!" "I want to do that!"

Vada swung around. "Y'all have a long way to go before you're ready to gallop a horse like that."

They quieted, faces falling in disappointment, and she felt compelled to add, "But it's easy to learn. Just keep practicing."

Mutters echoed behind her. "But we only ride here…"

Vada ignored the twinge of guilt between her shoulder blades as she turned to Cress. "Everything good at the rear of the line?"

"No problems at all!" Cress patted her horse's neck. "This girl is steady as a rock. And she keeps the horses around her calm, too."

Something nagged at the back of Vada's mind. She'd picked her own horse and Son's as well for the same reason. Which made Clover's unexpected bucking of Son that much weirder. "I'll have to check Clover over tonight. Make sure she doesn't have a rock in her shoe or something." She swiped at her sweaty forehead. "Do you see anything off about her gait?"

"Not at all." Cress studied the sedate chestnut mare tied to Vada's pommel. "If it's not her shoe, then something must have spooked her."

With a glance over her shoulder, she caught Preston eyeing them. He looked away quickly when Vada turned toward him. If something was up, he would be the ringleader. She was certain of it.

But for now, there was nothing to do except get these horses to the barn and the kids off safely. As they trotted into the barn, Son emerged from one stall, pitchfork in hand, and a smile on his face. Doing a double take as she rode past, she glanced at the stall behind him, a pleasant thrill of surprise running through her at its clean interior. After his splash in the creek, she wouldn't have blamed him if he'd just sat in the shade to relax. As her eyes swept back over him, she had to admit to herself, he looked good in a white t-shirt stretched tight over his muscles. Around them, kids buzzed in and out of various areas, toting hay and dragging the water hose.

Vada slid down from Cinnamon and tied her outside her stall. She eyed its spotless interior with clean hay already on the ground, another product of Son's handiwork. "If I'd known you were this good of a stable hand, I'd have hired *you* a long time ago."

Son's laugh did something to her insides, like a mix between a warm hug and indigestion. "You can put me to work anytime." He rested an elbow on the pitchfork. "Honestly, it's a pleasant change of scenery from my desk."

"Hey, don't tempt me. I'll take all the free labor I can get."

He grinned at her. "As long as you keep giving me popsicles, I'm yours."

Vada smirked. "Sorry, all out of popsicles." She pulled a cooler from the tack room, where she'd stashed it earlier. "Will an ice cream sandwich work?" Holding up a box with a white bear on it, she waggled her eyebrows.

His eyes lit up. "I loved these as a kid!" As he bit eagerly ripped off the silvery wrapping of the sandwich she handed him, Vada snickered at his adoring gaze at the sweet treat.

Behind him, Ellie paused with a wide grin on her face. She made a heart with her hands and pointed at them. Cress joined her making a puckered-up face. Vada waved them off.

Son glanced up. "Everything all right?"

"Fine," she lied, turning her wave into a fanning motion. "Just a pesky fly."

* * *

Vada ran her hands over Clover's smooth side, lifting each hoof gently to check it for rocks, cuts, and inflammation. She stood looking at Clover in the dim evening light of the barn.

The echo of footsteps behind her made her look. Mahalia stepped up onto a slat of the railing but didn't enter. She eyed the horse quizzically.

"What are you doing?" She draped her torso over the top of the rail.

Vada paused a second then waved her into the stall. With a grin, Mahalia hopped down and swung the door open. Vada slid her hand along Clover's back, checking for… burs, pulled muscles? She wasn't sure what she was looking for, exactly.

90

"I'm trying to see if anything could have caused Clover to buck Pastor Riser off."

Mahalia stood at her elbow. "I thought it was just one of those freak things."

"Definitely could have been. But anytime a well-behaved horse acts strangely, it behooves us to take a closer look."

"Behooves?" Mahalia teased.

Vada swatted at her. "Smart aleck." She turned back to Clover. "Here, let me show you what I'm doing."

For the next several minutes, Vada walked Mahalia through checking over a horse. As she showed her Clover's clean hooves, healthy teeth, and strong back, she watched in approval as Mahalia drank it all in.

Stepping back, she watched Mahalia pet and whisper to the horse with a glow of pleasure. But she still had no idea what had caused the day's fiasco. And that worried her.

Chapter 11

Vada trudged into the kitchen the next morning, wrapped in her terry cloth robe. For once, she felt well-rested despite the drowsiness still clouding her eyes. Beelining to the coffeepot, she poured herself a huge mug of the nectar of the gods.

As she sighed in happiness, her mom, sitting at the counter, piped up. "Now that you've got your morning caffeine, can I talk to you about something?"

Vada glared at her mother over her mug as she took another sip. Her family knew not to disturb her in the mornings until she'd had her first cup. In its entirety. With a *thunk*, she set the mug down. "Depends on what it is."

"Maybe it's time to let all this go." Her mom waved a hand toward the barn. "I'm afraid that all this—what you and Eve created together—is causing you to stay stuck in the past. Is this even what you want, or are you just holding onto Eve's dream?"

"But this is my dream too!" Vada sucked in a panicked breath.

"Can't you see…" she trailed off, realizing that she'd felt more alive these few weeks than she had in years. And it was all because she took one phone call. Hearing her mother's doubts clicked the last piece of a broken mirror back into place. She could finally look at herself and what she wanted.

Vada rubbed a hand across her forehead, considering what her mother had said. And, if she were honest with herself, that she was afraid. Afraid of what life looked like without the sister she adored, her partner in crime, her best friend. But it was time to brave and live the life that she'd found herself in.

"I want this. Really."

Her mother frowned at her, not convinced. "Then why aren't you doing anything to keep it going? Beyond this…" she bobbled her head. "…Windfall?"

Vada rubbed at her eyes. Her parents had put off retiring and moving to the mountains for years to support her "startup phase." That support had been not only letting her use their land for free but had also meant putting them to work as stable hands. And she'd totally neglected to safeguard their trust in her by pushing the equestrian school to the back burner.

"Things are looking up." Vada wrapped her fingers around her mug to still their trembling. Knowing what she wanted and knowing how to pursue was different.

"That's not enough, sweetheart, and we both know it." Her mom stood and walked over to her. She reached out and rubbed Vada's arms. "It takes more than blind luck to run a business. If you don't start pursuing… What I'm trying to say is. We want what is best for you. And this limbo you're in…" She shook her head. "It has to end. One way or another." She took a breath. "Your father and I have decided that if you haven't made some serious progress in getting steady revenue by December… we're going to sell the farm."

"You can't!" Vada gasped. She clutched the mug to her chest. Now that her mother had laid matters out so starkly, she trembled at the thought of losing her lifelong dream. "You promised—"

"You promised too. We've been more than fair."

Vada swallowed at her mother's words. How could she get the equestrian school going again? And with only half the year left?

"Sweetheart, it's not that we don't want you to succeed like we know you can. But it's been five years. And you're still not giving this your all." Her mom waved her hand. "Sometimes, I think you're trying to fail."

"I just… I don't know how to do this by myself," Vada whispered.

"No one knows how to go after their dreams until they start." Her mom pulled her into her arms, smelling of shea butter and vanilla. "We just want to see you start."

"Ok," Vada murmured against her mother's shoulder. "I'll try." She couldn't imagine a world where she got her dream while Eve was… gone. But as she thought of the barn and the rolling pasture with horses grazing placidly in it, plowed under by some farmer, she knew it was time to act.

Resolve steeled in her chest, straightening her back. She wouldn't lose the school. She owed it not only to Eve but to herself to see it thriving.

The only problem was that she still didn't know how.

* * *

Vada parked her truck outside the Co-Op. Somehow, even on

her day off, she'd ended up here. But she needed sweet feed for the horses and her mom needed a bird net for the garden. So here she was.

Slamming the truck door behind her, she loped into the Co-Op, determined to get in and get out before Lewis spotted her and put her to work. Like he was her boss or something.

Vada had rounded the end of the gardening aisle when she nearly ran over Mayor Patty.

"Goodness, child. You scared the living daylights out of me." Mayor Patty pressed a hand to her chest.

"Sorry, Patty." Vada tried to slide by her. The bird net was a few more steps down the aisle.

"Vada…" Mayor Patty's smooth tone made Vada halt. She turned to see what the mayor wanted. "You wouldn't happen to know the best fertilizer for tomatoes, would you? I'm bound and determined to beat Leora at the Fall Festival this year."

Exhaling, Vada pointed at a bag on the shelf. "The Dr. Earth fertilizer ought to do the trick. It has more available micronutrients in it than the Miracle Grow that Ms. McBride uses. And it's extended release so you don't have to re-fertilize as often." She ran her tongue over her teeth. "But if you really want to supercharge your tomatoes, get some bags of the Black Cow fertilizer we have outside in the garden center."

"Could I use both together?"

Vada thrust her hands into her pockets. She was not escaping Mayor Patty anytime soon. "You can, but I'd go easy on the granules in that case. Too much is not a good thing when it comes to gardening."

"You always know best, Vada." Mayor Patty grabbed the bag. "I'll get some of both." She looked expectantly at Vada. With a groan, Vada led her to the register, rang in, and totaled her up.

"Take this ticket to the loading dock and they'll put it in the back of your car for you."

Dewayne watched them, clearly annoyed that Vada was horning in on his shift. She didn't have time for his theatrics when she hadn't even punched in.

"Oh, Vada." Mayor Patty turned on her heel and faced her again. "The Business Chamber is meeting tomorrow night at the courthouse to welcome all the new businesses in town and explain the perks of membership. You should join us."

Vada's mind spun to her mother's words. This could be her first step: becoming a Chamber member. "I'll see you there." Vada turned to ring herself off the register.

"Oh, and Vada."

"Yes, Patty?"

Mayor Patty stood, squeezing her bag of fertilizer with one arm and clenching the strap of her purse with the other. Vada looked at her more closely. "What is it, Patty?"

"It's not my place… but I think you should know." Mayor Patty closed her mouth and shook her head. "You should know that Sheriff Swales has had to run a group of teens away from the quarry several times."

Vada rubbed a hand over her mouth. She had nearly drowned in the quarry as a teen—it was a popular swimming hole because of the rainwater that collected in a deep blue pool along its bottom. Vada had been a victim of the sudden drop-off in the middle until Eve, the stronger swimmer, pulled her out. "And I can assume Mahalia was with them?"

"That would be a good assumption." Mayor Patty nodded. "Like I said, looking after other people's kids isn't my place. But if she was my cousin… I'd want to know."

"Thank you, Patty." She fumed as the mayor walked away.

How many times had Vada warned Mahalia not to go near the quarry? How many times had she told her about the crumbling cliffs, submerged equipment, and sheer drop-off? And Mahalia had straight-up ignored her, putting her own life in danger. She jabbed at the register, signing out her code.

As she stepped out of the Co-Op into the sunshine, Vada looked up and down the quiet street. Her anger simmered lower. As picturesque as it was, Midnight Bluff was a sleepy, boring place to grow up. There was simply nothing to do for kids during the summer, outside of the church's camp. She could understand why Mahalia was drawn to the quarry.

But that didn't make her foolish decision better. She dialed Mahalia's cell and listened to it ring for what felt like an eternity before she hung up.

As the noon sun blazed overhead, Vada squinted down the road. Mahalia always had her phone glued to her hand. If Mahalia wasn't answering, then she was probably avoiding Vada. Or where she couldn't answer it. Like if she was out swimming.

With a huff, she cranked her truck and headed past the town limits toward the quarry.

* * *

Son stared at the stack of applications on his desk for the youth minister position and rubbed at his thigh. It was depressingly small. And he was still ridiculously sore from his abbreviated trail ride then mucking out stalls yesterday. With a sigh, he began spreading the papers out, ignoring the protest in his muscles. He'd eliminate the obvious stinkers and go from there. Tonight, he could work on stretching out his kinks.

To his dismay, not a single candidate met his expectations. They either lacked experience, were obviously looking for a chance to "climb the ladder," or wanted an exorbitant salary. None of them were suitable. He propped his head on his hand and stared at the papers spread before him as his favorite jazz album hummed behind him.

A knock on the door drew his eyes up. Lou Ellen stood frowning in the entryway. "Mrs. Langford just called again about Preston. Apparently, Sheriff Swales is concerned."

"What am I supposed to do about that?" Son groaned as he leaned back in his chair. He talked to the teen as much as he could at camp, but he simply didn't see what they expected him to do on the off days.

Lou Ellen tapped her nails on the doorframe. Today they were bright blue with little white polka dots. "I heard that..." She bit her lip.

Son sighed and tilted his chair back down. "What did you hear?"

"I heard Sheriff Swales has been having to run a bunch of kids off from swimming at the quarry." She crossed her arms and leaned against the doorframe.

"And why is that a problem?" He knew nothing about the quarry. His eyes widened in surprise as Lou Ellen described the dangers of the popular swimming hole.

"Snap." He stood from his desk, reaching for his keys. "They're going to get themselves killed." He paused. "Where is this place again?"

Lou Ellen scribbled out instructions using his notepad and handed them to him. With a nod of thanks to her, he rushed out of the church.

He shook his head as he zipped down the road, looking for

the unmarked turnoff by a lightning-struck oak tree in Lou Ellen's directions. Of all the things he'd imagined doing as a preacher, corralling empty-headed teenagers had never made the list.

Chapter 12

V ada eyed the small cluster of beat-up trucks and four-wheelers parked around her. She headed toward the path that wound down the steep cliff to the water just as the crunch of tires sounded behind her. Expecting more boneheads to be arriving, she turned to give them a good talking to.

Instead, Son's dust-covered sedan slid into the space next to her truck. He popped out, his white button-down blazing in the afternoon sun, and gave her a quizzical look.

"What are you doing here?" she asked.

"Probably the same as you." The slam of his car door echoed around the small gorge as he strode over to look down the cliff where kids played in the foggy water below. "Figured I'd try to head some trouble off."

"Amen to that." She began walking down the trail, gravel crunching underfoot. "You comin'?" With a snort, he hurried after her. She eyed his shiny leather shoes. "Not exactly the best footwear for this."

"Didn't know I'd be hiking when I headed out." He glanced over at her with a smile. Light filtered through the young trees shading the path. Reaching out, Vada steadied herself against one as they clambered over an especially treacherous switchback.

Vada gestured down the trail, surprised he'd risk his expensive shoes on a few kids. "This is about half a mile before we get to the water."

"What are a few more blisters?" He shrugged as he grabbed a limb above their heads and swung himself down.

Eyes on the uneven terrain, Vada listened to the quiet huff of his breath behind her. Son never stopped surprising her with his willingness to help those around him. Even a bunch of idiotic teenagers.

"If it's such a hazard, why hasn't this place been fenced off?" Son panted out.

Vada shrugged as she stepped over a log and eyed a swath of kudzu covering the path in front of her. "There was a fence that fell down a couple decades ago. Since then…" She lifted her hands in a questioning gesture. "Lack of funds. No one cares that much. Plain, old negligence. Take your pick." She gingerly tested the ground as she worked through the kudzu. "Besides the company responsible for this mess is long gone."

"Ah," Son grunted as his foot slid and finally caught on a slick spot. "Still seems like someone should do something about it."

Turning to glance at him, Vada shook her head. "Wouldn't matter. The Delta is riddled with spots like this from before land conservation practices were in place." She sighed as they scrambled down a relatively clear section of the trail. "If not here, then people would just go to older, more remote places to swim." Places where it would be even harder to get help when someone inevitably got hurt.

"I see." Son clambered down behind her, barely stopping himself from slamming into her with his broad chest.

She steadied him, her hands on his shoulders, before quickly pulling away, her breath coming even faster. Trying to put the muscly, panting man behind her out of her mind, she spotted the end of the trail with relief.

As they emerged onto the small, rocky beach, breathless and sweating, Vada drank in the sight before them. Half a dozen teenagers stood in front of them, staring at them in varying states of shock. Out in the cloudy blue water, the whooping and hollering died down. A quiet, "Oh shit," echoed through the quarry.

Son stood behind Vada, his arms crossed. A twinge of gratefulness for his solidarity flitted through her before she planted her hands on her hips and stared them down. "I heard *from the sheriff* that a bunch of hooligans was risking their necks out here."

It wasn't exactly true, but Patty had heard it from the sheriff, so it also wasn't exactly a lie. She spotted Mahalia, floating a few yards from shore, and pinned her with a furious glare. "And those hooligans are about to be in a world of trouble if they don't clear out right now."

The teens spun into motion, clothes flapping and coolers slamming as they scrambled past Vada and back up the hill. Mahalia waded out of the water, a scowl on her face.

"How could you!" she shouted, her face contorted with rage. "You're embarrassing me!" Water slung off her arms as she shoved her feet into sandals and pulled her shirt over her head.

"Truck, now!" Vada pointed sternly toward the trail. If

Mahalia tried to fight her now, she was pretty sure she was going to combust into a cloud of steam.

"I have permission…"

"…To be at Carmel's!" Vada shouted over her. How dare she try to pull that flimsy excuse with her? "Not risking your neck to hang out at *the one place* I specifically told you *not* to go!" Spit flew from her lips as her chest heaved.

Mahalia froze, shocked as Vada screamed at her. As much as she and Vada fought, Vada had made a point never to shout at her. Carmel stood behind Mahalia, nervously rubbing her elbow as Vada and Mahalia stared at each other. Preston shook the water out of his hair on the other side of Mahalia, the dynamic trio alternating between shades of worry and anger.

"You won't tell my parents, will you?" Carmel crossed her arms, anxiety on her face. Preston shot a nervous glance at Son and then back at Vada. They were all in deep trouble and they knew it.

Of course, Vada was going to tell the girl's parents. With another point, she ordered them up the hill, completely done with this nonsense. They climbed in silence, the only sound birds twittering mockingly in the distance.

They puffed out into the clearing at the trailhead, the crowd of cars already dispersing. Vada put a hand on Mahalia's shoulder to steer her toward the truck. With a violent shrug, Mahalia shook her off, scowl still in place.

Son cleared his throat. "I'll take Preston home if you've got the girls?"

Vada nodded, and Son waved at Preston to follow him, leaving the clearing eerily quiet. With a huff, Mahalia climbed into the truck and slammed the door. Rolling her eyes and praying for a miraculous amount of self-control, Vada held her door open for Carmel to clamber up onto the bench seat.

The silence clung to them as they sped down the road, each lost in their own thoughts.

* * *

The crunch of gravel echoed through Son's car as he carefully navigated around potholes. Preston glanced at him sidelong like a spooked horse preparing to bolt. Lost for what to say, Son let the silence hang.

Finally, as the edge of town appeared before them, Preston burst out, "Are you going to tell my mom?"

Son exhaled thoughtfully. "No. At least not right now." This could really backfire on him.

Eyes wide, Preston stuttered, "Why?"

Son chewed at his bottom lip and considered the co-ed sleepover mishap of his teens. "Because I remember what it was like to be your age. And how I wished for a little understanding when I made mistakes."

Preston wrinkled his nose but remained silent. Gripping the steering wheel tighter, Son explained, "Look, we both know you're not supposed to be at the quarry. More importantly, I'm sure you know *why*."

"Nothing's ever happened!" Preston looked out the window sullenly.

"Yet. Nothing's happened yet." Son sighed. An idea came to him as they passed one of the sidewalk improvement sites. "Think of it like walking through a construction zone without a hard hat… or the foreman and crew even knowing you're there." He pointed at a backhoe reversing beside a ditch.

104

"They're not going to be looking out for you. And, yes, you might dash through a couple times unharmed, but you're taking a colossal risk."

"The quarry isn't like that. We were just having some fun." Preston muttered. "This crappy town is so boring."

"C'mon man, use your head." Son huffed, his chest tightening at the thought of his kids getting hurt. Were all teenagers this mulish? "I'm not trying to take a bit of fun away from you. But I'd be giving you this same speech if you'd been exploring a rundown building or lighting off old fireworks."

Preston stared at his hands. "Are you just saying all of this because my mom asked you to?"

With a start, Son realized this was more important to him than keeping a promise to a congregant. "I was at first. You're scaring the bejeezus out of her." Preston looked down, the tips of his ears reddening. "But I care about you too. Not like your mom or dad. But I don't want to see you get hurt. And I'll do what I can to keep that from happening—even at the risk of annoying you."

He looked over at Preston, whose brows wrinkled in consideration. "So, I'll make a deal with you. I won't tell your mom—this time. Because I'm going to trust you to make better decisions about the fun you have in the future. Deal?"

With a nod, Preston agreed. "Deal." He sat for a minute as Son pulled up outside his house. "I don't understand why you would do this though. Don't you have better things to do?"

"Nothing is more important to me than your safety." Son hit the "unlock" button. "Not even one of my snooze-fest sermons." He grinned at the boy, and Preston smiled back at him.

"See ya around, Pastor!" Preston swung out of the car with

the sort of carefree lope only the young and unburdened have. Son chuckled as he watched him run into the house. Kids never changed.

* * *

The windows in the entire house shook as Mahalia slammed the door closed. Slamming it right into Vada's nose as she followed her up the steps and across the porch.

With a snort, Vada twisted the handle and swung the door open. "You're not getting away from me that easily!"

"Just let me go!" Mahalia spun as she stomped up the stairs. "We both know you don't want me around anyway, so just let me go!"

Vada stood, gobsmacked, one foot on the bottom stair. With a click, she shut her open mouth. "What on earth are you talking about?"

"Girls!" Vada's mom stood in the doorway to the sunroom, a thunderous expression on her face. "What in tarnation is going on?"

"Vada's sticking her nose in my business again!" Mahalia balled up her fists on her hips.

Vada rolled her eyes. "It's my business if you get yourself killed being stupid."

"You had no—"

"Stop." Vada's mom held up her hands, her voice ringing out. "I want to know what happened and I want to know it now."

Mahalia crossed her arms and stared at Vada, triumph on her face. "Vada embarrassed me in front of my friends for no reason."

Her mom nodded and turned to Vada, waiting. Grinding her teeth together, Vada counted to five before she spoke. She was the adult in this situation; she couldn't sound like a bratty teenager herself. No matter how much she wanted to shake some sense into Mahalia.

"I heard from Mayor Patty who heard from the sheriff that kids were swimming out at the quarry. Apparently…" She cut her eyes over to Mahalia. "…They've been sneaking out there a lot this summer." Swinging her arm toward her cousin, she continued. "And that's exactly where I found this one after she didn't answer her phone."

Her mom frowned, nose flaring, as she stared down at her bare toes silently. A twinge of guilt shot through Vada as she realized they had disturbed her one peaceful afternoon with this idiocy. Looking up, her mother enunciated slowly. "Mahalia, give me your phone and go to your room. Stay there until I tell you otherwise."

"But…" Mahalia fidgeted.

"No buts or you will lose your phone for the rest of the summer." A flinty look flashed through her mom's eyes as she looked at the now-cowed teenager. With a huff, Mahalia slapped the phone into her hand and bounded up the stairs with a glare at Vada.

Vada turned to her mother, cringing. Any second now, she expected a torrent of words to crash down on her head as they used to when she and Eve fought.

Instead, her mother wiped her hands slowly over her face with a groan. "I need some tea. Want some?"

Suspicious, Vada followed her to the kitchen and watched as she opened the fridge and poured glasses of sweet tea. "No lecture for me? That I should keep a better eye on her?

Handled things differently?"

Her mom pressed a cold glass into her hand, her eyes meeting Vada's tiredly. "No." She took a long sip from her own glass. "You're an adult, Vada. And while your tone could use some work..." A small smile lifted the corners of her lips. "...You did the right thing. We've told her a half-dozen times to stay away from that quarry." She shrugged. "But she's fourteen in a small town. I'm not surprised she didn't listen. And now she has to deal with the consequences of that."

The back door creaked open, Vada's dad hallooing as he entered. Rounding the corner into the kitchen, he halted, looking back and forth between their tense expressions. "Am I interrupting something?"

Before Vada could tell him the story, her mom spoke. "Mahalia went to the quarry. Vada retrieved her." A muffled thump echoed upstairs, the slam of a door.

"Ah." Her dad sucked his teeth for a second then asked, "And I take it a meltdown ensued?"

"Yep." Vada scratched at the bridge of her nose, longing for a nap.

"Then I'm going to need some tea too." He pulled a glass from the cabinet. A stereo clicked on upstairs and blasted a pulsing beat that made the plates rattle.

Vada studied her parents as they moved about, unfazed. "How are y'all so calm about this?"

They hooted with laughter, her mom wrapping an arm around her dad's waist. "Honey, teenage girls ain't nothing new to us." Her eyes glimmered. "This storm will pass. She might or might not learn her lesson. That's up to her." She waved a hand.

Her dad piped in, "Young 'uns always need to stretch their

wings, test their limits. You and your sister sure gave us plenty of heartburn."

Vada frowned, remembering the haze of loud discussions and slamming doors from her puberty. "How did you handle us?"

Her parents glanced at one another and smiled. With a broad grin, her dad looked at her and said, "How old were you when you got your first horse?"

Eyes widening, Vada glanced up the stairs. "Oh!" Behind her, her parents doubled over laughing.

Chapter 13

Lights glowed from the courthouse window as Vada pulled into a spot on the curb. Resting her head on the steering wheel for a second, she longed to curl up and take a nap right where she sat.

The day's youth camp activity had been marred for Vada by Mahalia silently glowering at her all day. She'd banged a hammer on a lopsided birdhouse so forcefully that Herb had finally taken the hammer away from her and passed it to Carmel.

The scowl only disappeared when Vada told her she could grab a soda with Carmel and Preston at the diner afterward—with a stern warning not to wander off. Having deposited a slightly less crabby Mahalia back at home, Vada had rushed out the door back to town for the Chamber meeting.

She looked at the time on the dash: 7:15. She was running late. Great. That meant she could sneak into the back row, and no one would see her. Solid plan.

Steps echoing down the dim hall, she hurried toward the conference room. Voices echoed through the open door. Trying to move quietly, Vada slipped into the room, and leaned against the back wall a few paces away from Lester. She couldn't remember a time she'd seen the long-faced man outside of Southern Comfort.

Maybe it was time to scale back how much time she spent at the bar.

Sweet T, the owner of the boutique, stood up at the podium, Mayor Patty sitting in a chair to the side with a serious expression. A projector flashed slides up onto the wall.

"And here you can see how investing in a locally targeted mail-out increased our February sales, a historically low month for us…" As Sweet T continued, Vada stared bewildered. Had she wandered into some sort of marketing symposium?

Giving up, she leaned toward Lester, who also stood slouched against the back wall. "What's all this?"

He visibly jumped. Eyes widening, he looked her up and down to her mucky boots. "Vada! How long you been a Chamber member?" His whisper carried to the back rows, causing other people to turn around and stare. From the side of the room, Dottie grinned and waved vigorously. Mayor Patty straightened in her chair with a smile as her eyes fell on Vada.

Heat flooded through her face. This was exactly the reaction she'd hoped to avoid. "First time," she whispered back, much quieter.

"Ah. Well, then this…" Lester gestured to the projector and the room. "…Is our latest series on local marketing efforts. Each month, a couple members volunteer to present how they've recently promoted their businesses and what effect it had on sales." He grinned. "My turn's next month."

"And you do this voluntarily?" Vada couldn't fathom why a business owner would willingly give away a successful strategy for free. Wasn't the point to compete?

"Rising tide lifts all ships." Lester patted her arm. "You'll see."

Silently, Vada nodded and continued to watch Sweet T's presentation. She had to admit, she'd never considered using a local mailer before. Fascinated, she listened as Sweet T explained how she pulled it off, detailing all the way down to the company she used and how much it cost. As Vada frantically typed notes into her phone, Lester shot her another grin.

At the end, Mayor Patty stood up and thanked Sweet T. "And now, the part we all enjoy! Pull out those cards, flyers, and pamphlets, and let's get to swapping!" Surging up, town members began rushing back and forth shoving materials into people's hands. Vada blinked as Dottie shoved a flyer into her hand with a wink and then trotted over to another knot of people. A stream of business owners did the same, all shaking her hand or hugging her as they passed. Vada shook her head. She hadn't realized that Midnight Bluff had so many businesses, much less—she glanced down at the colorful, growing stack in her hand—that they were all so… professional.

Gulping, she looked around. Suddenly, her "business" seemed pitiful by comparison. How had she ever thought she could do this on her own? Not wanting anyone to notice that she had nothing to swap, she began sliding back toward the door. She shouldn't have come tonight. She could see that now. She was a pitiful excuse for a business owner—

A hand grabbed her elbow and stopped her in her tracks. Mayor Patty looked up at her with a knowing smile on her lips and a twinkle in her dark eyes.

"You goin' to leave without saying 'goodbye?'"

"I don't have anything to—" Vada tried to explain. But Patty was already waving her words away with a *shush*.

"Nobody cares about that, sugar. This is strictly on a 'if you have it, bring it' basis." Mayor Patty glanced at the people bustling about. Vada noticed a few other outliers like herself who had come empty-handed. "We do this to practice our networking. And sometimes, to test out new flyers and whatnot. Get some honest feedback before they go out in public."

Nodding, Vada ran her tongue over her teeth. "Is it always like this?"

Mayor Patty peered up at her. "Some months we have more or less."

Vada wasn't sure if she meant people or pamphlets. Either way, her stomach sank at the realization that she didn't belong here. "I don't even have a business card."

"Didn't expect you to." Mayor Patty's earrings quivered as she shook her head. "Besides, there are people here who can help you with that. Networking, remember?" With a tug, Mayor Patty guided her to the front of the room, where she shoved yet another pamphlet into her hands. "Look at this. The Chamber provides not only access to the equipment you might need for day-to-day business functions—like copiers, fax machines, and even a virtual business address—but we also list and promote all our members."

Scanning the bullet points, Vada quirked an eyebrow. "Billboards?"

Patty nodded enthusiastically. "Higher-tiered members receive some exclusive advertising, but most of our promotions are available to all."

"Hmmm." Vada refolded the pamphlet. "It's tempting, Patty, but I'm not sure if I'm ready for this."

"Nonsense! You own a business, don't you?"

Vada wasn't sure she owned much more than an LLC listing. She shook her head ruefully. "Kind of."

"There you go then! You're ready for this." Patty touched her arm. "I know getting started is daunting, but that's why I'm so passionate about the Chamber. One perk of being an entry-level member is access to our business guides and templates. We don't leave you in the dark."

Lester sidled over to them. "Ladies." He nodded at Vada and shook her hand. "Good to see you here, Vada. Can't wait to hear more about that equestrian school of yours. Got a grandkid who'd be mighty interested."

Vada blinked as he walked away. Mayor Patty beamed up at her. "See?" She folded Vada's hands around the pamphlet. "You're where you're meant to be."

* * *

Vada had the Friday Feeling, and she had it bad. With a huff, she decided she needed to blow off some steam. And preferably, it would involve food.

That morning—her one day a week to be truly off—the sound of a slamming door had woken her up early. The noise was quickly becoming Mahalia's signature.

Robbed of sleep, she had come to town to have breakfast

with Ellie at the diner where she'd run into Mayor Patty just as Mira was bringing her first cup of coffee. Now, she stood on Main Street, a laminated Chamber Member card in her palm. It had all happened in a blur—Ellie shoving her out of the booth, Mayor Patty leading her at a trot to the courthouse. Now, she was somehow, inexplicably, an official Chamber Member.

A Chamber Member sans breakfast and with no idea what she was doing with her life. Her heart thumped wildly, and her throat burned every time she looked at the card, tangible evidence *things were happening*, so she shoved it into the pocket of her jeans and looked around for a distraction.

Son's car over at the church drew her attention, and an idea popped up in her mind. It was time to take her camp counselor role more seriously. She headed toward the bakery for supplies.

* * *

Lou Ellen lounged in the chair before Son's desk, one leg crossed daintily over her knee, swinging her foot back and forth. "Ok, start from the beginning and tell me what happened."

"When I got to the quarry, Vada was already there, and we got the kids out of the water together. Vada took Mahalia and Carmel home. I took Preston. The rest skedaddled." Skedaddled? Was he really using such folksy terms now?

"And nothing else happened?" she pried.

"Nope. Very anticlimactic." He didn't tell her of his talk with Preston. He couldn't imagine any teen being thrilled if word got out that he'd been "hanging out" with the preacher. Even if the boy had quietly followed him around the next day at camp.

A look of disappointment creased Lou Ellen's forehead before she wiped it away. "I suppose that's for the best. Sometimes boring is good." Her face said boring was never good, but Son let it go with a repressed smile.

She shifted in the chair. "How's the hunt for a new youth minister going?" He rolled his eyes. She would not get off his case about this.

"It's not." All his leads had turned into nothing, and now he was left with a disconcerting pile of less-than-stellar resumes.

She arched an eyebrow at him, lips pressed together. "You can't keep doing this."

"I'm trying," he protested.

"You've thrown out most of the resumes without even calling them." She waved at the stack on his desk. "It's like you don't want to find a replacement." He looked at her askance. Why would he *not* want to find a replacement? Shaking her head, she crossed her arms. "If you will not take these applicants seriously, why are you looking at all?" She frowned at him, waiting for an answer.

Son stared back at her. "What do you want me to do?"

With an eye roll, she shoved the stack toward him. "Pick two of the least offensive...and call them."

He considered the teetering pile skeptically. She wasn't wrong. He had eliminated a lot of contenders rather perfunctorily. "Fine. I'll try it your way. Just not today. I've got a sermon to write."

"Good." The swish of boots on the carpet sounded behind Lou Ellen, and a second later, Vada's face popped up behind Lou Ellen's shoulder.

Chapter 13

"Am I interrupting?"

"Not at all." Son waved her in with relief. Lou Ellen shook her head at him and turned to leave. "Have a seat," he offered.

Vada shook her head as she surveyed the detritus of applications on his desk. In one hand, she held a basket. "Nope. You're coming with me."

He stared up at her, confused, as she pulled on his arm, tugging him out of his chair. "What's going on?"

"As your camp counselor, I officially declare that we are playing hooky today."

Lou Ellen looked between them with a wide grin on her face. At his glare, she held up her hands and left the office.

He turned back to Vada. "Hooky?"

"Hooky. The time-honored tradition of youngsters skipping out on school and other responsibilities to have a day of fun." She grinned at him, her hand warm on his arm. Her lips looked incredibly soft. He felt an impulse to lean in and kiss her to see if her lips tasted as good as they looked. Blinking, he drew his arm away from her.

"I know what hooky is. Why are we doing it?" He stammered as the suggestive words fell out of his mouth.

Ignoring him, Vada grabbed his hand and towed him toward the door. "Because everyone deserves some fun now and again." She looked over her shoulder with a sly grin. "Even pastors."

"But I'm working…" His sermon notes stared up at him accusingly from his desk.

Vada shushed him. "Your work will still be there when we get back. I'm the camp counselor and I decide what the day's activities are. And we…" She held up the basket. "…Are going on a picnic."

117

He looked at her and then at the piles of paper on his desk. A sudden wave of fatigue washed over him. He could use a break. Reluctantly, he allowed her to pull him by the hand down the hall. "Fine. Where are we going?"

She hefted the basket. "Ever seen the Mississippi River from the bluffs?"

"What does that have to do with hooky?" He studied the basket, the lid barely closed against its contents.

"Because that's where we're going!" Her eyes sparkled at the words.

Son clasped his fingers around hers. She laughed and pulled him out into the parking lot. A second later, they were in her truck, flying down a backcountry road with a blazing blue sky above them.

Chapter 14

A gentle breeze ruffled the surrounding grass. Son leaned back on his elbows on the picnic blanket and took a deep breath. At the foot of the bluff on which they sat sparkled the Mississippi River, wide and dark with silt. The scent of peaches warming in the sun drifted to them from the surrounding orchard.

Son hadn't been this relaxed since... Well, it had been a long time.

Beside them lay the scraps of their lunch, paper wrappers from the chicken salad croissants and empty bottles from the grape soda with which they'd washed the sandwiches down. A picked-over fruit tray was the only remnants of food left.

Beside him, Vada lay on her back staring at the slowly drifting clouds through the branches. A content smile hung on her lips.

"I can't imagine a better day than this."

Vada sat up at his words and wrapped her arms around her knees. "I can. But it would involve a wedding."

He laughed. "Your own or someone else's?" For the amount of time they'd spent together so far this summer, he still didn't know that much about her. More surprisingly, he wanted to know everything that hid behind her veiled eyes.

She smiled at him and then looked at the rippling river. "My own."

With a nod, he followed her gaze as a barge drifted past them. "What sort of man do you imagine marrying?"

"Oh, you know." She grinned. "Ruggedly handsome, good with his hands. A real stud."

Son chuckled. "And Christian?"

She nodded. "That's a given. Don't want to raise kids in a split household."

His ears warmed at the mention of kids. "I can see him now." He waved his arms in front of him, conjuring an image. "A 6'7" Adonis with abs of steel and a heart of marshmallow fluff."

Vada's lips twitched as she tried not to laugh. "And an unflagging work ethic."

With a fake groan, he laid back on the blanket. "That rules me out then because I'm never leaving this spot. I can die here fat and lazy."

She pinched his side, and he yelped, bolting up. "Nope. Not fat. Just full," she teased.

He laid back down and draped an arm over his eyes. "And here I thought we were friends."

Vada's words drifted to him, soft and indistinct. "We are friends. I hope."

She lapsed into silence, and he lay there pondering her words. Had she doubted that they were friends before? Women—and people in general—were a mystery to him, saying one thing then something else a second later. But unlike most people, he wanted to unravel Vada's meaning.

"What was your mom like?"

The question made Son sit up in surprise. "My mom?"

"Yeah." Vada studied him, her eyes boring intently into his. "I've found that talking about people we've lost brings them back to life. So, tell me about her."

He swallowed as he put one hand gently on hers, knowing just how true the words were for her. "My mom was amazing."

The words flowed out; he'd never talked about Mom with his dad. He imagined it was too painful for him. A week after the funeral, his dad had put away all the pictures of her in the house, gone into his office, and basically not come back out. At the time, Son had been too young and timid to ask, but now… He wished he had pressed him more. She'd become such a buried subject that some days he wondered if she'd been real. Except he was here.

"She read me a bedtime story every night, even when I was too old for it. And she gave the best hugs. But what I really remember is all the time I spent with her at the church." He took a breath and realized Vada had scooched closer to him, entwining their fingers. He squeezed her hand. "She was the women's pastor, and she led VBS every year, and was the head of the prayer committee. If it happened in the church, she was a part of it. Which meant I was right there with her, helping."

Son lit up as a memory of his family gathered around the dinner table flashed through his mind. "And her cooking! That woman could have been a world-class chef and, instead, she was a preacher's wife in the suburbs of Atlanta. Absolutely incredible."

Vada whistled. "Sounds like she was the perfect Proverbs 31 woman."

Warmth flooded through his chest. "I hope my wife someday is even a speck like her."

With a small smile, Vada shook her head. "I'm sure *someone* like that is out there." She pulled her palm from his and stared over the water, rubbing at her arms.

Son had the feeling he'd said something wrong, but he couldn't pinpoint what it was. In the silence, a chickadee chirped overhead, its song lilting and sweet.

"Tell me about your sister," he blurted. As Vada glanced at him with a raised eyebrow, he resisted the urge to kick himself. Trying to explain, he offered, "I saw a picture of you two at the house. You looked very close."

"We were. Practically inseparable." Her words echoed her mother's and the same sad look rose in her eyes. "She was more than my best friend. We planned everything together." She whispered, "Everything."

"It must have been hard to lose her. What happened?"

"Tongue cancer."

Son blinked at the odd words. "Tongue cancer?"

Vada shrugged. "Most people don't even know it's a thing. But yeah, tongue cancer. No smoking or anything, just genetic luck of the draw. She had a sore on her tongue that she thought was a lie bump she kept biting. By the time we got it checked out, it had metastasized... everywhere."

Shuddering, she continued, "She didn't last six months after the diagnosis. It devastated Jake."

"I knew he was a widower. I didn't realize he'd been married to your sister." Shock rippled through him.

She gave him a sad smile. "High school sweethearts." She sat forward and crossed her legs in a meditative pose.

He chewed at his lip. "And what about you?"

She looked at him oddly. "What do you mean?"

"Well, you said Jake was devastated. But you lost your best friend and your sister. Weren't you devastated as well?"

"Still am." She wriggled her nose. "Still pretty pissed at God about it too." She sighed, the sound whooshing out gently. "I think that's why I'm so…" She waved her hands in a gathering motion. "…Uptight? About Mahalia. Why take risks when life is risky enough?"

Son looked down at the grass as he ran his fingers through it. "I get it. My dad wouldn't let me out of his sight for years after my mom died." He rubbed at his jaw. "Sometimes, I wish she was still around to tell me what to do. Especially with this youth group situation."

"What do you imagine she would say?" Vada turned toward him, her eyes curious.

"I don't know. But my dad keeps reminding me that being a pastor is not about being perfect. It's about listening to the hurting and lost." He inhaled. "That just being there for them is sometimes the most powerful thing we can do. But it's frustrating." He exhaled and laughed. "I just want to *do* something!"

"Like shake some sense into them!" Vada chuckled as she nodded her head in agreement.

Son laughed at her intense expression. "Look. I don't know what to tell you about Mahalia. Except to be there for her. That seems like a pretty good place to start."

"I suppose." She swiped at her face then glanced at him. "You know for a 'not-youth' pastor you're pretty good at this stuff. I've seen you with Preston."

Son shrugged, pleased by her compliment. "I'm trying. That's about all I can do."

"Amen to that."

* * *

Vada picked at her nails. This conversation had gone in a weird direction. Instead of a relaxing day by the river, they were baring their souls to each other. Getting Son out of his stuffy office had been the goal, but apparently, he couldn't leave the pastoring behind in the building.

They needed a change of topic and fast. Good thing she'd planned ahead.

"C'mon. Next camp activity." She stood and began gathering up their picnic supplies. Son followed her lead slowly.

With a confused look on his face, he accepted the basket when she handed it to him. "What are we doing?"

She grinned at his consternation. "You'll see." Plucking a couple of ripe peaches off a nearby tree as a snack later, she headed toward the truck.

"Were you supposed to take those?" Son huffed as he hustled to keep up with her.

"Supposed to? No." She smiled at him as he scooted into the seat beside her. "But will Mr. Nettles mind if we take just a couple? Also no." She handed him a peach that was so ripe and juicy that it was practically glowing. He took it and held it up to his nose with an appreciative sniff. With a smile, she cranked the engine and headed them back toward town.

A few minutes later, they stood staring at the side wall of PlantedWorx, the co-working space in the old catfish plant. Yards of colorful graffiti stretched to either side. Son stared at an oddly spelled name.

Disbelief flickered across his face. "This is what kids do

around here for fun? Defacing private property?"

"That and cow-tipping and skinny dipping. But I didn't figure you were up for either of those." Vada couldn't help grinning at him as she wiggled her eyebrows. Rustling through the bag in her hand, she tossed him a can of spray paint. "I think green is your color!"

Muttering, Son shook up the can. "Let's get this over with and get out of here." He was already glancing over his shoulder nervously.

"That's the spirit!" Vada turned back to the wall and got to work. Not long into her project, she felt Son's eyes on her. Turning, she asked, "What?"

He pointed at the horse coming to life before her on the wall. "That's pretty good." He smiled teasingly. "But it doesn't hold a candle to mine!" Beside him glowed his name in neon green. In what Vada was pretty sure was a terrible attempt at calligraphy. Her heart flipped as he continued to smile at her, creating a ripple effect of shivers through her body.

"However will I catch up?" Nervously, she turned back to her creation and added a touch of black as shading. "There. All done. That wasn't so bad, was it?"

"C'mon. Let's get out of here before Sheriff Swales gets here and lectures *us*." Son tossed her the can of paint.

Vada laughed. "Oh, you don't have to worry about that." She pointed to an old egg crate nearby, filled with old cans of paint.

At Son's confused look, she explained. "It's tradition! Kids 'deface' the wall as much as they want, but no one gets in trouble as long as..." She pointed at a mailbox randomly mounted on an old post beside the crate. "...We give a little token of appreciation." She pulled out a couple of dollar bills from her pocket and shoved them into the box. "Every spring, we get a fresh new wall and begin again."

"So… it's a system?"

"Yep. Mischief managed and everyone's ok with it." Vada smiled at him. "Don't worry. I wouldn't try to get you to do anything seriously wrong." She winked. "Like skinny dipping."

Son chuckled as they climbed into her truck. "I would hope not."

"You're safe with me!" Gravel pinged against the side of the truck. Vada glanced at Son, his face split with a grin. Mischief managed indeed. She pressed down the accelerator and whooped as they raced back toward Midnight Bluff, Son's voice rising to meet hers.

The deflating feeling of a letdown zipped through Vada as they drew into the parking lot of the church. As fun as the afternoon had been, she still had Mahalia to deal with at home.

As Son slipped out of the passenger seat, peaches in hand, she was already putting the truck back into gear.

"Vada!" His voice made her pause. She looked up and Son shuffled the peaches into one arm as he reached across the seat and touched her hand on the steering wheel. Instinctively, she flipped her palm up to meet his. She sucked in a breath as Son looked at her, his eyes sparkling.

"Thank you for… today. I didn't know how much I needed to cut loose." He squeezed her fingers and sparks shot up her arm and into her chest, kick-starting her heart. "It helped me see things from… a more youthful… perspective."

Vada swallowed, her mouth suddenly dry. "Anytime."

Another small squeeze and he released her fingers and then backed away from the truck with a little wave. As Vada slid the gearshift back into drive, she spotted a flicker of blinds behind

Son. Lou Ellen peered out of the office window, grinning like the cat who ate the canary.

Vada's eyes flicked back to Son as he stood waving at her. So, Lou Ellen had been up to something all along.

With a little start, Vada realized she wasn't mad about it.

* * *

Vada stopped at Carmel's house on the way home. After a few irritating text messages as the minutes ticked by, Mahalia finally emerged from the front door.

Her hair was freshly coiled into little knobs all over her head. Cynically, Vada wondered how many times she hadn't noticed her cousin's changing hair as a coverup for swimming at the quarry, thinking it was just girls being girls. She snorted as Mahalia reached the car. Well, she wasn't blind anymore.

Mahalia slid into the passenger seat, phone already back in her hand. "Let's go!"

Vada snorted. "Sure."

Her cousin looked up, eyes wide. "What's eating you? Wasn't this your day off?"

Vada shook her head. "It's nothing." She looked at Mahalia's wide eyes and realized she couldn't bring the hammer down on her without breaking their fragile truce. "Just got up on the wrong side of the bed."

"Ah." Mahalia went back to her phone. "Want me to put on some tunes?" She grinned impishly at Vada, and she couldn't help but return the smile. If Mahalia could let their argument go, she could too. But that still left Vada at an impasse on how to keep her cousin out of trouble. As the fields streamed by on either side of them, first the gold of ripe corn left to stand, then the blown-out white of cotton just starting to bloom, Vada considered what to do.

"Why don't you help me around the barn some more? Start learning how to work with the horses?"

"Really?" Mahalia looked at her skeptically. "We've tried this before and it hasn't worked out."

It would mean yet more shuffling of her schedule, but at least this way she could keep a closer eye on her without being obnoxious. "If you don't want to, that's up to you! I've just been thinking it over, and I could use the help."

That part was painfully true. The only reason she'd been able to take today off was that her parents had volunteered to do the chores.

"No! I want to!" Mahalia's voice inched up in excitement. "Oh, this is going to be good. I can't wait to saddle-train my first horse."

"You're going to have to learn a lot before then, chickadee." Vada patted her leg. "But we'll have you stomping broncs in no time."

"I thought you didn't like that method of training?"

"See! You're learning already."

Vada laughed along with Mahalia as they turned down the long drive to the farm, relief flowing through her. She was going to keep her cousin safe this summer one way or another.

Chapter 15

V ada yanked the aluminum table leg down and slid the lock into place. With a heave, she flipped it upright and then slid it into in a row of folding tables. Outside the Loveless Bakery, the stars shone on a placid square. But inside…

Willow hefted another table into place. "How is setting up workstations harder than laminating dough?"

"Well, we changed our minds about the layout fifty times." Vada grimaced. This was the… fourth?… time they'd moved all the tables, with their accompanying equipment. She picked up a stack of bowls and baking sheets and set them on the table in front of her.

"At least we're learning." Willow wiped her sweaty hands on her apron. "Let's just hope the kids like what we're baking tomorrow."

Willow always worried about details like that which was why Vada loved her so much. "If they don't, we'll just feed them some brownies and it will be fine," she said breezily.

Vada fiddled with a holder full of whisks and mixing spoons. "But enthusiasm hasn't been a problem so far."

She thought with chagrin about the boys going to town with hammers on the birdhouses they'd built last week while the girls argued over paint colors. Learning to canter had been equally... stimulating. She'd had to chase down three runaway horses when the kids got overly excited and attempted a gallop.

The jingle of the bells above the front door interrupted her thoughts. Lou Ellen stormed in; she fixed Vada with a stern look. "All right, I have to know. What happened with Pastor Riser last Friday? He came back looking satisfied as a tick on a deer and he still won't tell me a thing."

Vada looked at Lou Ellen, flabbergasted. They hadn't had a conversation this open in years. It was almost like... they were friends again.

Willow turned to Vada, setting her hands on her hips, with a smirk. "Yes. What did happen with Pastor Riser?" Her raised eyebrows signaled to Vada that she was in trouble for failing to keep her informed.

"It was nothing!" They met her weak protest with looks of deep skepticism. She tried again. "We just went on a picnic by the river."

Lou Ellen's eyebrows shot up. "And the peaches?" That was Lou Ellen. Always pressing for more.

"Peaches!" Willow leaned toward Vada with a grin. "You didn't, Vada!"

Reluctantly, Vada nodded. "We *might* have snuck a few peaches from Mr. Nettles' orchard on the way to the mural." A very liberal name for the graffiti wall at PlantedWorx.

Lou Ellen clapped her hands. "Ooh, girl!"

Willow's grin turned sly. Holding up her hands, Vada protested, "I just wanted him to have a day to relax, cut loose a little. No shame in that!"

"No, indeed." Lou Ellen her head, curls bouncing. "Great idea. He needs to get out of the office more." Her eyes glimmered with success.

Everything clicked into place. "You set this up, somehow…"

Lou Ellen grinned. "I wasn't sure how it might happen. But I thought you might get through to him."

"So, wait, what was your plan exactly? That I would have pity and act as a life coach to Son?" Vada stared at her in consternation.

"He asked you to call him Son?" Lou Ellen gaped at her.

"Obviously." Vada looked between Lou Ellen and Willow. "Did you know about this?"

Willow held up her hands. "Hey! All she said to me was that Pastor Riser should consider your idea."

"Look, Vada, you're always the one with a plan. And when you see someone who needs help, you don't hesitate." Lou Ellen held up her hands in mock surrender. "All I did was facilitate the right circumstances."

"Facilitate," Vada scoffed. "Played matchmaker more like."

With a bob of her head, Lou Ellen assented. "Kinda?"

Vada rubbed the bridge of her nose. "Unbelievable. I knew you were up to something."

Willow touched her arm. "Hey. Only good things have happened. You've got an opportunity to grow your business. And Pastor Riser… gets to learn how to loosen up. Before someone chunks a coffee pot at him." She looked at Lou Ellen.

Lou Ellen's skirmishes with Son over having a coffee pot in the church were legendary. He advocated they shouldn't feed caffeine addictions. Lou Ellen espoused that he'd have a lot more grumpy members if he took it away. The coffee pot had stayed. So far.

Vada clenched her hands. "So what, this is some sort of intervention for him?"

"Look at it that way if you want to." Lou Ellen turned toward the door. "But don't thank me or nothing for sending business your way. I don't need it."

Vada felt like a heel. "Thank you, Lulu. I really do appreciate it."

Lou Ellen nodded, with a soft smile, and let the door fall closed behind her as she stepped out into the night. Vada stared after her as she disappeared down the dark sidewalk.

"I think that was her way of offering an olive branch." Willow grabbed a rag and began wiping down the tables for the fifth time that night.

"I think so too." Vada stared after her old friend, wondering if this meant the past was forgotten.

* * *

The song of a thousand crickets hummed through Son's window. He leaned back in his office chair, exhausted from trying to knock out an entire sermon in one day. He'd barely scraped together something acceptable on Saturday after his excursion with Vada.

Playing hooky had not been a good idea. Except he enjoyed it so much…

Rising from the chair, he stuck his head out the window, surveying downtown Midnight Bluff. In the distance, he could just make out the lights left on at Loveless Bakery. With a sigh, he wondered if Vada was there setting up for tomorrow.

He sank back down in his chair, too tired to head home or go in search of anything to eat. This malaise that had fallen over him the last few days concerned him in a detached sort of way. He'd dealt with ennui before, especially in seminary. But usually, it went away after a day or two.

His thoughts drifted back to Vada the other day, and how she'd laughed even as she chased down stray horses with teenagers clinging to them. They hadn't spoken much that day, content to work in companionable silence. At least, he hoped it was companionable for her.

Son stared at the phone on his desk. He hadn't called his father in days. With a sigh, he dialed the phone. His dad picked up on the first ring, his voice booming over the line.

"Son! I was beginning to think you'd died in this heat."

Son laughed. "Not quite. Although to be fair, I'm pretty sure I've sweated out my body weight several times over now."

"Like father, like son." His dad's chuckle rumbled, warm and endearing. Son fell silent for a minute. "What's on your mind, Son?"

The words were out before he realized this was the question he'd called to ask. "Dad, how did you know Mom was the one?"

"Now what makes you ask that? Is there a woman I should know about?"

Son gulped as Vada's smile flashed through his mind. "Not really. Just curious."

His dad *harrumphed*. "Imma let that lie go." One of his most annoying traits, Son's dad always knew when he was fibbing. "But as for your question, I just knew. I always looked forward to seeing her and hearing her voice. She was such an amazing woman, and I respected the things she did. How hard a worker she was." He blew out a breath, his words cracking with nostalgia. "I felt at home with her, and I'd never felt like that with any of the other girls I'd dated."

"But how did you know?" Son pressed.

"She looked at me one day, when I stopped by her shop, and told me I'd been on her mind all week. And I thought 'no one can be happier than me right now.' Knowing she thought of me as much as I thought of her."

Son mulled over his words. "Mom had a shop? How come I don't remember that?"

"You wouldn't." His dad sighed. "She sold it out of the blue when you were about two. Said she wanted to focus on her family." He murmured, "That shop meant the world to her. I've never known a more selfless person."

"And she just gave it up because you asked?" Son couldn't believe what he was hearing.

"I didn't ask her to. When it came to her business, your mom kept her own counsel and made her own decisions. I never tried to interfere." He sniffed. "No, she did it because that's what she wanted to do. What she thought was right."

"Wow." Son stared at the clock above his door, ticking slowly past nine.

"Yeah. Like I said. She was the most impressive woman I knew." They sat on the line together for a moment.

Son's eyes watered. He had to know. "How come you've never talked about her before?"

"You never asked. And… thinking of her is very painful for me. I don't like to drag it up without a reason."

"But she was my mother." Son wiped at his eyes.

"I'm sorry." His dad inhaled. "For years, I couldn't see past my suffering. And you were so young, I thought you'd bounce back quickly if I didn't keep dragging up the past. It wasn't until right before you left for college that it occurred to me, that you might need the past. And by then, it felt too late."

Son sniffed and wiped at his face again. "I needed it."

"I am so sorry. I'm happy to tell you whatever you want to know now."

Son leaned his head back, barely noticing the water-stained ceiling tiles. "Another time. I got a lot to consider right now."

"I'll be here whenever you're ready."

Son agreed, and they hung up, promising to talk soon. As the crickets' song whirred on, Son turned out the lights and walked home, his full mind whirling with thoughts of horses and a certain sunny smile.

Chapter 16

K ids filled every inch of the Loveless Bakery, milling around makeshift workstations. Son's heart thudded just looking at them from his spot behind the counter. This was so much worse than the birdhouse building workshop. What if someone burned themselves on a hot baking sheet or sliced open a finger with a pastry knife?

Before he could spiral any further, Vada tapped him on the shoulder. "We can get started in just a sec." She scanned his face with a smile. "Don't worry. Everything's going to be fine." She brushed past him into the fray.

Willow lugged forward containers of flour and sugar and various other ingredients, depositing a set on each table. A smile lit up her face as she chatted with the kids while she worked. Vada wandered among the groups as well, laughing and talking. He took a steadying breath. If Willow and Vada weren't worried about anything happening, then he shouldn't be.

His stomach growled loudly in an unexpected lull in the

conversation. Vada looked at him, eyebrows inching up. He patted his stomach as it growled again, willing it to shush.

"So, that's why you're antsy this morning." Vada strolled over, looking amused.

"I'm fine." Despite his protest, he was pleased to be noticed. And while he almost never skipped breakfast, he'd been so worried about today's activity, that he'd clear forgotten when he got ready this morning.

"You weren't this strung out when we handed them hammers and told them to hit things," she retorted. She bent down and grabbed a Ziploc bag out of her purse which was stashed behind him. "Here." She shoved a fudge brownie into his hand. "This should perk you up."

She handed him the bag. "In case you want another. But go easy on them."

She stepped over to a nearby table with a wink and began to fill a small canister with flour as he stared at the brownie. It wasn't his usual fare of toast and eggs. He wasn't really a sugary breakfast food sort of person. But he supposed it would have to do. He'd eaten two whole brownies and was halfway through another delicious fudgy square when he noticed the quiver in his hand.

In front of him, Willow barked out an order, and the kids turned toward him.

"With her pastry school experience, Willow can be a little scary when she takes charge," Vada whispered to him. With a wink, she walked away to set out the last of the supplies.

Swallowing the last bite of brownie, he began the day's lesson at Willow's command, hoping he didn't have chocolate on his teeth. As he prayed, his heart began to race. Bullets of sweat broke out on his forehead.

Something was wrong. As the kids turned with a cheer to make cookies, Son grabbed a bottle of water from the cooler and began chugging it. Alarmed, he placed his fingers over the pulse in his neck. His heart pounded, and he felt like he was about to jump out of his skin. Was this a heart attack? Despite hours at the gym, were his years behind a desk finally catching up with him?

Vada glanced over at him from where she stood next to Carmel then snapped back to stare. Trotting over to him, she asked, "What's wrong?"

"My heart is pounding and I… feel jittery. Like I'm going to explode." He shook his hands trying to get the weird sensation out. "I think I'm having a heart attack."

Vada glanced at the bag on the counter next to him and then burst out laughing. "How many of those did you eat?"

"Three? What does that have to do with anything?" Irritation ran through him at her mirth while he was dying.

"You've got a caffeine high!" She picked up the bag. "These are espresso brownies. Each of them has the equivalent of like four cups of coffee."

Mouth open, he stared at her. "How have you not died already?"

"I drink coffee like it's water. I'm sorry. I forgot you weren't a coffee drinker." She shrugged and handed him the bottle of water. "Keep drinking water. It will help flush it out of your system soon enough."

He sat down on the cooler and drank like it was his job. Vada glanced back to the kids who were most definitely looking at him with wide-eyed expressions.

Great. Now he was entertainment for all the teenagers of Midnight Bluff. With a sigh, he took another sip from the water bottle.

* * *

Vada pressed her lips together, trying not to giggle, as Son mopped at his forehead with… a handkerchief? She snorted. Of course, he had a handkerchief.

She really shouldn't be laughing at him. But as his knee jogged up and down, she couldn't help another chuckle. The man had never had caffeine before.

"How did you make it through college and seminary without coffee?" she asked. She couldn't imagine getting through school without her coffee by her side.

"Eight hours of sleep every night and lots of prayer." He swiped at his forehead again. "Does caffeine always make you this sweaty? How do you manage?" He squinted up at her, obviously studying her for signs of excess perspiration.

She cleared her throat to cover a laugh and ignored his question. "So, you didn't have a social life there either. Got it. Explains a lot." Turning back, she watched the kids measuring and mixing.

"Be sure not to overwork your dough or you'll get tough cookies!" Willow called out. She flashed a thumbs-up to Vada.

"It explains how I got a doctorate of ministry." He stood, leaning against the counter. "Still, sweat?" His exasperated expression made Vada focus.

"If you're sensitive to caffeine—or never had it before—it can trigger your fight-or-flight response." She pointed at his face. "Your pupils dilate, your heart rate speeds up, and you can even sweat more." Tilting her head, she added, "I'd say you've hit all those points."

"That's just great," he groused. "Just peachy. I get to be strung out all day."

While he didn't direct the words at her, Vada winced with guilt, like she'd given him pot brownies instead of espresso. "I'm clearly not helping matters, so I'm going to check on the kids."

She walked away before he could say anything else. As she edged up to Preston and Mahalia's station, the kids looked up at her.

"Preacher all right?" Preston's eyes with wide with worry. Mahalia leaned around him to look at Son.

"Just not feeling great. Too much caffeine." Vada left out her part in the matter. "He'll be ok in a bit."

"Should we do something to help him?" Mahalia asked.

Vada pursed her lips. "Like what?" There wasn't much they could do for a caffeine high.

"I dunno…" Preston replied for Mahalia. "Like pray or something? That's what he's always doing when we don't feel good." Surprised, Vada looked at him. Apparently, Son was leaving more of an impression than she'd guessed. Preston shifted his gaze away, embarrassed. "It couldn't hurt."

"No, it couldn't," Vada agreed. "I think he'd like that."

Mahalia turned to the table behind them, and Vada watched as the news traveled around the room. The power of teenage networks never ceased to amaze her.

In just a few minutes, the kids set aside their mixtures and drifted to the back of the bakery, circling around Son. He looked up startled and glanced at Vada to learn what was happening.

Vada shrugged with a smile. The kids were leading this, not her.

Mahalia clasped her hands. "We know you're not feeling ok. Would you mind if we prayed for you?"

He nodded. "I'd be honored."

Slowly, the kids reached forward and placed their hands on his back and shoulders. Preston began the prayer, asking for Son to feel better soon before letting the prayer pass from him to another teen. Vada looked on, impressed by how much they'd picked up. Her heart swelled as she realized just how much these teens had grown over the summer, despite some bumps along the way.

As Preston prayed, Vada reached out and grasped Son's forearm. Without opening his eyes, he placed his hand over hers and squeezed her fingers.

* * *

Anxiety bled away from Son as the kids prayed over him, their hands hot and sticky where they touched him. If every day in ministry bore such obvious fruit, all ministers would want to work with youth despite the challenges. They'd be knocking down his door for the job.

Joy at their caring nature bloomed in Son's chest as they said "Amen." They left back to their stations with light pats. Vada turned and walked away with them, his arm growing cold from where her hand had been.

Son wiped at his forehead and realized while the jitters may not have gone away, he felt much more at peace. He sipped his water for another couple of minutes before standing.

"Where can I help?" he asked Willow.

She pointed to Preston and Mahalia's table. "They're about to roll out their dough and cut shapes."

Mahalia brightened as he walked over. "Pastor Riser! What should we make our cookies? Preston is saying alien gingerbread men." She shot an indignant glance at him.

"It'd be funny." Preston shrugged, not bothered. He held up a paring knife with a grin. "We can carve them into some crazy shapes."

"Isn't this sugar cookie?" Son asked, peering at the flat oval of dough rolled out on the table.

"That's what I said!" Mahalia crowed.

"We could still make aliens." Preston sniffed, not impressed.

"Why not cut out circles and stars and then you both can decorate them how you want to when they come out of the oven? You can make alien planets." He patted Preston's shoulder. "And you can make flowers and faces and stuff."

Mahalia rolled her eyes. "But those shapes are so boring!"

"Works for me." Preston shrugged, apparently his default move. He set the knife down.

"Fine." Mahalia tossed her braids over her shoulder. "I'll go get the cookie cutters."

After she'd walked away to retrieve the cookie cutters from a pegboard wall in the back that held all sorts of utensils, Preston leaned over to Son. "Want to help me play a prank on Mahalia?"

Just as Son was about the squash the idea, he thought of Mrs. Langford and his promise to her. If playing a harmless prank would help him bond with Preston, then he should try it. "It's not like the ketchup incident, is it?" he asked.

"Nope! Just need a paper cup and a post-It."

Willow glanced at them as she strolled between tables. "You really think it's a good idea to play a prank in a bakery?" She glanced meaningfully at the knife.

"It won't hurt anybody!" Preston protested.

With a sigh, Willow nodded at him then rolled her eyes at Son. "Good luck."

Preston ran behind the counter and grabbed a cup. From beside the register, he grabbed a post-It and pen.

"Ok, what are we doing?" Son asked when he got back.

Preston scribbled on the post-it and stuck it to the cup. "We just need to put this where she's sure to see it." On the post-it he had scrawled, "Do not lift unless you plan to kill it."

Son nodded, easy enough. He set the cup, upside down on the baking sheet by his elbow.

"Genius!" Preston enthused.

Mahalia walked back toward them, cookie cutters dangling from her fingers. "These were all I could find. Everyone else is using them too." She set down the cookie cutters on the table.

"What is that?" She jabbed a finger toward the cup.

"Spider." Preston snickered.

Taking her shoe off, Mahalia reached for the cup. As she lifted it, Son half-expected a big, ole hairy spider to scoot out.

"There's nothing here." She slapped Preston with her sandal. "Jerk!" Setting the cup back down where it was, she turned to chew out Preston.

From the corner of his eye, Son saw Vada look up at the sound of Mahalia's voice and head in their direction. "What is going on over here?"

Vada looked at Son like he was a misbehaving kid too. Which was fair since he wasn't exactly doing much to help the situation. "It's just a…"

"Spider!" shouted Preston, pointing at the cup. Mahalia tried to protest, and he pinched her arm cutting her off with a squeak.

But Vada's face had already turned ashen. With a shudder, she turned and sped out through the kitchen, Preston laughing up a storm. Willow strode over and whacked him up the backside of his head. He quieted abruptly.

"I told you this wasn't a good idea." Willow directed the words at Son, not the kids. He supposed as the adult in this scenario, he was the most to blame.

"You got this for a few minutes?" He nodded at the kids around them.

"Go!" Willow shooed him away.

Son jogged after Vada, concerned about the way her face had paled. He found her outside sitting under an oak tree.

"You ok?" He sat beside her.

Head hung, she asked, "There wasn't anything under the cup was there?" He shook his head.

Sighing, she closed her eyes and leaned her head back against the tree. "I just..." She shuddered. "Really hate spiders. It's irrational, and I can't explain it. I just do. They're so creepy."

"They do have a weird number of eyes and legs," he conceded.

"Exactly! And those creepy little fangs." She shuddered again. "I just need a minute before I go back in."

He tugged on her arm. "C'mon. I have a better idea." Clasping her hand in his fingers, he led her down the street and into the cool, quiet interior of Southern Comfort. Her hand was small and callused in his, reminding him just how much hard, physical work this gorgeous woman did.

"I thought Baptist ministers would burst into flames if they entered a bar?" Vada looked at him, brows quirked.

"I'm not a vampire." He grinned back at her. "Besides, I left my crucifix at home."

They settled onto stools at the bar. Vada ordered a gin and tonic from Lester while Son got a club soda with lime. At her skeptical glance, Son explained, "I'm not against drinking in moderation. But as a pastor there are certain appearances I must maintain, a certain example."

Vada set her drink back down on the counter, untouched. "In that case…" She waved down Lester and sheepishly asked him to change her order to ginger ale.

"You don't have to do that for my sake." Son stared at her.

"It's not like it's a big sacrifice. Besides, the magic of a bar lies in the community, not the drinks." She sipped at her ginger ale.

They sat next to each other, enjoying the quiet. "Can I ask you something?" Son said after a minute.

"Shoot."

"How do you deal with spiders at the farm? I imagine there's a lot of them in the barn." Son studied her as she smiled down into the bubbles of her ginger ale.

"Have you ever seen one at the barn?" she replied.

Now that he thought of it, he hadn't. He shook his head.

"That's because I keep my barn spotless, so the critters spiders eat don't want to be there." She bobbled her head. "And if I see one, I smash it before I can think about it."

"Huh." He wouldn't have imagined that she could smash one of the little critters based on her reaction in the bakery.

"What about you? Any creepy crawlies you can't stand?" Vada tapped her knuckles on the bar.

"Not really. Well… caterpillars."

Vada snickered, "Caterpillars?"

"Hey! Some of them are toxic. And the way they move…"

He rolled his shoulders.

Vada tossed her head back laughing. "I guess we have something in common then. Not liking bugs."

He smiled and drained the last of his club soda. "I guess so." He was sure they had more in common than just not liking bugs, but she'd finally loosened up and he didn't want to make her feel like she was being scrutinized.

Vada set her own empty glass on the bar, and Son threw down a few bills and waved at Lester. They stood and, without a word, headed back to the bakery.

"Camp's almost over." Son wasn't sure what had prompted the declaration, but he leaned into it. "Just a couple more days."

"Yep." Vada nodded, her eyes staring into the distance. "It's flown by."

With a start, he realized he wanted more, to hear her voice and find out what she thought of the future. He was going to miss these moments with her. "Got any big plans for the fall?" Right now, he'd do anything to keep her talking.

She paused on the sidewalk, shuffling uneasily. "My parents…" She drifted off, blinking as she thought.

"Mmmhmm?" he prompted.

With an inhale, Vada spit out, "My parents have given me an ultimatum on the equestrian school. Start making revenue or sell." She bit her lip. "I went to a Chamber meeting the other night to get some ideas, but…" She waved a hand. "I'm still at a loss."

"Well…" He tilted his head. "What sorts of things did they suggest?"

"I dunno. Marketing stuff. Sweet T was doing some presentation on mailed flyers." She crossed her arms over her chest. "Not sure I have the cash to do something like that."

"Not a bad idea though. Maybe start smaller?" He pointed at the storefront windows stretching before them, sporting various posters. "You don't have to go big to make a big impact."

"That's what Lewis always tells me. Put up posters." She scoffed, the huff coming out gravelly.

"Don't know until you try." Son shrugged as they started strolling toward the bakery again. "There are other things you could try if that's not your speed. Ads with the Mississippi Farm Bureau. Facebook… stuff. I'm sure there are plenty of horse magazines out there you could put something in."

He patted her back, his hand lingering at the small of her waist. "My point is you have to get started somewhere."

Vada nodded, lips pulling down into a frown. "You're right. It's just nerve-wracking." With an empathetic nod, Son swung the front door of the bakery open.

Willow spun toward them as they entered, her head cocked curiously. "You sure were gone for a while." She nodded at the kids snickering behind them. Son caught Vada's eye and bit back a smile.

Vada glanced at his face, dimpling with mirth that mirrored her own, then, loud enough for the whole bakery to hear, said, "I just needed a few minutes to calm down." She eyed Preston. "I hate spiders."

The tips of Preston's ears turned red as he bent over a spatula and transferred sugar cookies to a baking sheet to cool. Son did not want to get in a staring contest with her. He was sure he'd lose, although it might be worth it.

With a smirk, Vada turned slowly and walked to a workstation to help. Son stood there for a second before he followed her example and returned to Preston and Mahalia's table, wishing he was two tables over with Vada instead.

* * *

The last of the cars left the church parking lot as the sun began sliding down the sky in a halo of pinks and purples. Vada rubbed at her back, the wear of a full day on her feet getting to her. Son stood next to her looking equally beat.

Vada groaned at the thought of more chores waiting for her at home. She'd give anything to put that off.

"C'mon. Let's go to Al's and get in the A/C. Let me return the favor of that drink earlier." She tapped his arm, and he immediately turned toward her, eyes bright.

"You don't owe me—"

She made a *pssh* sound and set off. "C'mon!"

She heard Son follow her, his shoes clopping on the sidewalk. "I don't see how you can stay in those all day." With a glance at his shiny loafers, she shook her head.

"They're not that bad." Son grinned then winced. "I've only got three blisters."

She laughed disbelieving. "My man, that's what sneakers are for."

"So, I'm yours, huh?"

Vada glanced at his teasing smile, her heart fluttering. "My pain in the butt, maybe." She swung the door of Al's open to hide her grin, and he reached to take the handle from her.

"After you." He waved her in before him. She had to give him brownie points for courtesy.

They had just settled in with the largest glasses of sweet tea Mira could scrounge up when the door swung open, and

Betty Coleman strode in.

The lady was tanned and lined from long hours in the sun working her fields. One of the few female farmers Vada had ever met, she had nothing but respect for Betty. The woman kept the farm going—and thriving—despite her husband being on the road two-thirds of the year for business.

Betty beelined in on Vada and was at their table in a heartbeat.

"Vada, I been meaning to talk to you." She nodded curtly to Son. "Nice to see you, preacher."

"You too, Betty." Before Son could say anything else, Betty turned back to Vada. "Jackie's in trouble."

Always to the point. Vada could appreciate that, even as worry at her announcement coursed through her. "I thought she was keeping things running pretty well." Son looked between them but wisely stayed silent. Betty wasn't the type to share in front of someone she didn't know that well, and she wasn't the most regular churchgoer.

Betty shook her head. "Just barely and not for much longer. Me and Clay are doing the best we can to help her, but she needs more." She leaned toward Vada. "Her two remaining farmhands are so burned out, I wouldn't be surprised if she lost them before the end of the summer. No matter how much they love her."

Betty straightened. "And then, there's this matter of the development. All that land the feds put to auction after Van…" She shook her head. "Well, Jackie's place is just a sliver in the middle of that. If things get much worse, she'll have to sell."

"But that house has been in her family for three generations!" Vada's throat constricted. As good as the development was for Midnight Bluff, she abhorred seeing one of their own get pushed out of the way for it.

"I'm just telling you what I'm seeing." Betty shoved her hands in her pockets. "Jackie's in a tighter spot than she knows. If things get dicey, she could lose everything."

Vada blew out a breath. "What did you have in mind?"

"I dunno. A…" She waved her hands. "Meal-chain but for farming help? A community fund to help keep her on her feet until she's stable? A miracle?"

Vada thought it over. "I can float the community fund idea by Mayor Patty. And we can put out the word that she needs help with the farm."

She pulled out her phone and started tapping in notes. Looking up, she asked Betty, "Can she turn a profit on what she's producing? Enough to live on?"

"The amount of debt Van left her in, I dunno. But if it weren't for that, I'd say yes. She has enough acreage to live on, barring any disasters."

They frowned meaningfully at each other. The Mississippi Delta was notorious for tornadoes, floods, and droughts.

"So, she needs alternative income," Vada stated.

Betty nodded. "The only reason she's made it this far is her nursing job. Poor thing is run ragged trying to do both."

"I can imagine." Vada chewed at her lip. "I'll call you when I know more." She grabbed Betty's arm. "But Betty, Jackie has to be smart about this. If she can't figure out another income stream, I don't know if any amount of help will fix this."

Betty nodded and patted her hand. "I know, sugar. But we got to try." She marched over to the to-go window and grabbed her takeout bags with a wave at Al. As she pushed her way out the door, she nodded at Vada and Son.

Son leaned toward her. "What are you… the town fixer?"

Vada laughed, despite her anxiety for Jackie. "More like the town switchboard." She took a sip of her tea. "I know everybody and their business and that means…" She cocked her forefinger and thumb at him. "That I know who to connect with who when something needs to happen."

"Kind of like what you've done for the summer camp and for the Nettles…" he trailed off looking speculative.

Vada sat forward and put her hand on his arm. "Because that's what neighbors do. They help." She looked into his serious, dark eyes, sparks pricking in her fingers.

He took her hand in his, the tingles running up her arm and into her chest. "I didn't realize you did so much."

She licked her lips, mouth suddenly dry. "You know now." Gratitude at his praise warmed her chest. So few people really saw what she did.

"You are one of the most incredible people… most incredible woman… I know." He pressed her hand gently between his, his smooth palms pleasant against her rough fingers. In response, her heart sped up, tapping out an excited rhythm.

The words of admiration sent a shock through her system. A pleasant, tingly shock. No man had ever expressed such open… feelings… toward her.

She sat back, extricating her hand before her heart could start dancing the macarena and clutched her glass. "Now you know." She swallowed against the dryness in her mouth, trying to stay calm.

"Cheers to neighbors!" She raised her glass. With a chuckle, he tapped his glass to hers.

"Neighbors," he echoed, but his gaze never left her face.

Chapter 17

V ada trudged around the kitchen, mind full. The kids would be here soon—along with Son. After her spider meltdown the other day, and their ensuing conversations, she didn't know how he would treat her. Did he think she was the crazy spider lady now? An over-sharer? A flirt?

The last one hung in her mind. If she were honest with herself, she'd relished his attention. But as for flirting—she hadn't crossed any lines, right?

Her heart sputtered at the thought of his face, softening in the late afternoon sun as he'd looked back at her in Al's. She stirred sugar into her coffee and stared out the window, willing the van to get there already and put her out of her misery.

"You ok, honey?" Vada's mom touched her shoulder.

"Huh? Yeah, I'm fine. Why do you ask?" She clasped her hands around her mug.

"Because that was the third time you've put sugar in your

coffee." Her mother's eyes sparkled. Across the island, Mahalia nodded at her with a grin.

Vada looked down at the muddy brown of her cup. Taking a sip, she screwed up her face at the obnoxiously sweet taste. With a laugh, her mother took her cup, dumped it in the sink, and refilled it—with one spoonful of sugar this time.

"Thank you." Vada gratefully accepted the cup and gulped down the hot brew.

"What's got your mind up in the clouds?" Her mom smoothed her hand down Vada's back in a soothing gesture.

"Don't you mean *who*?" Mahalia piped up. Her mother's eyebrows shot up.

Vada glared at Mahalia. "I didn't ask for commentary."

Mahalia stuck her tongue out and turned back to her bowl of cereal. With a chuckle, her mother turned back to her. "So, there's a who?"

"There is not. I'm just tired from everything going on." Vada inhaled as she thought of her evening spent with Son.

"Yeah, then where'd you disappear to Thursday for so long with the preacher?" Mahalia waved her spoon, splattering milk across the counter.

Vada handed a kitchen towel to her. "As I said, I just needed a few minutes to calm down after that prank."

"Oh yeah? Then why did you go to Al's with him afterward?"

Vada gaped at her. Mahalia was supposed to have gone to Carmel's after baking, not hung around downtown. Her mother looked between them skeptically, butting in before they could start sniping at each other. "You know, this could be a good thing."

"What could?" Vada looked at her in exasperation.

"Dating." The way her mother stated it made Vada inhale,

like her dating their preachers was already a done deal.

"I'm not with Son. We're just friends."

"Chile, I agree with Mahalia. It certainly looks like you're dating him. Goin' on picnics and slipping away together." Her mother's words were gentle, but they sent a ripple of alarm through Vada.

She hadn't even considered dating since Eve passed away. Because dating inevitably led to a breakup. And losing the most important person in her life had left Vada hollow for so long that she couldn't imagine going through it again. And not being with someone while they were still alive sounded like a new level of torture.

But the press of Son's hand had felt... right. His gentle words always hung in her mind, tickling her imagination of what could be. Maybe dating was worth the risk for the right person.

The crunch of tires on gravel outside saved her from having to reply. She rushed out the door and waved at the van as kids tumbled out.

Son smiled at her, his teeth brilliant in the morning light. No sign of avoidance or embarrassment at her expense. Her heart thudded in her chest as her mother's words echoed in her mind.

She ticked off all the time she'd spent with Son. On the river, the picnic, Southern Comfort, Al's... Were they dating? And if so, could she call it dating if it started so unassumingly?

There was only one way to find out. As Son checked kids off on his clipboard, she strode over to him and wrapped her hand around his arm.

"Hey, you." She knew she was testing her limits, but Son turned to her with a smile, delight dancing in his eyes.

154

"Hey." His voice was deep and warm, sending tingles through her. So quickly she wasn't sure it happened, he leaned in and kissed her temple.

A silly grin crept its way across her face. "Can we talk later?"

"Of course." He nodded with a smile. Behind him, Lou Ellen looked at her, eyes wide and a big smile on her face. As Son turned back to counting kids, Lou Ellen flashed a double thumbs up at Vada.

With a laugh, Vada walked over to the milling kids and began splitting them into their groups.

"Uh-huh. There's no 'who' for you." Mahalia brushed by her with a smirk. Vada really needed to consider her words more around that whippersnapper. She snuck a look at Son, who was looking at her from the corner of his eye with a smile, and decided she wouldn't worry about it today.

* * *

Son leaned on the fence as he watched the kids run through the course one more time. Poles lay flat on the ground or on low crossbars at intervals around the ring.

As he watched, Carmel loosened her reins and urged her horse into a trot. They rode over a set of poles, the horse precisely setting her feet in between the obstacles and then gently hopping over the low crossbar without balking. Carmel smiled and praised her with a pat on the neck. It was a major improvement from this morning, when many of the kids had nervously clutched and yanked the reins, causing the horses to balk at the obstacles.

"Great job, Carmel!" He called out. Pride flowed through him as he watched another kid do the same thing. It shocked

Son how strongly he felt watching these kids succeed and enjoy themselves.

Carmel turned around in her saddle, watching Mahalia go through the obstacles. "Loosen up on the reins, Hal!" she called out.

Mahalia nodded, not taking her eyes off the poles, but gave the reins a little more slack. With a snort, her horse trotted straight over the poles, delicately placing its hooves. Only a slight hesitation before the crossbars then Mahalia had cleared the course. The other kids cheered from their horses, urging each other forward.

Son's heart swelled as they wound down for the day. They really had come so far.

A few minutes, the kids were hard at work in the barn, brushing down their horses and filling buckets with water. Preston lugged a saddle over to Son. He handed it to Son, who took it with some surprise. The kids were responsible for cleaning and putting their gear up in the tack room under Vada's guidance.

"Vada said she needed your help with something," Preston shrugged. "Not sure what, but she's back in the tack room now."

"All right," Son replied, confused. Vada organized her tack room with military efficiency, so he couldn't imagine she needed anything, but he headed toward the room, anyway. Stepping through the door, he found Vada wiping down saddles in the dim room. She looked up at him in surprise. "Preston said you were looking…" Behind him, the door swung closed with a loud creak. The lone lightbulb flickered out overhead.

Vada sighed and glanced at the door. "Why did I think

having the light switch outside made sense?" She reached around him and tried to shove the door open. It wouldn't budge. "Looks like they're Parent Trapping us." She sounded more amused than upset.

His heart skipped at her words, tumbling in a joyful rush, but he tried to play it cool. "Does that scenario really apply to us? We're not divorcees." He set the saddle down on a sawhorse and put his shoulder to the door and strained against it.

"Kids pranking us into being alone together." She tilted her head to the side. "Close enough for my standards."

"Sure." He pushed against the door again. It was not budging. "Looks like we're really stuck in here."

"Not quite the way I wanted to talk to you. Being held captive and all." She picked up a long flat piece of metal that Son couldn't name and edged around him. "But it'll work."

With that, she wedged the metal piece in the crack between the door and door sill.

* * *

Vada's mouth went dry as Son hovered behind her in the dark, so close she could feel the heat from his body and his breath on her cheek. If she'd had any doubts earlier, now they were all dispelled. She glanced back at him, in the small slivers of light filtering in from around the door.

In the gloom, he towered over her, pecs rippling temptingly under his shirt. It wasn't fair that a preacher had muscles she wanted to run her hands over.

With a start, she realized she'd stopped working to jimmy the door open and was staring at him. She swung back around and pried with the metal, trying to catch the latch.

"So…" her voice trailed off. Now that they were at this point, she didn't know how to ask her question.

"Vada." Suddenly, his hands, large and hot, were on her arms, gently spinning her to face him. "Are you all right… after the other day?"

Her mind spun, grasping for what he meant. "You mean with the not-spider?" She blinked up at him through the dimness.

"That and…" He cleared his throat. Dropping his eyes to the floor, he cleared his throat again. "With what you said about me being yours."

It had been a slip of the tongue at the time, but now… now she meant it with every muscle of her body that was straining against her self-control. "I'm fine and…" It was her turn to stammer. "I meant what I said. But if that's not what you—"

He was already nodding. "It is." With one last tug, she was in his arms cradled against his chest, every delicious fiber of him pressed to her. "I can't think of anything—anyone—I want more than you."

His lips skimmed over hers tentatively, asking a question she had one, enthusiastic answer to. Pressing up onto her toes, she crashed her lips against his. Against her chest, she felt him inhale then his arms wrapped around her waist, lifting her off her feet. He pressed kisses from her lips down to the hollow of her throat, making her throw her head back with a little moan.

Vada had never kissed anyone like this before, with so much unbridled passion. Her head spun, as he returned to her lips and teased them open, and they tasted each other in one heady rush. Vada sunk further into bliss as she jumped up and wrapped her legs around him. He gasped and pressed her back against the door.

"It's mighty quiet in there!" Mahalia's muffled voice echoed through the room. Vada's eyes flew open. In one ungraceful motion, Son set her down and backed away, panting.

"Ahem." Vada cleared her throat, heat flooding her cheeks, and turned back to the door, frantically working the metal piece. Within seconds, it swung open, and Vada stepped out into the blaze of the late afternoon sun. Before them, kids scattered, pretending nonchalance. Only Mahalia remained, arms crossed and a cheeky grin on her face. Lou Ellen peaked out of a stall, a pleased expression on her face.

"You were right. They were Parent Trapping us." Son stepped out and wrapped an arm around her shoulders.

Vada shook her head at her cousin, who continued to grin at them as she strolled away. "Looks like it worked!" Mahalia called over her shoulder.

Vada glanced up at Son's glowing face and stifled a giggle. "Looks like," she agreed.

Chapter 18

Vada fiddled with the settings on her social media ad once again. Why wasn't she getting any clicks? Was it the photo? Vada thought her mom's snapshot from her horseback riding championship five years ago looked pretty good. She rubbed at her forehead. Maybe her targeting was off?

She stared at the screen until her eyes burned. With a groan, she slapped her laptop closed. This was useless. She wasn't a marketing guru.

Mahalia traipsed down the hall, singing, "Vada and Soo-oon sittin' inna tree. K-I-S-S-I-N-G!" Vada tried not to smile at the sound, but she could already feel her cheeks dimpling. Mahalia poked her head in Vada's room and grinned at her. Chunking a throw pillow at her, Vada shouted, "Will you stop that already, brat!" With a giggle, Mahalia dodged the pillow and continued down the hall.

The singing didn't stop. Just like the smirking hadn't stopped at dinner.

As steam rose from her mom's poppyseed chicken casserole set between them, Vada had done her best to ignore the gloating as her parents exchanged amused glances. Nothing was going to wreck the glow she still felt from this afternoon.

Except for the dang ads. She snatched up her computer and clicked furiously. She just didn't know what she was doing wrong.

After another five minutes wasted, Vada set her computer aside again and clomped downstairs to stare moodily into the fridge. Giving up on her quest for a snack, she settled for a glass of sweet tea instead. With a sigh, she settled with her drink on the porch swing and stared at the darkening yard and the wide-open sky, stars winking overhead.

The screen door creaked open, and her dad slipped outside, easing onto the swing beside her.

"Big day today." Her dad's classic opening to a serious "talk."

Vada quirked an eyebrow at him. "Camp went well."

"Especially for you." The corners of his mouth flickered up as he glanced at her.

"Yeah… about that…" She inhaled trying to figure out how to explain.

He held up his hands. "I'm not worried about that. You're an adult." He sniffed and swiped at his nose. "What I am worried about is that you're rushing into this."

"We're barely dating—we're not rushing anything!"

"I didn't even know you liked him," he said softly.

Vada wrapped her arms around her knees. "I didn't even know I liked him until last week. Then…" She shrugged, thinking of his hand in hers as he helped her up from where she sat beneath the oak tree. Her dad nodded, waiting silently for her to continue.

"He's amazing." Vada sniffled, emotion stronger than she'd felt in a long time suddenly welling up. "He puts me at ease. Makes me laugh. This is the first time I've felt truly happy since…" She trailed off, and she knew he understood. Eve might be gone, but her presence loomed large over all of them. She swiped at her nose. "I just want to enjoy… whatever this is… for now."

"I can't tell you how happy I am to see you happy." He sighed. "But being with a preacher comes with certain expectations that I don't think you fully realize." He held up a hand as she opened her mouth. "Whether or not they're fair. You will be watched more closely. Judged more sternly. Slip-ups won't be tolerated nearly as much. It's just the reality." He shook his head. "Are you ready for that?"

"I know all that, Dad." She tilted her head back. "We'll figure all that out as we get to it. We're partners." As the words left her mouth, she realized how naïve they sounded. Of course, she was going to be under a microscope now. It made sense to think ahead about it a little. Her stomach flipped at the thought of being the subject of constant gossip—not just in Midnight Bluff but in larger church circles as well.

She nodded, trying to reassure herself. "We'll be fine."

Her dad studied her, one eyebrow lifted, before nodding. "If you're sure, then that's good."

"I am." Vada stared out into the yard, where lightning bugs flickered in and out, feeling exhausted. If this was how everyone reacted to them dating, she wasn't as ready for this as she thought. She stared at the dancing flashes of light, wondering what she should do.

* * *

The smell of sizzling bacon and fresh-brewed coffee wafted over Son causing his stomach to growl as he stepped into Al's Diner the next morning. After last night, he could use a hearty breakfast. His head had been so full of thoughts of Vada after they spoke on the phone that he'd hardly slept, and the fatigue he already felt in his joints told him he would pay the price for it today. But food would help.

Clay waved to him from a corner booth, and Son stepped over, happy to join his friend. Before he could even open the menu, Clay was talking, one eyebrow arched.

"Heard there were some shenanigans yesterday."

Word spread devilishly quick in this town. Son set down his menu, lips working against a smile. "It was nothing."

Clay took a sip of his coffee. "I have a feeling it wasn't nothing." He took another sip. "You don't strike me as a fellow who takes things lightly. Or acts rashly."

Son felt his cheeks dimple as he grinned. Everything about yesterday had been rash and unplanned. And he couldn't make himself regret any of it. In fact, he was positively ecstatic about Vada. "I'm not." He tented his fingers. "But with Vada, I just feel freer."

Clay smiled at him. "I've been told the right woman has that effect."

"It's not just that." He rubbed at his jaw. "I'm more than just a preacher to her." The words swelled in his chest making him feel six inches taller.

"She makes you feel like a man," Clay summed it up nicely.

"Exactly. I'm more than my job." Being a preacher was exhausting. That Vada didn't look at him like he was a creature in a zoo was a breath of fresh air. "I can relax around her."

"Amen to that," Clay murmured as Mira set down a glass of

orange juice for Son and took their orders. Son considered Clay. The man was a gifted doctor, had the silver fox thing going on, and was respected by everyone in Midnight Bluff.

"Why haven't you ever settled down?" Son cut into his pancakes. "You seem like a family sort of guy."

"Oh, I always wanted a family. But I never found the right woman to tie me down." Clay laughed, but it sounded hollow, his smile not reaching his eyes. Son decided not to push the subject; the man's reasons for not marrying were his own.

"What do you think of… Vada's job?" He asked hesitantly, Vada's words ringing in his head. Running an equestrian school wasn't exactly what he'd imagined his wife doing.

"The Co-Op?" Clay blinked up at him.

"The barn." Son stared back at him curiously. "Her equestrian school?"

Clay waved a hand. "*Pssh.* I wouldn't worry over that. Vada's been 'starting' that school for years. I'd be shocked if anything came of it."

Son relaxed back into his seat. So, the equestrian school wasn't a big deal to the folks around here. But something about how dismissive Clay talked about it rubbed Son the wrong way. "What do you mean by 'shocked?'"

Clay scooped up a forkful of eggs and held them up consideringly. "It's not that I think Vada can't run the school. She's the most capable person in town. If anyone was going to be successful running their own business around here, it would be her." He chewed on his eggs for a minute. "But she's had opportunities to do more with it, and she hasn't taken them. I think the wind got knocked out of her sails when Eve died. They were supposed to run it together."

Son rubbed at his lips. Vada's mom had said something

164

similar, painting her in a whole new light. While Vada knew what's what around town, under the layers of bravado she wore, she was hurting.

Clay nodded. "Yep. I wouldn't worry about the school if that's what's holding you back." He scooped up more eggs. "She'll make a good partner."

Son turned back to his pancakes, more thoughts and questions spinning through his head than when he sat down.

Chapter 19

S on's heart thumped in his chest as he swung the van into a spot on the grass next to Vada's car at the Wilder's house. Vada was nowhere to be seen, but that didn't stop his traitorous heart from speeding up anyway. After the torment of the last day apart, he wanted to see her, touch her, hear her laughter ring out in that bold, brassy way that gave him chills. No late-night phone call could make up for that.

Kissing her again was probably off the table with all the kids around.

He ushered them out of the van, and they streamed behind Lou Ellen toward the ramshackle house. Following their laughter, he found Vada talking to Ruffin on the back deck which was crowded with picnic tables, Adirondack chairs, and shady umbrellas. A series of stairs led down to a long dock on the river with a roped-off area next to it.

Sunlight sparkled on the water in brilliant flashes of light while a host of birds sang around them. It was picturesque and peaceful and just what Son needed.

Ruffin shook his hand. "Hey, man! Glad you brought the kids out today."

Son looked over the heads of the laughing and jostling crowd of teens. "They've been excited for this all summer."

"Well, we won't keep them from it long then." Ruffin turned to his mom, Cynthia, who had stepped out of the house to say hello to everyone. She gave a friendly wave to Son but concentrated on talking to the teens around her.

Amid the kids swarming Cynthia, Vada slipped over to him and squeezed his arm. "Hey." She smiled up at him shyly and he grinned back at her, heat spreading through his chest.

"Hey yourself." He stared into her dark, warm eyes. "Ready to get things going?"

"Mhmm." His heart fluttered at the sound. This was going to be a glorious day even if they couldn't spend it fixated on each other.

Vada held his gaze for another second, lips pressed together in a flirty smile, then turned to the teens milling around the deck. "All right, everyone! Listen up! We got some rules to go over today."

Slowly, the kids quieted down and listened to Ruffin give the safety spiel. Ruffin stepped up onto a picnic table to be heard better. "Ok, first things first. *Nobody* gets in the water until you've applied sunscreen. That means nobody. We're not sending you home sunburned and sick today." Grumbles resounded around the group, but the kids nodded.

"Second, life vests! You'll notice we've got a couple of canoes and kayaks out for you today. If you get in one, you must have your life vest on and buckled. Same goes for anyone who isn't a strong swimmer—even in the swimming area. I don't want to pull you out and neither do Pastor Riser or Miss Vada." The kids chuckled as they glanced to where Son and Vada stood together. Lou Ellen drifted behind them, already rubbing sunscreen onto her pale cheeks.

"And if we say out of the water, that means out of the water, no dawdling!" Ruffin glanced around sternly, looking every inch the fire chief that he was. After a minute, he broke into a smile. "Let's go have some fun!"

The kids cheered and rushed down the steps toward the dock, towels and tubes of sunscreen in hand. Ruffin trailed after them, like a golden retriever with a group of puppies. Son smiled as he saw them pause at the water's edge to slather on sunscreen, the distinct smell of coconut and zinc filling the air as Vada and Lou Ellen helped a few of the girls rub lotion into their backs.

He strolled down the dock and settled into a chair, enjoying the sun. It was going to be a beautiful day indeed.

* * *

Vada couldn't help watching Son as he strode by them. She hated they hadn't talked in person yet, but it would have to wait until they weren't surrounded by teenagers. Mahalia turned and grinned at her meaningfully. With a shake of her head, Vada turned back to Carmel, unable to resist smiling as she smeared a generous amount of sunscreen onto her back.

"It's cold!" Carmel exclaimed.

"It'll only feel cold for a second." Vada concentrated on rubbing the lotion in. Around them, the girls chattered as they helped each other.

"Preston, now there's a boy who's cute *and* godly!" declared one girl. Vada rolled her eyes. That boy was a few sticks short of a fire, but whatever worked for them.

Mahalia snickered. "He'd die if he heard you say that!"

"If you know so much about him, then why don't you marry him?" retorted the girl, her voice sing-songy.

Carmel looked over her shoulder at her. "Someone's jealous." She smiled, the words light.

The girl sniffed. "At least I don't hang out with a bunch of boys." Her eyes sparkled as she watched the taunt land.

"No, you just make out with them." Carmel's tone had gone from teasing to nasty in a split second.

Vada cut in. "Girls! No boy is worth fighting over."

They grumbled and changed the topic. "So, who are you dating, Miss Vada?" Carmel looked at her with an enormous smile. The girls tittered.

She glanced at Son then back at the group suddenly closing in around her like a school of piranhas. "For now, I'm married to my work." The girls laughed and looked at each other, eyes wide.

"Sure you are," the troublemaker piped up.

Vada rubbed the extra sunscreen on her palms into her hands. She needed to distract them fast. "Everybody got sunscreen on? Good. Let's go!"

With a *whoop*, the girls charged the water, argument forgotten.

Teenage girls could be brutal. With a sigh, Vada pulled off her T-shirt and began rubbing on sunscreen. It had been so long since she'd taken any time for herself that she'd dug her swimsuit out of the bottom of her drawer and was surprised the dark blue halter still fit. She should really get out more.

When she looked up, the little spit of beach she stood on was deserted, all the teens laughing and splashing in the water.

In his chair on the dock, Son looked like he had already fallen asleep in the warm sun. She hoped for his sake he remembered to put on sunscreen before taking a nap.

Wading into the tepid water, Vada cringed against the mud of the river bottom. She walked out farther, and with a gasp, felt the water temperature change from warm to deliciously cold. She sank in up to her shoulders, enjoying the refreshing chill. Around her, the kids splashed and sang out, already embroiled in games of chicken fight and Marco Polo.

The water flowed around Vada, inviting her to enjoy this rare experience. Deciding it would be worth washing her hair, Vada turned onto her back and stared up into the bright blue sky, weightless. Her muscles loosened, and she breathed deeply enjoying the peace of the river.

Her thoughts drifted to Son and the golden light glinting on his toned chest. She sighed as she drifted further out into the water. He was gorgeous and kind and thoughtful. And the feel of his lips against hers made her whole body tingle. How he'd run his hands up her sides. The memory made her close her eyes against the blazing blue of the summer sky, thankful no kids were nearby to see the grin sprawled out across her face.

After several minutes of daydreaming, she realized someone was calling her name. Flipping up, she treaded water as she looked around. A group of girls was calling to her from the shore to go fishing with them. She smiled and waved that she was coming.

With a few quick strokes, she pulled herself to shore. As she felt the water turning warm again, she set her feet down in the mud and began wading. Emerging out of the water by the dock, she stood up straighter and felt something sharp slash through the pad of her foot.

With a gasp, she stumbled against the dock, wincing back curse words as pain blazed up her leg. She squeezed her eyes shut as she struggled to breathe.

Dimly, she heard her name being called, then two strong hands pulled her up and set her on the rough, warm dock. Son peered at her, alarmed, as he took in the blood spreading on the weathered boards.

"What happened?" as he half-shouted the question, Ruffin appeared by his side.

"I stepped on something sharp." As air filled her lungs again, Vada looked at her scarlet foot, feeling woozy as she watched blood ooze from a deceptively small gash.

Ruffin gently lifted her ankle and set it on his knee. "Looks like glass. I'll need to get it out and clean the cut." He turned to Son and sent him to fetch his med-kit from the house. With a pat on her knee, he reassured her, "No need for stitches though, I think. If you can stay off it for a day or two."

Vada nodded as they waited for Son, closing her eyes so she wouldn't see the blood. She'd always been queasy at the sight of it, and seeing her own... She forced back a gag and pressed her eyelids tighter. In just a couple of minutes, Son came running back, followed by a huffing Cynthia.

She took one look at Vada and called the kids out of the water, her voice ringing out clearly over the river. With a flurry of splashes, the kids came tumbling out of the water, heading for the picnic tables on the deck.

With a gentle squeeze, Son wound his fingers into Vada's as Ruffin worked, pulling small shards from her foot and dabbing peroxide on the wound. Son's chest pressed against her back, warm and reassuringly solid.

"We'll need to check the shoreline again before the kids go back in the water." Cynthia's voice drifted over Vada as Ruffin wound gauze around her foot. "Your dang uncles must have been down here again. I could just strangle them!"

"Mom!" Ruffin interrupted. "Could you get Vada a coke? It will help the jitters."

As Cynthia stalked off muttering about men who knew better, Son slid an arm around Vada's shoulders and helped her shuffle over to the chair he'd been sitting in.

"You ok?" His warm hands were gentle on her knees as he knelt in front of her. Even with the pain throbbing in her foot, Vada inhaled at the sight of his eyes, dark as the river, looking up at her.

"I'm fine," she mumbled.

He glanced over her shoulder at the sound of approaching footsteps. "I'll be back in a few minutes to check on you." He wrapped a towel around her shoulders and pressed a kiss to her forehead before he turned away. Cynthia settled into a chair next to Vada, handing her an ice-cold can of coke, as Ruffin handed Son a mask and snorkel. The two men headed down to the water.

Vada rested her head back against the chair, irritation licking through her. The day had been so full of promise, and she had to slash her foot open. Just like her luck.

She stared after Son, hoping this incident wasn't a sign of what was to come with their relationship.

* * *

Cynthia sat smoking menthol cigarettes on the dock, a magazine spread over her lap. Vada glanced over at her, wondering what to say.

Vada pulled the towel a little closer around her shoulder as the wind cooled the drops of water on her skin. "Thank you. I don't know what I would have done without you and Ruffin."

"Oh, you're welcome, chile." Cynthia nodded decisively, her eyes twinkling. "But I have a feeling that young man of yours would have taken right good care of you too."

Vada frowned as she thought the statement over.

Cynthia glanced up at her then chuckled. "Chile, you keep frowning like that and your face is going to get stuck."

Vada chewed her lip. "Hard not to worry, considering…" She waved at her foot.

"Oh, you'll be fine. Just put some ointment on it to keep infection away and you'll be right as rain in no time."

Vada nodded absentmindedly as she watched Son wade into the water. He looked confident and in charge of the situation. So far from how Vada felt—about anything.

Cynthia took a drag of her cigarette, letting out a stream of smoke that hovered out over the water. "You ain't worrying over that preacher, are you?" She looked at Vada knowingly.

"That preacher just had to pull me from the water like a drowning kitten." Vada wrung her hands together.

With a cackle, Cynthia tossed her head back. "Oh, he don't mind, believe me. I saw the way you two looked at each other. Hot enough to boil water."

Vada blushed right up to her hairline. "Is it that obvious?"

"Only to a blind man." Cynthia continued to laugh.

Vada pressed her palms to her burning cheeks, foot forgotten. "Oh my God! How…"

Cutting her off, Cynthia set her magazine aside. "I'm a little sharper than most."

"But we…" Vada trailed off, thinking of Son's face looking up at her adoringly. They would have to be more careful. The way gossip would fly if anyone saw them! "But Son's a preacher. I can't be… There's already so many expectations, and I don't even know what we are yet."

Fixing her with a stare, Cynthia tapped the can of Coke clasped in Vada's hands. "Here. A little sugar in you will perk you right back up."

Grateful, Vada cracked open the ice-cold can. "What am I supposed to do?" Vada hadn't even realized she'd spoken the question aloud when Cynthia answered her.

"There's not much to do except enjoy the ride." Cynthia took a swig of her own Coke. "New love is so exciting. Makes me remember when I met Warren. Couldn't keep our hands off each other."

Vada stared down at the can in her hand. "I don't know if it can go anywhere with pressure like this."

Another laugh made Vada look up. Cynthia's eyes were sympathetic. "Of course, it can't go anywhere if you're too afraid to even step on the path."

The two of them drifted into silence. "Can I make an observation, sugar?" Cynthia leaned over and touched Vada's arm.

Mutely, Vada nodded.

"You are putting far more pressure on yourself to make this be perfect than anybody else ever could. Nobody can live up to that." She leaned closer. "All you have to do is appreciate what you've been given. Let go and let God handle the rest. He's got more of a handle on our situations than we ever will."

"I suppose." Vada struggled against the doubt bubbling in her chest. The last time she'd really trusted God for anything was when Eve got sick and look where that had gotten her. But Cynthia's words echoed in her mind.

No, Vada decided, forcing the doubt down as Son dove into the water, it was time she had a little faith again.

* * *

Son glanced over his shoulder at the dock as he emerged from the water, bone tired from trawling the bottom. At the end of the dock, he and Ruffin had found a rash of beer bottles, which had cut Vada. It had taken them ages to gather all the bottles and shards.

Vada had been sitting on the dock an awfully long time. Maybe he should make sure everything was all right? Beside her sat Cynthia, and they appeared to be in a serious conversation. He might not be the most welcome person right now.

He tried to concentrate on the kids sprawled across the back deck. It was getting close to lunchtime, and he would need to get everyone something to eat…

So far, Vada had taken charge of all the meals and snacks. But he was a grown man; he could figure it out. And knowing her there would be a couple of coolers stashed somewhere.

Sure enough, he found the coolers stacked in the Wilder's kitchen. Wheeling them out onto the deck, he began passing out sandwiches and drinks to the anxious kids.

"What's wrong with Vada?" Mahalia asked him as she grabbed her lunch. Preston hovered at her elbow, worry pinching his eyebrows.

"She cut her foot on some glass. She's all bandaged up, and we've got the glass out of the water." Son tried to keep his tone light and reassuring even as he glanced down toward the dock. Mahalia stared at him a moment longer, with her lips pressed together in a frown that said she wasn't quite convinced, before walking over to sit beside Carmel.

A step sounded on the wooden staircase behind him, and he spun around. Vada limped up onto the deck, smiling cheerfully, Cynthia's arm wrapped around her waist steadying her. "I wanted to make sure the kids were getting fed." She grinned as she sat at a nearby picnic table. "But it looks like you've got that all taken care of."

As he looked at her, hair curling in the humidity, tingles of admiration worked their way up his arms. So many people would be upset at what happened, railing and demanding to go home, and here Vada was laughing it off.

He took her hand, her fingers warm and rough in his, and pressed a kiss to her knuckles. "You are extraordinary, you know that, right?"

She threw her head back laughing. "I'm extra all right."

He chuckled and turned back to the waiting line of hungry teenagers.

A few minutes later, Son sat next to Vada on the deck, the kids spread out in the shade around them, enjoying a cold-cut lunch. They chatted over the nice weather, the lovely water, how well the kids were doing, and whether she would need stitches. Everything except themselves and the one thing that was on their mind.

At one particularly terrible pun of his, Vada tossed her head, snorting with laughter, and Son watched her face transform with beautiful dimples. Today might not be ideal to have the serious conversation they needed to have, but he was grateful for the time nevertheless.

Chapter 20

T he last car was leaving the parking lot when Son turned to Vada. Their little... kiss... was only two days ago, but it may as well have been printed up in the morning paper the way everyone seemed to know about it already.

Fortunately, all the moms seemed to have a sense of humor about the situation, throwing smirks and outright grins at Son and Vada as they pulled away in their mini-vans.

"Want to go get some sweet tea?" He nodded at Al's Diner.

Relief crested over Vada's face. "God, yes." She bit her lip. "I mean, yes, I would."

He chuckled. "Me too."

Before they could take a step, Son's cell phone rang, bells trilling through the air. He glanced at the caller ID and groaned. "Sorry, I have to get this."

"Go ahead. I need to put this away, anyway." Vada picked up her bag stuffed with towels and sunscreen and headed to her car, hobbling.

"Hey, Dad." Normally, Son would have been glad to talk to his father, but the man had chosen the worst timing possible to call.

"Where are you?"

At his father's direct tone, Son pulled the phone away from his ear and looked at it before answering. "Just finishing pick-up for the day at the church. Why?"

"Ah. So that's why you're not at home by now." His dad's tone lightened. "I'll just wait for you then."

"Wait! Are you at my house right now? As in this instant?" Bewildered, Son tried to piece together what was happening.

"Of course!" His dad laughed. "It sounded like you were having so much fun with *the camp…*" The words trailed suggestively. "…That I had to join you for the big overnight trip. Plus, I haven't seen you preach in a while. Thought I'd make a long weekend of it."

Son groaned under his breath. His dad always announced his visits well in advance, like months in advance. Something was most definitely up. And he had an idea after their talk the other night exactly what it was. Or rather who.

"I'll be there in a sec." As Son hung up, he muttered under his breath about nosey parents. Vada stood in front of him looking quizzical.

"So, my dad is here. As in waiting for me at the house as we speak." He grimaced at the words knowing full well that his dad was there to scope out Vada.

"Oh!" Her eyebrows shot up.

Son hated the disappointment that clouded her face. He pulled her into his chest and kissed her slowly. Her smell of coffee and sugar, mingled with sun and river water, washed over him as he inhaled against her lips. She felt so perfect in

178

his arms, he never wanted to let her go. And from the way she clung to his T-shirt, he knew the feeling was mutual. "We'll talk soon, ok? I promise."

Vada nodded, pursing her lips. With one last peck, Son turned and jogged to his car. He waved at her, where she stood as if frozen, as he drove out of the parking lot. Finally, she raised a hand in return. His heart clenched at the thought of letting this thing linger unspoken between them any longer.

Why did his dad have to choose today of all days for a surprise visit?

* * *

Vada stared out the window while she waited for Son in the Loveless Bakery, a cup of coffee cooling at her elbow. She propped her foot up on her opposite knee. It almost didn't hurt anymore, but she was still taking it easy. Nervously, she thought of hiking on it next week and hoped it would heal enough in time for the camping trip.

She'd spread before her on the table all her lists of supplies, the camping registration, and a stack of permission forms for the trip. Willow clattered a baking tray behind her as she put the afternoon bake into the display case.

Vada had no clue if she and Son would have a chance to talk today. As she stared out the window at the looming rain, she took a deep breath to steady herself. Whatever happened, it would be all right. They would be all right. She just had to believe.

A few minutes later the bells over the door jingled and in walked Son. As he held the door open, he mouthed "Sorry" to her just as his father trailed in. With a sinking stomach, she realized they would not be talking today. Vada stood up to shake the older man's hand. She had only seen him once or twice before when he came to visit and hear Son preach, and she wanted to leave a good impression.

"How are you, my dear?" His voice boomed through the bakery causing Willow to jump. She looked at them, eyes wide, and scurried into the back.

Vada would not be intimidated by Pastor Riser and his overly large voice. Some men just dominated a space without even realizing it. She shook his hand firmly as they sat, Son wedged in between them.

"Son tells me you've been doing a marvelous job with the youth this summer." Pastor Riser glanced fondly at Son. Underneath the table, she felt his fingers slip into her palm. It took every ounce of restraint not to smile like a giddy schoolgirl. "I have to say, for the short notice you had, and such a small town, you seemed to have pulled it all together quite well. I just had to meet this miracle worker."

Son smiled at her encouragingly and squeezed her fingers. Drawing another deep breath, Vada told herself to relax. "Everyone was eager to help the kids. When we all pull together, things get done around here." Vada leaned forward onto her elbows, releasing Son's hand.

"Well, she's modest too!" Pastor Riser slapped Son's chest with the back of his hand. "You got a good helper here, Son." Vada didn't miss the meaningful look he gave him, or Son ducking his head and rubbing at the back of his neck.

So, the old man knew. Heat flushed through her cheeks as she glanced at Son who sat staring daggers at his dad.

Pastor Riser sat back in his chair, looking pleased as punch, as he studied the two of them. "So, Vada, what made *you* decide to help?"

She shot another glance at Son before answering honestly, "I had several reasons. Obviously, it's been good for my business. But my cousin is also in the group, and I know how important it was to her. I'm sure it's important for a lot of the other kids as well. They need a safe place to go during the summer, and what safer place than church?"

The older man nodded, looking satisfied. "Nothing else?" He stared at Son who sighed, loudly.

Vada tried to bite back a smile. "Nope."

A twinkle in his eye, Pastor Riser sat forward. "Well, I'm glad you've been able to… keep an eye on him… as well."

"Dad!"

Vada laughed. "I can see where Son gets his sense of humor." Son huffed at her as she grinned back. For an interrogation, this was turning out to be fun.

Pastor Riser sat back again with a chuckle. "Well then, I won't take up any more of your time. I know you've got to get down to business." Pastor Riser gestured at all the papers before them, giving them a break from his questioning.

Vada tried to focus on the lists as she ran over the last supplies they needed to gather before Tuesday, but Son's warm hand resting on her knee distracted her. Despite her brain wanting to melt under the heat from his hand, she kept going. They didn't hit any hiccups until they got to the permissions forms.

"The few holdouts we were waiting on all promised to give me their forms on Sunday, including Preston." She tapped the stack. "And then we should be good to go." She picked up the camping registration. "We just have to verify our reservation in the cabins for seventeen people."

"Eighteen," Son murmured.

"Eighteen?" Vada flipped through the pages. "Did I miscount?"

Pastor Riser shifted in his seat. "I'm afraid you have me to blame for the last-minute change. I begged Son to let me come along." Son's pressed lips and drawn-out sigh said something completely different. Pastor Riser shot him a look, and Vada wanted to giggle at the image of a teenage Son scowling at his father. "It's been a long time since I worked with youth, but I figured you could always use another chaperone."

"That's no problem. We have a couple of extra spaces in the cabins. Just need to let the park know we have an updated headcount." Vada made a note on the sheet. Her heart sank as she realized Pastor Riser was there to scope out a potential daughter-in-law.

Even though she and Son still hadn't determined what they were yet or if they were in this for the long haul. Her stomach fluttered at the thought.

"Well, if that's all." Pastor Riser stood. "Come on, Son. Let the lady get back to her planning and prepping."

Son rose reluctantly from his seat. As his father strode out the door, he quickly bent and furtively kissed Vada's cheek. "Sorry," he whispered in her ear. His warm breath sent tingles down her neck.

As the door swung shut behind them, Vada stared out the window, frowning. It was going to be a long five days.

"Girl!" Willow's perky voice drew her out of her stupor. "How're you gonna make it through that camping trip with him breathing down your neck?"

"Oh, he seems nice enough. I'm sure it will be fine." She was not at all confident that it would, in fact, be fine. She spiraled as she thought of all the ways the trip could go wrong, like when she cut her foot, with *Son's dad* watching. Maybe she could ask Lou Ellen to distract Pastor Riser with her endless chatter.

Willow shrugged as she set a fresh cup of coffee for Vada down on the table and slid into the chair next to her. "If you say so." She punched Vada's shoulder. "Also, that must have been one heck of a kiss. Because, *whooo*, I could cut the tension between you two with a knife. Holding hands under the table and stealing looks."

As Willow chattered on, Vada stared out the window toward the church through the drizzle which had finally started. Despite what she said, and despite the growing attachment she had to Son, she wasn't sure she was ready for this at all.

Chapter 21

After an unending weekend with his father, Son was eager to get on the road. Even if that road included fourteen, overly enthusiastic teenagers and four disenchanted adults.

That was still better than his dad staring up at him from the front pew as he struggled to grasp just the right words to impact the congregation. Anything short of astounding and he would hear about it later. He'd sweated through his shirt so bad that he'd immediately changed in his office afterward.

As they bounced over the road to Leroy Percy State Park, Son sighed in relief that he was no longer the sole object of his father's scrutiny as the kids began another round of "Ninety-Nine Bottles of Coke on the Wall."

He glanced in the rearview mirror to see Vada and his dad singing along with the boisterous group. From the passenger seat, Lou Ellen shot him a long-suffering smile. Finally, the entrance to the park appeared, and with relief, Son gave their reservation sheet to the gate attendant as the kids cheered.

A few minutes later, they pulled up beside two rustic cabins that looked like they had seen better days. Sagging screen hung on the windows of the porches and moss grew thickly on the roofs. Son studied the cabins skeptically.

"I know they look sketchy, but they're clean and won't leak in a rainstorm." Vada appeared beside him, startling him. A huge duffle bag was slung over her shoulder. "My family likes to come out here sometimes." Swiping at her forehead, she frowned. "Although, usually when it's cooler. We'll have to leave all the doors and windows open, so we don't sweat to death tonight."

Son swiped at his own face as he felt moisture prickle behind his ears. "Let's pray we get a nice breeze." A gust of wind blew through the clearing, stirring the long grasses around them.

Vada glanced at him, a grin on her lips that made his heart gallop. "Looks like someone heard you." She tapped his arm. "C'mon. Let's get everything unloaded, so we can get going." He eyed her as she walked away, concerned about her foot, but her gait was smooth, her steps sure.

While Lou Ellen and his dad took the kids to the cabins to choose their bunks, Son followed Vada back to the van. Vada swung the back doors open and stepped forward, creating a screen around them from prying eyes. With a grin, she chunked down her duffle bag and grabbed the front of Son's shirt.

As her lips crashed into his, Son sighed, relieved to have her in his arms again. With a groan, he pulled her close, exploring every part of her mouth. She gasped and slid her arms around his neck. With cicadas thrumming around them, he clung to her, not wanting to ever leave this blissful moment.

With his dad there and monopolizing his attention, he

wasn't sure how many of these moments he'd be able to steal with Vada. Wrapping his arms around her waist, he kissed her even more fiercely as her hands slid up to the back of his neck.

Footsteps crunched over old leaves behind them, and they leaped apart, straightening clothes and grabbing coolers and boxes from the back of the van.

Lou Ellen popped around the open doors, peering at them with a knowing smirk. Son's heart thumped with relief. "I came to help you two, but it looks like y'all already have it handled." She looked between them, lips pressed together in amusement.

Son tried to scowl at her as he drug a large cooler down. Plunking the handle in Lou Ellen's palm, he quipped back, "We've just about got it wrapped up." His face heated as he realized his shirt was still bunched up where Vada had grabbed him.

Lou Ellen snickered while Vada pressed a hand to her mouth as he smoothed it out. Glancing over her shoulder, Lou Ellen dropped her voice, "Pastor Riser is preoccupied with the kids. They're trying to convince him to take a top bunk."

Son could just imagine his father clambering gamely up a bunk, then getting stuck with his bad knees. He winced. "I should probably go see what's happening." He picked up a couple of cords of firewood to take with him. "Thank you, Lou Ellen."

"No problem. Just keep the make-out sessions to a minimum, 'k?" Her laughter mingled with Vada's as he strode away.

Already, they had been busted. This trip was going *great*.

Chapter 21

* * *

"I'm impressed."

Son looked over at his dad as they trecked down the trail. The muggy air swarmed with the sounds of crickets, frogs, and birdsong. Not to mention mosquitoes. He swatted one of the pesky bloodsuckers away from his ear as he asked, "What's got you impressed?"

His dad smiled as they clambered over a log. Up ahead, Vada was surrounded by a gaggle of the girls, who chattered and horsed around. "At this." He waved a hand. "In less than an hour, we've gotten unpacked, the fire pit set up, and on the trail." With a shake of his head, he added, "Even in my heyday as a youth minister, I could never do that."

Son nodded at Vada's back. "It's all her."

His dad swept him with an appraising look. "I know. Vada is a fearsome woman. I haven't met one like her since your mother."

A rumbling in his stomach warned Son they were on dangerous ground. "She's impressive all right."

His dad shot him another look. "When I met your mother, I just knew I'd found my match. She didn't put up with any of my self-indulgence. I wanted to be a better man to deserve her." He clapped Son on the shoulder. "I'm glad to see you with someone who does the same for you. I've been wanting a daughter to dote on. And it doesn't do for a pastor to stay unmarried too long."

Son looked back at his dad wide-eyed. He hadn't expected him to attack the topic so blatantly. He stuttered as he searched for the words. "We're not… We haven't even…" he stuttered.

His dad held up a hand. "I know what I see." He nodded

toward Vada. "And if you love her, you shouldn't beat around the bush. A woman like that doesn't stay single for long."

"Can I ask you something?" Son skirted around a washed-out section of the trail.

"Sure." His father gazed up at the leaves swaying overhead.

"How did you and Mom make it? As a couple, I mean. You two were so different. She had the shop, and you had the church." The question had been bugging him ever since his dad had told him about his mother's store. It was an eerie echo of him and Vada.

"I'm not going to lie, it was hard at first. We were always so busy that we hardly ever saw each other. And I was a jerk sometimes about my wife not being as devoted to the church as I was." His dad scratched at his nose. "Eventually, we learned how to make time for each other. And I realized your mother had her own calling, and it was my job to support her as much as she supported me." He shrugged. "And then you came along, and she sold the shop, and it wasn't an issue at all anymore."

"So, it resolved itself?" Son asked. It seemed to him, that his parents' problems all stemmed from the store.

His dad shot him a look. "Yes, but that's not my point. Your mother was her own person, not an extension of me. Once I learned that things got better." He stared into the distance. "I've always wondered if she would have kept the shop if I'd been less... well, pardon my French, but less of an asshole about her being there so much when we were first married. She never said a word about the late hours I pulled at the church." He shook his head. "What I would do differently."

Son nodded as he chewed on his lip, thinking about Vada's nascent equestrian school. Up ahead, Vada looped her arm through Lou Ellen's, their laughter floating back to him on

188

the breeze.

* * *

Vada laid out the fixings for s'mores with a sigh. Why had she decided that everything they brought to eat on this camping trip had to be grilled or cooked over the fire? She'd already had to fend off three kids from playing in the bonfire. Preston had even tried to leap over it. Thankfully, only his shoes scorched.

As she handed out straightened coat hangers for the marsh-mallows, she eyed Son and Pastor Riser where they set together on the opposite side of the fire, laughing and joking.

She hadn't missed that they'd hung back from the group on their hike, ensconced in an intense-looking conversation. Now, Son kept shooting her looks that were a mix of pensive and speculative, his brows quirked together. Whatever he'd been discussing with his dad earlier, it must have had something to do with her. She would pry it out of him later.

"All right, everyone! Grab your s'mores and settle down." She shooed all the teenagers into a loose ring around the fire pit. Elbows jabbed and pushed as the kids tussled for the best spots. Son stood and grabbed some graham crackers and marshmallows with a wink at her.

As she settled onto a log in front of the fire, she felt a presence at her elbow. With an *oof*, Son sat down next to her, dangling his marshmallow over the blaze.

"If you're not careful, you're going to turn it all black," she teased.

"Maybe I like it that way." He waggled his eyebrows at her.

She sniffed and turned back to the fire. "You can have it any way you like." His head swiveled toward her at her sassy

189

words.

Giggling, Mahalia stood and came over to her. "I made you a s'more!" She handed the treat to Vada and scurried back to her friends.

"Oh, that was sweet of her." Vada raised the s'more to her lips.

"I don't think—" Son began, but she'd already bitten into it. Whipped cream exploded out the sides and all over her face. Across the fire, Mahalia and her friends cracked up. Vada shot a glare at them as she shook the sticky stuff off her hands.

"Here, let me." Son leaned over and dabbed at her face with a paper towel. His hand seared into her skin where he cupped her jaw, his deep gaze sending a shiver down into her core. Vada froze, mesmerized by his dark eyes and gentle touch. "There." He swept away the last remnant of whipped cream and sat back. Noticing her stare, he cleared his throat and rubbed the back of his neck.

"Why don't I grab my guitar?" He broke the silence as he turned away. Her skin tingled, suddenly cold, where his hand had been.

Around them, the kids rustled as they shifted in their seats from where they had been openly ogling them. Vada glanced at Pastor Riser and found him studying her, his head cocked to the side. As Son returned with his guitar case, the kids cheered and began shouting out song suggestions.

"All right. You should know this one. We've sung it plenty on Wednesday nights." Son strummed a few golden chords then launched into "Awesome God." His rich baritone rumbled through the circle as the kids joined in, clapping their hands and stomping their feet to the rhythm. Radiant faces, bathed in the warm light of the fire, surrounded Vada.

Son's voice pulled her deeper in, the song she'd once sung in youth group as familiar to her as her dreams. With a laugh, she clapped and stomped along.

As Vada watched Son's strong fingers fly over the shining strings, she gulped against a rising knot of emotion. She loved him. She loved him with all the blood in her body and the breath in her lungs.

In the flickering glow of the fire, Vada sat next to Son in the late summer heat and shivered.

* * *

Son flipped the light switch back and forth several times to get the boys' attention. "Bedtime!" he hollered. A chorus of groans rose. "It's well past midnight. Scoot!" The kids grumbled as they drifted into their bunks, but Son just chuckled. His dad shook his head with a smile and then rolled into his bunk as well.

In the sudden quiet, Son flipped the light off one last time as he stared out the window. Vada was still outside cleaning up, having entrusted the girls to Lou Ellen. The memory of her gorgeous eyes and soft skin earlier made him suck in a breath.

Easing out the door, he slipped down the cabin steps into the cooling night air.

"Vada," he called softly, not wanting to startle her as he strode over. She glanced up at him, a small smile on her face as she poured a bucket of sand over the dying fire.

"Quite a night," she called back, her voice husky and low. The moonlight spilled down her, gilding her curves and lighting up her eyes. She was the most incredible woman he had ever seen.

"A perfect night." He stepped up to her and wrapped his arms around her waist, holding her close. Lowering his lips to hers, he drank her in, savoring the brush of her soft mouth. Feeling her melt against him, he leaned in, ravaging her mouth with all the passion he'd kept banked the last five days with his dad around. She pressed into him, her hands running down his back then looping into his waistband, her knotted fingers pushing against his stomach as she rose to meet him.

This woman lit every part of him on fire. From her deep eyes to the way she took control of every situation, he adored all of her. He couldn't imagine another woman in his arms. He was hers completely.

He sighed in ecstasy against her lips.

Gently, Vada pulled away from him, her hands still on his chest. He tried to draw her to him again, but she pressed him back. "Don't you think we should talk first?"

He cradled her chin. "I thought our lips were already saying it all."

She lightly slapped his chest. "You know what I mean."

"All right." He stepped back and shoved his hands in his pockets to keep from reaching for her again. "You're right. Let's talk." He sat on one a log beside the dead campfire and waited for her to join him.

As she settled in with a sigh beside him, he studied her serious face, his stomach knotting at the way she hunched her shoulders. "How come I get the feeling that this is about more than us dating?"

Vada clasped her hands. "It's not!" She cast her eyes down to the ground, frowning. "Or maybe it is. I dunno."

He took a steadying breath. "Why don't you tell me what's

on your mind and we'll take it from there?"

"It's this." She pointed between them. "How is this supposed to work? I'm a farm girl, not a pastor's kid. I've never been to seminary. I know nothing of being a preacher's wife!"

"You're the woman I'm in love with." He reached for her and took her hand. "You're the most incredible person I know." Her eyes sparkled with tears as he rubbed his thumb across the back of her hand. "And we've barely started dating—we haven't even been on a proper date yet—why are you really worried about being a wife?"

"Because…" She slipped her palm from his and spun her hands in the air. "*You* have to be. The woman you date and marry has to be a leader in the church. She's gotta be all upright and submissive and stuff—like your mother."

She whispered, "I'll never measure up."

He knew now that his mother had grown into her role, just as Vada would in time. Son grabbed her hands again. "There is no measuring up. I'm not dating my mother; I'm dating you. You're more than enough to me." Gently, he shook her arms to get her to look at him. "Hey, I mean it. Trust me."

Vada stared at him, tear tracks slick on her face, as her breath hitched. After a few seconds, she inhaled deeply. "Ok." She repeated, "Ok, I trust you."

He wrapped an arm around her shoulder. "Good. You know we'll figure all that stuff out. The leadership stuff and whatnot."

She breathed in through her nose. "It's going to be tough fitting in anything more with my schedule."

Seeing an opportunity, Son leaped in. He remembered Clay's assertion that the school was going nowhere. How things had eased between his parents when his mother gave up the store. They didn't have to make the same mistakes. If Vada could just see that it was holding her back… "Maybe it's time for you to rethink the school. Open up your possibilities."

Under his arm, Vada stiffened. "What do you mean open up your possibilities?" Her face went still as she looked up at him.

He swallowed, already regretting his words. "It's just that… You see… Well, your school isn't doing much right now, is it? You could look for something new to do."

"Something new." Her voice was flat, like her stare.

"Something new," he agreed, knowing he was walking into a trap of his own making.

She sat up away from him. "How come a couple of weeks ago you were telling me to go after my dream, give it my all—but as soon as we're…" She raised her hands exasperatedly. "…then I'm the one who must walk away from my life's work? Why don't you come help me at the school instead?"

Son didn't point out that they'd both be broke if he did, or that his years of studying for his doctorate in theology would be for nothing. Instead, he grabbed at the most obvious idea. "I'm a pastor!" His voice ticked up. Why did he even have to spell this out for her?

"And my calling couldn't possibly be as important or God-given as yours?" Her eyes blazed at him.

He sputtered, his own temper flaring. "It does kind of take precedence, yeah."

"I minister to those kids just as much through horses as you do through sermons." She stood abruptly. "God, if this is what you think of…" She choked back a sob.

He could feel her slipping away, not just in the way she pulled back, but in the look in her eye. "I'm not saying… I didn't mean you have to give up your job if you don't want."

"Just that it's not as important as yours."

"That's not what…" He clenched his fists. "Gah. Have you ever considered that the school is what's holding you back, Vada?"

"Back from what?" she hissed.

He gestured sweepingly around the clearing. "From more!"

Shaking her head emphatically, she bit back, "Your idea of more! Not everyone is called to work in a church."

"I'm not saying…" He pressed his lips together, suddenly seeing that they were at an impasse, and he had no way to solve it. "Maybe, you're right. If this is how we handle every little thing… No compromise… We'll never work."

Vada's shoulders slumped. "Maybe."

Hands hanging limp at his side, Son asked, breath hitching. "So, is this it? We're done before we've even begun?" Hot tears slid down his cheeks at the words.

"I guess." Vada swiped at her cheeks. "I'm sorry." Covering her face with her hands, Vada spun and ran into the girls' cabin.

Son stood alone in the moonlight, his heart cracking in his chest, wondering what he had just done.

* * *

The sun rose the next morning as Son stared up at the ceiling of the cabin. His dad snored away beneath him, oblivious to Son's tossing and turning. Around him, teenage boys snorted in their sleep, the whole place smelling like a locker room.

The shock had finally worn off as Son hunkered down in his sleeping bag last night, replaced by anger and an ache that ran so deep beneath his breastbone, that he didn't think he'd ever be rid of it. Vada was being unreasonable. Of course, she'd see he was right about the equestrian school if she just took a minute to think. She'd come around.

But his aching heart told him he'd messed up big. That this was more than a simple fight. He loved Vada so much it was giving him heartburn at just the memory of her defeated face last night. She was like the sun, and he craved her warmth, wanted her soothing touch. His whole body ached for her.

But she was right. How would things even work between them? They couldn't.

Grunting, he rose and began petulantly rolling up his sleeping bag. He wasn't sleeping anyway, so why pretend anymore now that the sun was up? Flinging the rolled bag over his shoulder, he stomped out of the cabin.

And immediately halted on the steps. Vada sat with her back to him on a log in front of the dead fire. At his step, she glanced over her shoulder and rose, spinning to face him.

Son tightened his grip on the strap of his sleeping bag. "Good morning." He strode by her to the van, willing himself not to reach for her.

Tentatively, she trailed behind him. "Can we talk? After last night…"

He couldn't do this with her. They could never work this out; they'd always be pulling each other away from what they were meant to do. And if they got back together it would just hurt that much worse when they broke up for real. He ground out. "There's nothing more to say after last night. You made yourself perfectly clear."

She sucked in her lower lip, eyes pleading. "I just wanted you to understand that it's nothing—"

"Please, Vada." He rubbed at his face, the lack of sleep and the gnawing anger making him sharp. "Please don't say it's nothing to do with me. Because that will not make this situation better."

"But it's not—"

"Vada!" he growled. "What do you want from me? To not feel guilty because you broke up with me over nothing? Because if that's it, then I forgive you."

"You forgive *me*? I didn't break up with you!" she blurted, hurt clear in her eyes.

"You're the one who walked away!" He brushed past her back toward the cabin. "You made it clear there was nothing to work out. So, please, leave me alone."

As he slammed the cabin door behind him, he looked back. Vada stood where he'd left her, hands clasped over her chest and head bowed.

Chapter 22

T he ride back was subdued. Vada crawled to the back bench of the van, leaving as much distance between Son and herself as possible. As Lou Ellen slid the door shut at the engine's rev, she shot a worried glance at Vada.

With a shrug, Vada leaned back in the seat. There was nothing she could do about the awkward situation. She'd already tried explaining things to Son, and that went as well as a lead balloon at a birthday party. Thank God this was the last summer camp excursion of the year. They wouldn't have to see each other anymore except in passing at church.

And that thought made her want to double over, the breath whooshing out of her like she'd plunged into icy water and been socked in the stomach all at once.

"You got this, Son?" In the front, Pastor Riser leaned toward Son with a concerned look on his face. Vada tried to ignore the dark circles beneath Son's eyes and the way he gripped the steering wheel.

"I'm just tired. I can drive," Son responded tersely.

Lou Ellen shot Vada a grimace from where she sat in the first row of seats. "You ok?" she mouthed. Vada shrugged. Lou Ellen frowned and turned forward as Son cranked the van.

As they pulled into the parking lot later, Vada sighed in relief. She'd imagined this moment as more celebratory. Instead, she stared dejectedly out the window at the waiting line of cars as the kids began clambering out of the van, then moved to follow them.

Handing a duffle bag to Preston, she turned to find Mrs. Langford hanging right by her elbow. "Vada, dear, I've been meaning to get your number. Preston just loved horseback riding so much, I figured I would see if I could sign him up for some lessons this fall." Suddenly, a chorus of mothers closed in, voices raised as they all demanded her information.

Numbly, Vada typed her number into the cellphones they shoved into her hand. "I'll have to get back to you about availability." What she wouldn't give for a stack of business cards right about now.

Mrs. Langford winked at her, "No problem, dear. Just trying to get some after-school activities lined up." With a finger wave to Vada, she ushered Preston into the waiting sedan. The other mothers all murmured similar sentiments and dispersed.

Just a second later, Mahalia flounced up to Vada. "Can you take me to Carmel's?"

With a mechanical nod, Vada threw their bags into the back of her truck. The minute she closed the door, Mahalia started in on her. Because, of course, the kids already knew by some osmosis that she and Son had split.

Vada clenched the wheel as Mahalia railed on, "And after all that hard work we put in, you blow it!"

"All that work?" Suddenly, Vada felt the beginnings of a migraine. Mahalia went quiet.

"Mahalia, what work?"

Biting her lip, Mahalia muttered, "We might have tried to help you two out?"

"What do you mean 'we'? And what do you mean 'help'?" Vada bit out. "Have you been meddling in my relationship all summer?"

"Not all summer." Mahalia couldn't hide the smirk but wiped it away as soon as she saw Vada glaring at her. "The ketchup packet was just a fluke! But then we saw the way you look at each other…"

Vada cut in. "So, the entire youth group has been what matchmaking us?"

"I mean, sort of?" Mahalia pursed her lips. Vada curled her toes against the sudden desire to shake the information out of her like a piggy bank with a few coins left.

"Mahalia—"

"It was just a few pranks!"

Suddenly, things clicked into place. "So, the door and the stream?"

"The stream wasn't supposed to go like that." Mahalia shook her head. "The horse was just supposed to buck a little, so you'd have to come and ride beside him."

Vada bit her tongue, trying to tamp down her response. "He could have gotten really hurt, Mahalia."

Mahalia looked down at her lap, contrite. "I know. I'm sorry."

Vada pinched the bridge of her nose. "It's ok. It's over now."

"But why? You two clearly still like each other. I mean, he

totally digs you." Mahalia looked at Vada like she was a sweater that had unexpectedly shrunk in the wash.

"It's complicated. You wouldn't understand." The last thing Vada wanted to do was talk about her love life with her fourteen-year-old cousin. Especially when her heart was still so raw. The breakup—if she could even call it that—was only a few hours old.

"What is there to understand? You like each other, so be together." Ah, for the logic of a teenager.

Vada shook her head. "Just, please, be quiet. It's not happening and there's nothing you can do about it."

Mahalia sniffed and crossed her arms. "Blew it, man."

Deep down, in some part beneath the hurt and anger, where a saner version of Vada sat quietly waiting to be let out, she agreed. A second later they pulled up outside Carmel's, and Mahalia ran out of the truck without another word, shooting a sulky look at Vada as she went.

With a sigh, Vada turned the truck back toward town and the over-air-conditioned refuge that was the Southern Comfort bar. She desperately needed a drink.

* * *

Under the dim lights of the bar, the whiskey glowed golden in Vada's glass. She tapped the bar, getting Lester's attention, and raised her glass for a refill. It was a two-drink kind of day.

Next to her, a barstool squeaked. Leora smiled at her as she primly crossed her legs. "I thought it was you I saw over here, sugar."

"Hey, Leora." Vada took a sip at the melting ice in her glass as Lester finally worked his way down the bar toward her.

She shouldn't have been surprised to see Leora here; everyone came through Southern Comfort at some point in the week, whether for after-work drinks or karaoke night. It was just Vada's luck that even here, someone wanted to talk to her.

"I had something I wanted to ask you." Leora tugged at the string of pearls around her neck.

Wanting to get this conversation over with, Vada leaned her elbows on the bar. "Shoot."

"We're recruiting new members for our Women's Committee." Vada opened her mouth to protest, but Leora laid a gentle hand on her wrist and continued. "And I thought of you because of all the good you do in our community. I couldn't tell you how happy it would make us to have you as a member."

Vada swallowed against the rising knot in her throat. What Leora wasn't saying was that now she was the pastor's girlfriend, she should, of course, act like a church leader. Except she wasn't and never had been, not really. She licked her lips, trying to think of how to explain everything to her.

"Now…" Leora held up a hand. "…before you go telling me no and how busy you are, why don't you just come to one meeting and see what we're all about? You'd be surprised at all we do. I'm sure there's an area that would be a good fit for you."

Any other day, an invitation to join one of Midnight Bluff's most important committees would have thrilled her. Vada's fingers tingled at the possibility, the ability to do more around town. But she drew back at the thought, eerily echoing Son's words.

She loved Leora and knew that whenever she was behind something big things happened. But she just couldn't be around the church more now. Not when she would be there gabbing over finger sandwiches with Son just down the hall from the ladies' parlor.

"Leora," Vada began. "I'm touched you would think of me. But that kind of thing really isn't for me." She held up one of her booted feet as she tried to laugh it off. "I'm more of a working girl, not a planning girl."

"Oh, we get our hands dirty!" Leora said with a smile.

"Still, what you're offering, it's just not for me." Her cheeks hurt from the plastered-on smile. "I'm not…" How to tell her tactfully? "Me and Son… we're not a thing," she blurted, tears stinging her eyes.

Leora's face melted into sympathy. "Oh, here I am bothering you, and you're going through a breakup. Oh, honey." Her hand moved to Vada's back, rubbing in slow, motherly circles. She pressed a napkin into Vada's hand. "I am so sorry, sugar. Is there anything I can do?"

Vada sniffed back her tears. "No. I'm all right. I just can't…" She waved a hand. "I'm just trying to wrap my head around it."

Patting her hand, Leora slipped off her barstool. "Of course, sugar. I'll leave you to it. If there's anything I can do, just let me know." And with that, she slipped away, leaving nothing but the faint scent of Chanel No. 5 behind.

Vada rubbed at her face, sniffing. Leora's abrupt about-face told her everything she needed to know of her offer. She hadn't been after Vada; she'd been after the pastor's girlfriend. Vada herself had nothing to recommend as just herself.

And that thought depressed her more than any other.

Chapter 23

S on leaned back in the Adirondack chair on his back patio, enjoying the quiet. After two full days with the youth group, the peace was much needed. As his dad bustled around inside, Son stared over the pristine flower beds into the fields beyond.

This year, they were full of sunflowers, six feet tall and bursting with light. With soft tweets, birds dipped down and then rose from the field. The entire scene was so bucolic it sent a pang of longing through him.

Son had hoped that Vada would sit here with him, drinking a celebratory glass of lemonade. Instead, she was miles away across town, probably cursing his name.

He knew he would.

The screen door behind him creaked open and his dad settled with a groan into the neighboring chair.

"What a day." His dad handed him a glass of lemonade, beads of condensation running down the side, and it took all of Son's self-control not to snort at the irony.

They rested in silence for a few minutes. His dad cleared his throat. "So, what's got you brooding out here by yourself?"

"Nothing." The lie was instinct. Son didn't have the words to describe the ache in his chest, how his bones felt heavy. His tongue felt so heavy with regret he wasn't sure it could dredge up the syllables needed to explain.

"Wouldn't have something to do with that pretty cowgirl leaving in a huff today, would it?" With a twinkle in his eye, his dad turned to him. "Seemed like you two weren't speaking."

"It doesn't matter, Dad." Vada kept her face turned from him at pickup at the church. He had reached out for her, wanting to say anything to soothe the hurt between them, but she had stayed stubbornly focused on slinging bags out of the van with unnecessary force.

Not that he knew what to say anyway.

Snorting, his dad sat back in the chair. "Stop your sulking, Son. It doesn't suit you."

Startled, Son looked at his father. "What would have me do then? Beg her to be with me? She's made it pretty damn clear we won't work."

"Watch your mouth, young man." His dad's look was stern. Feeling chastised, Son slumped in his chair, and they sat in the quiet for a moment. He asked gently, "Would you two really not work, or are you afraid to put in the work?"

Son was too tired for cryptic suggestions. "What do you mean by that?"

"Remember the story of how I met your mother? Well, there's more to it than what I told you." Rubbing his hands together, his father paused. "Your mother had much the same reaction—that we couldn't work. And she was so strong-willed." He coughed out a laugh. "Took me the better part of a year to even get her to go out on a date with me. She used to say to me, 'How can a pastor and shopgirl make it work?' But I could see that she ministered just as much from her register as I did from the pulpit."

He held up a finger. "Do you hear me? A whole year before she said yes to a *date*." Son shifted. All it had taken to derail him and Vada was one argument. His dad continued, "But it was that spark, that determination, that I adored."

"And once we were married, it didn't stop being hard overnight. We both thought we knew what was best, so our arguments were excruciating." He sighed. "It took us years to figure out that until we were fighting for our marriage together, we would always be at odds. In the end, I never tried to pastor a large church, so we could stay in that little town she loved. And your mother, bless her, never tried to grow her boutique. And I hated that for her as much as I was grateful. That she had so much potential, and she spent it on me." His gaze drifted off, contemplative.

Son prompted him, "What made you stick it out?"

His dad's eyes snapped back to him. "Perspective. We came to see those sacrifices not as things we were giving up, but as opportunities to grow together." Laying his head back against the chair, he concluded, "Falling in love... that's the easy part. Staying in love takes focus, commitment."

Son mulled over his words, about his mom ministering through the boutique. Vada had said something similar, though he'd been too angry to hear it. Ministering through the everyday. With all his Bible degrees, the thought had never occurred to him. To him, serving God meant studying and striving, always alone. But Vada just got it.

She was so sure of herself and her purpose. And he... had

been trying to change that about her under the guise of "making it work." Guilt wound through them. In truth, if he was more assured of his calling, hers wouldn't unsettle him so much.

Son stood and strode restlessly around the yard, paying no attention to the flowers in their glory, his father watching over him from the porch.

* * *

Vada plucked at a rip in the red gingham tablecloth. Willow swatted her hand as Lou Ellen leaned toward her over their steaming cups of coffee.

"Are you sure you don't need anything, sweetie? Xanax? Ice cream? To go key his car?"

Vada exchanged an amused glance with Cress, who sat picking at a croissant beside her. Only Ellie was missing from this little tête-à-tête, stuck showing a tract of land on the backside of Cleveland.

God, she'd forgotten how nice it was to have Lou Ellen in her corner. Lou Ellen was a force of nature, and Vada hadn't realized how exhausting it had been to tiptoe around each other all these years.

Willow shook her head. "Probably not the best idea to key your boss' car, babe."

"We totally could though," Lou Ellen took a sip of her coffee and then snapped her fingers. "I know! We'll get a bunch of smelly fish and dump it in his office." She pulled out her cell phone. "Lonny over at the catfish plant owes me a favor—"

With a laugh, Vada put her hand over Lou Ellen's phone. "I appreciate it, really. But let's not get arrested for defacing private property."

She lifted her cup of coffee to her lips. "Besides, I might have gotten a little creative with a can of spray paint the other night." After drinking her sorrows away at Southern Comfort, she'd swung by the Co-Working Space and… embellished his name.

The ladies around her hooted with laughter, breaking off abruptly with the ring of the bells above the door. Willow stood with a smile, then froze.

Vada followed her stare and jolted as she met Son's eyes. His father wavered in the doorway behind him. The moment stretched long and tenuous as a strand of over-pulled taffy. Then Son smiled, his face strained, and her heart screeched back into action with a painful thump.

Vada slouched in her seat as they passed her, Willow scrambling to the register.

"Why does he have to show up now?" she whispered to Cress.

"I have no idea." Cress didn't bother to lower her voice. Beside her, Lou Ellen's gaze at Son was acidic.

Order placed, Son sidled up to their table, change jingling in his pocket. "Ladies." He nodded. Gazing straight at Vada, he sucked in a breath, his chest rising with effort. "Vada, I didn't get a chance to thank you. For all your help this summer."

Around them, the women had stilled, watching their exchange with rapt attention. Vada shifted in her chair. "It was nothing, really."

He exhaled heavily. "But it was. I couldn't have done it without you. You're a natural leader." He gazed meaningfully at her. "And I enjoyed having such an experienced camp counselor."

The words dug into Vada's flesh, stinging like rubbing alcohol on a paper cut. Her heart kicked her ribs painfully as she tried to smile back at him.

"You are an inspiration." His dad took her hand, a kind expression on his face. "I'm sure God has a bright path laid out for such a determined young lady like you."

"Thank you," Vada murmured. With a little pat on her hand, the older man turned and slipped out the door, Son throwing an enigmatic look at her as the door shut.

Willow came up and gripped the back of Vada's chair as she stared out the window, watching them walk away. "What was that all about?"

Vada blinked quickly. "Nothing. Just being polite." She waved away their concern.

A bright path. She felt it calling to her as clear as the wind. "So, I'm thinking about taking that Business Basics class with the Chamber." She picked up her mug as all three of her friends chimed it was an excellent idea.

Willow squeezed her arm. "I'll go with you." Across the table, Lou Ellen stole the second half of Cress' croissant and winked at her.

It was time to claim her God-given dream.

Chapter 24

S on studied the young man peering back at him from the Zoom window. "I must say, your qualifications are spectacular." Burying himself in the hunt for a new youth pastor had been Son's saving grace this week. Every empty moment filled itself with spinning thoughts of Vada and what he should have done differently. "What interests you about Midnight Bluff Baptist, Travis?"

Travis fiddled with something off camera. "I've always been drawn to small towns. You can get to know the people on another level, you know?"

Smooth answer. The whole interview had been smooth, even before today. The moment Son had resurfaced Travis' resume from the stack on his desk, things had just flowed. Another pastor would have taken it as a sign that this was ordained to be.

But something still bothered Son. Maybe it was Travis' shifting eyes or how he kept fiddling with things off-screen. "Youth ministry is an interesting career choice for someone with your background. Why youth?"

A pause followed, and Son frowned wondering if the connection had frozen. "I think I lost you." He clicked to check his Wi-Fi signal. Sometimes it got a little flaky.

"Sorry, I was just thinking." Travis tugged at his cuffs. "Youth ministry is such an overlooked part of our church. It's these kids' most impressionable years. We can have a real impact on them for the rest of their lives, but most churches relegate it to a Bible college student who is using it as a stepping stone." Son resisted the urge to point out that Travis was a recent graduate himself; he wasn't that far off from being a student. "I see it as an area of need, and I want to make a difference."

A feeling of satisfaction spread through Son at the perceptive answer. Few people Travis' age would see such a low-glory position as something worthy of pursuit. At the beginning of the summer, Son hadn't even seen it that way until he'd gotten to know his kids on a more personal level.

"I like your outlook." He smiled at the younger man. With his exceptional seminary record and recommendations, Son couldn't imagine a more tailor-made fit for a minister to hand the reins over to. "Sounds exactly like what we need here in Midnight Bluff. Would you be interested in coming for a trial run?"

Travis nodded eagerly. A few minutes later, Son hung up the phone, after discussing the start date and salary. They'd settled on a probationary period of six weeks with pay and then a full-time offer pending a congregational vote. Sighing with relief, Son sat back in his chair, relief washing through him.

Finally, he'd gotten one thing right.

Vada shrugged on her vest as she surveyed the shelves stretched out before her. They could use a good straightening up. Dewayne didn't care about how things looked if everything was where it was supposed to be, and the carelessness showed. Same with the break room in the back. Walking through the Co-Op, she made a mental tally of all the things to do.

The back door chimed, and she waved at Lewis as he entered and headed to the office while she loaded the cleaning cart. She added talking to Lewis about going back to her usual schedule to her growing list.

Just as she wheeled the cart to the middle of the store, the bells on the front door clanged and Mayor Patty bustled in.

"Vada!" The older lady rushed up to Vada, chest heaving like she'd sprinted to the store. "The fire ants are back in my kitchen again. I need the best poison you got. Spray, granules. All. Of. It."

Vada grimaced as she spied angry welts across Patty's feet and legs. That had to sting. "We've got several things that should help." She loaded Patty's arms down with enough bug poison to last a year. "And for those bites…" She nodded her head. "…put some Windex on them. Or a touch of ammonia if you have it."

"You're a lifesaver." As she rang Patty up, the mayor took a few calming breaths. "I've been meaning to ask you how you're doing. You've been so busy this summer then when I saw you last night at the Business Basics class you looked a little blue…"

Vada let Patty trail off, avoiding the dig for information.

The whole town knew about her and Son's split by now, and Patty was sure to be in the vortex of the gossip gang. "Just a little overwhelmed with this whole running my own business thing."

As she waved a scanner at a bag of fire ant granules, she added, "And the social media ads I'm running are kicking my butt. Not sure what I'm doing wrong."

"Social media?" Patty wrinkled her brow. "Why are you bothering with that when you have people banging down your door right here?" She waved her toward the front windows and Midnight Bluff beyond.

"I wouldn't call a couple of mothers being polite banging down my door." Vada tucked the items into a bag for Mayor Patty.

"If they asked you, instead of you asking, then they're interested, sugar." Patty leaned forward and grasped Vada's forearm. "Honey, most people start with the good old-fashioned methods to reach people starting out. A little in-person salesmanship so to speak."

Vada nodded, unsure of how effective hitting her neighbors up for business would be. "I'll keep that in mind, Patty."

Patty gathered up her bags and headed for the door. "Remember what I said!" she called over her shoulder. With a bob of her head, she disappeared out the door, headed back to wage war on some ants.

Lewis appeared at the door to his office. "Want to look over your schedule now?"

With a glance at her abandoned cleaning cart, Vada followed him into the tiny closet of an office and perched on a wobbly swivel chair.

"Aight, I was thinking you could take back some morning

shifts—" The ringing of Vada's cell phone interrupted him as he slid a paper schedule toward her.

Vada glanced at her caller ID. "It's Mrs. Langford. Preston probably lost something on the camping trip. Mind if I get this?"

Lewis nodded agreeably. Stepping outside the office, Vada didn't bother to shut the door behind her. With the school year starting, she had been waiting on beleaguered parents to call her about the heap of lost and found items she'd collected during camp.

"Vada, honey! I was just calling to see if you'd still be able to give Preston some lessons. He's still talking about the day y'all cantered... or something like that."

A pit formed in Vada's stomach. "I'd be happy to work him in. Just give me a couple of days to get my schedule set and then I'll see when I can squeeze him in." She did not know how she would work at the Co-Op, take care of her boarders, and teach Preston, but she'd figured it out.

"Ok, dear. But don't wait too long. Because if you can't take him, I've got to get him signed up for some after-school activities by the time the semester starts."

"I'll let you know," Vada promised. She rubbed at her forehead as she stepped into the office. Her life just got more complicated. "Where were we?"

Lewis stared up at her with a strange expression. "You're fired."

Shock rippled through her followed by numbness. "What? Why—"

He held up a hand. "Vada, you're a good worker. One of the best I ever had. But I'm not going to be the reason you don't run after your dream."

Her eyes misted as he took her hand and guided her back to the chair. "I wouldn't do this unless I believed to the very marrow of my bones that you have what it takes." She sniffed while he tore up the schedule in long shreds. "This store is my life, but it's not yours. It's time for you to see that even if I have to shove you out of the nest."

He held out his hand, and her heart swelled as she handed over her vest, a weight she didn't realize she'd been carrying lifting from her shoulders. "What are you going to do to fill my position?" Her days stretched before her, bursting with potential.

Lewis grinned at her. "Got a couple of young 'uns that have been asking around about jobs. Probably will take on a couple of them." He patted her hand. "I expect you to put up that poster like you been promising."

"I will." She nodded as she wrapped the old man in a hug. "Thank you, for everything, Lewis."

He beamed at her. "Now get out there and go make your dreams happen."

As Vada stepped out into the blazing afternoon sun, she stretched her arms above her head, easing the ache in her shoulders and laughed up at the sky. For the first time in years, she felt light. Even though she should worry about her next paycheck and health insurance and all the burdens that came with adult life, her heart spun around as giddy as a child.

A sign in the store's window caught her attention, and a grin crept across her face at a sudden, crazy idea.

She pulled out her phone and dialed the number. "Mr. Nettles, hey! It's Vada. Do you still have that horse for sale?"

* * *

Vada slipped off her boots as she entered the house that evening, excitement thrumming through her. Her family had already gathered around the dining table for supper.

"Where have you been all day? Your shift ended hours ago." Her mother glanced at Vada as she spooned casserole onto her plate.

Vada slipped into her chair. "Well… I got fired today."

Everyone froze, staring at her. Mahalia was the first to break the silence. "What did you do?" she asked at the same time her dad rumbled, "I'm going to call Lewis and give him a piece of my mind."

Vada laughed and quickly told them the story, their expressions molding from alarm to worry. "But how are we going to take on more students?" her mother objected. "We spend all our time on the boarders."

Grinning, Vada said, "I gave Benny a call. He's been looking for a part-time job to fill the days he's not on at the fire station."

"And how are we going to pay Benny?" Her dad leaned forward, looking thunderous.

"I don't think that will be an issue." Vada popped a bite of food into her mouth while her family stared at her incredulously. She savored their curiosity. "I also called Mrs. Langford and…" She enjoyed the surprise and happiness that lit each of their faces as she told them about her discussions with the mothers. "We've already got a nearly full after-school schedule, and I haven't even called the referrals they gave me."

"If we open some early morning lessons as well, we should break even and then some by the end of September. Even with Benny's salary." She finished with a flourish.

"And that's with paying yourself, right?" Her mother studied her, pride mingling with anxiety on her face.

Vada nodded. "I calculated that first. I can pay myself a little more than my hourly rate at the Co-Op, or I can stock the extra cash back to reinvest."

Her dad sat back in his chair. "Sounds like you got this all figured out."

She shrugged. "Still got a few details to iron out, but it's coming along."

"Well, then." Her mother lifted her glass. "Here's to you then. You deserve all this and more."

As they settled back into their supper, Vada leaned over to Mahalia. "After dinner, I have a surprise for you. In the barn."

Mahalia looked up, eyes wide, as realization dawned on her face. She bolted from her chair, squealing, Vada on her heels.

It was worth dipping into her savings to see the look in Mahalia's eyes when she saw the tiny bay mare for the first time.

Mahalia cried as she kissed the horse's soft nose, the mare already nuzzling her shoulder affectionately, babbling out her thanks.

Vada hugged her, delighted by her happiness. "I just thought that if I got my dream, you should too." She picked up a couple of curry brushes and tossed one to Mahalia. Together, they began grooming the horse as Mahalia chatted away about all she was going to teach her to do.

Chapter 25

T he sky hung overcast and heavy as Vada's heart as she slipped into her place in the pews. Despite the thrill of seeing her equestrian school grow in a matter of days, this was one Sunday service she would rather have missed. The thought of seeing Son sent an ache shooting through her, salt on the open gash that was her heart.

But Mahalia had pleaded and begged, eager to see her friends react to news of her horse. And with her parents taking off on a much-deserved weekend away, no one else could take her.

As soon as she stepped through the door, a whirlwind of teenagers surrounded her, eager to tell her of their school year plans. Carmel hung onto her arm, chattering about cheerleader tryouts while Preston pretended not to care what she said. Clearly, he was smitten as he kept hovering to the girl's side.

Vada snorted. Even with all their clamor, she hadn't realized how much she'd missed these kids. She eagerly looked forward to the start of after-school riding lessons with many of them.

Perhaps, one or two would even show enough talent for competition riding. The thought bloomed, warm and edifying, in the center of her chest.

"Did you hear about the new youth minister that's coming?" Preston asked her. She looked back at him, startled. Neither Lou Ellen nor Son had given her a heads-up about this development. Although, there was no reason to keep her in the loop now that she wasn't working with the youth group.

The kids quieted, listening expectantly for her answer, hoping she'd have a choice bit of gossip about the new minister. Carefully, she replied, "I'm sure he's going to be awesome." They deflated, sensing her evasion.

"Yeah, but he won't be anything like you and Pastor Riser," Carmel groused.

"You know that we're always around if you need us," Vada tried to reassure her. A bell tolled, long and stately, and as suddenly as they had flocked to her, the teenagers dispersed to their families in the pews.

With a whisper of air, Willow slipped into the pew beside her. "Looked like quite the mob."

"They're just excited about the new youth minister and were asking me about him." Vada looked at Willow. Shock rippled across Willow's face. So, she hadn't known either. Vada hadn't been left out of any official announcement.

"That was fast," Willow murmured as the organist fired up the morning's first hymn with a brassy bellow.

"Seems like he's ready to get back to normal." A normal that didn't include Vada. From the front pew, she spotted Son's dad as he turned around, scanning the fullness of the sanctuary. Spying Vada, he waved at her, a grin stretching across his face.

She sighed. No matter how hard the people around them

might pretend, she and Son would not get back together. She would never sit in that front pew where one day his wife would preside. A deep ache began throbbing in her bones as the vestry door opened, and Son strode out, resplendent in his Sunday suit.

Placing his Bible on the pulpit, she watched in mute agony as he asked the crowd to stand and join him in song praising their Lord, his strong fingers grasping the sides of the pulpit until the tips turned pale. As she listened to the deep timbre of his voice belting out "When We Gather at the River," her heart threw itself against her ribs as her breath hung in her throat. There was something about seeing him in his element, behind a pulpit, where he belonged, that unraveled her.

Seeing him look every inch the pastor that he was rocked her as she realized how foolish she had been to ever think they could be.

"I've got a headache. Tell Mahalia I'll meet her in the truck." Before Willow could respond, Vada turned and slipped from the pew, hurrying as unobtrusively as possible down the aisle. Despite her stealth, heads still turned and looked at her.

She bit her lips, holding back tears as she shoved open the side door and bolted out into the storm. The rain stung her face as she cried into a gale. But her heart lifted.

She had seen him and survived. All these years, she'd been just fine on her own; she didn't need a man to hold her hand. Even as her heart argued that Son wasn't any man, she brushed away her tears and dashed for the truck. As she slid into the cab, soaked to the bone, she promised herself that the worst was over, and now she could move on with her life.

* * *

Son's breath hitched as he watched Vada slip out the door, her face knit in misery. His voice fell flat as he led the congregation into the chorus, and he struggled to reclaim the notes.

In the front pew, his dad gazed up at him, eyebrows drawn together. He'd noticed the stumble. Son would receive a concerned question about it later. Pressing his palms into the cool, dark wood of the pulpit, he straightened his back and launched into his sermon, reciting his points by rote as he walked through the lesson of Isaiah 62.

Vada's back as she hurried down the aisle, away from him, flashed through his mind and his throat caught. He coughed to clear it. Still, his voice stubbornly rasped out despite frequent sips from his bottle of water. Would he and Vada ever be able to stand in the same room again? Or were they destined to circle each other warily for all eternity?

Focusing his thoughts on his sermon proved impossible as the quiet click of the door behind Vada echoed again and again through his mind.

Blessedly, the service ended quickly as Son skipped many of the embellishments and illustrations he would usually add. Today, his heart just wasn't in it.

His dad might not understand, but he hoped God would.

Hurriedly, he flipped his Bible closed and dismissed the congregation. Vacantly, he shook hands and hugged bodies as the crowd slowly filtered out of the sanctuary. He noted the number of sympathetic pats rained down on his shoulders until his face ached with the smile he held.

Exhausted, he finally slumped down into his office chair what felt like hours later, the last congregant issued out into the lingering drizzle. With a quiet squeak, his father settled in the chair across from him.

"You all right? Sounded a little hoarse up there." There it was, the dig for information, gently prying into Son's state of mind.

He sighed and shook his head at his dad, out of words. Son let the silence linger. Everything there was to discuss, they'd already been over. What good would it do to revisit it?

His dad harrumphed and slapped his hands against his knees as he stood. "Well, guess I'll head out then."

"You're leaving already?" Son looked at him startled.

"Would like to get to Atlanta before the dinner rush." His dad held out his arms for a hug, and Son rounded the desk to embrace him. Now that the moment had come, he was reluctant to see his dad go, to have his supportive if stern presence disappear and leave him alone with his thoughts.

"Thank you. For being here." He swallowed against the knot in his throat.

His dad patted his arm. "I know I can't make you see reason on my own, but I trust that you'll work out where the Lord is leading you." He inhaled through his nose. "Sometimes, we just have to stumble onto the path."

Leave it to his dad to get in one last parting shot. Son shook his head with a smile as he watched his father stride out of the office and down the hall.

He looked around the room, the only sound the ticking of the clock on the wall. Not even Lou Ellen lingered in the building.

For once, he cherished the silence as he settled into his chair to think.

Chapter 26

Mahalia bounced out of Vada's truck with a wide smile on her face. As she melded into the stream of teenagers headed into Cleveland High School with a wave over her shoulder, Vada sighed. Some days, she felt more like Mahalia's mom than her cousin.

And today, first-day-of-school moroseness threatened to envelop her as she watched Mahalia disappear into the building. With her parents gone on vacation, that left Vada to her own devices, except for the short periods when Benny joined her. The boy was hardworking, but not very talkative. She couldn't decide if he was shy or not a big talker.

Either way, the day promised nothing but hard work and boredom until the kids began arriving for the lessons after school let out.

A bubble of worry popped up in her stomach as she mentally ran through that morning. Had Mahalia tucked all her art supplies into her backpack? Had she given her lunch money?

Her parents had drilled every detail of Mahalia's new class

into her before they left. "She has to be at school by 7:50." Her mom had jabbed a finger at a printed-out schedule. "She has to have a little time to make it to her locker and socialize…"

Vada had held up a hand. "I remember the drill, Mom. I've got it."

Sacia had exhaled. "I'm sorry. This is just her first full school year with us, and I want it to go well for her."

"It will," Vada reassured her. "She's already made some great friends. She's signed up for the art class she was dying to take. We got her all the 'in' school supplies." Vada made a face at the memory of Mahalia's ridiculously specific back-to-school list. "She's going to be fine."

Her mother held her breath, unconvinced. Finally, as her dad rubbed a hand across her back, she exhaled, the breath escaping from her like a popped balloon. "You're right. I'm just worrying to worry."

The next day, her parents had headed off on their much-deserved vacation, and Vada and Mahalia had lived it up on junk food and late-night movie fests.

With a yawn, Vada threw one last glance at the school doors and put her truck into gear. She was worse than her mom, sitting here fretting. Mahalia would be fine.

That afternoon, as Vada sat in the slow crawling pick-up line, she watched Mahalia reluctantly peel off from Carmel and Preston. Her face was wreathed in smiles, and the tension Vada had held in her chest all day slowly unwound. But just as Vada relaxed into her seat, Mahalia's expression changed once her back was to her friends.

Her bright eyes fell to the sidewalk and her shoulders slumped. With a whoosh of muggy air, she slammed the door behind her.

Vada examined her, wondering if she'd had some sort of falling out. Silence hung in the car as Mahalia settled her backpack at her feet. "So, how was your first day?" she prompted.

"It was a day." Mahalia stared out the window with a glare. No babble of who was dating who, or what teachers were cool or lame. Not even a complaint about the amount of homework she already had, which Vada could see from her backpack was a lot.

"Seems like you had a full day." Vada tried to pry a little more out of Mahalia.

"God, can we stop with the interrogation already!" Mahalia threw up her hands.

"What's gotten into you?" Vada asked as she pulled out onto the highway. "Did someone pick on you today?" Alarm flared through her as she imagined her sensitive cousin being mocked... or worse.

"No! The day was fine. Everyone was fine." She waved a hand. "I'm just tired."

"Ok." Vada dropped the subject as she noticed the set of Mahalia's mouth, in a stubborn line. Sometimes, teenagers just needed a little space after an overwhelming day. That was all this was. She tried to reassure herself as they pulled up to the house, her first lesson already waiting for them.

Mahalia ran into the house, Vada calling after her, "Don't forget to exercise Fletch!" Waving Vada off, her cousin vanished inside with the slam of a door.

Concern lit up flares inside Vada's brain as she stared at the door, but with people already waiting on her, she didn't have time to chase after Mahalia. With a deep breath, she turned, ready to kick off her first lesson.

Vada hung the bridle on the wall of the tack room, breathing in the cool, dusty air gratefully. Her last lesson of the morning had just left, leaving the rest of the day gloriously wide open. Saturday stretched before her filled with freedom.

Just as she was reveling in this newfound feeling, she turned to leave the room. A breeze caught the door and swung it shut. Plunged into sudden darkness, she pressed a hand to the wood and breathed against the knot in her throat. The last time she'd been in here...

The memory of Son's hands on her skin sent a flush through her cheeks. No matter where she went, she couldn't escape memories of him. Yanking the door open, she strode out. Suddenly, the day's emptiness yawned before her, threatening to swallow her in memories she didn't want to relive.

Nope. She wasn't going there. Only misery lay in that direction.

A few minutes later, she yanked the covers off Mahalia, still curled up in her bed despite it being dangerously close to noon. "C'mon! We're going!" She threw a pair of jeans at her cousin.

Mahalia's mood had only intensified throughout the week, her sullen brooding almost comical. They both needed a break, and Vada knew just what Mahalia couldn't resist.

Mahalia stared up at her groggily. "Going where? It's Saturday."

"C'mon, lazy bones." She shoved a shirt into her hands. "We're going to miss the 1:30 showing if you don't start moving."

Vaulting out of bed, Mahalia rushed to the bathroom. "Why didn't you tell me earlier? I would have..." Vada grinned at

226

the chatter. Finally, something had broken through the dark cloud hanging over her.

As they pulled into a parking spot a block down from the Cleveland theater, Mahalia was still talking. "And after the movie, I want to go to Cotton Row Books and then get a coffee."

"Whatever you say!" Vada stepped up onto the broiling sidewalk, eager to escape from the heat in the quiet coolness of the theater. Mahalia grinned at her agreeableness.

Just as they headed towards the door, a *yoohoo* sounded down the sidewalk. Leora hurried up to them, her hair coifed perfectly despite the humidity. How much hairspray had that taken?

"Vada, dear, I've been wanting to talk to you!" Leora's fingertips brushed Vada's arm.

It was sweltering on the sidewalk. Vada glanced longingly toward the theater door as she shoved a few bills in Mahalia's hands and sent her to get their snacks.

"What can I do for you, Leora?" She edged into a sliver of shadow, unsure how long this conversation would take.

"I was reflecting on our... discussion about the Women in Ministry group, and I realized that I may have come across the wrong way." Leora touched the base of her throat.

Vada looked at her in surprise. "It was nothing, Leora—"

The older woman touched her arm, cutting her off. "But the timing... It looked like I was asking because..." Leora shook her head. "Every woman deserves to be measured on her own merits. Not the status of the people she is associated with." She took a breath. "What I'm trying to say is, we would love to have you on our team. For your own sake. Nothing else."

Vada drew the soupy air into her lungs, touched by Leora's

thoughtfulness. "I would be honored, Leora." She paused. "But I'm not sure why you want me." She laughed, trying to shoo away her awkwardness. She wasn't ministry material.

Leora waved a hand. "Honey, you are a natural leader. I can't think of anyone more capable than you." She squeezed Vada's arm. "Come to a meeting and see what we do."

"Ok," Vada agreed hesitantly. A little thrill of pride straightened her spine. Leora wanted her, not Son's girlfriend. The satisfaction of the realization refreshed her like cool water.

Quickly, they exchanged information, Vada promising to be at the next meeting as they went their separate ways.

* * *

Son folded his hands together as Travis settled into the squeaky chair. "Thank you for meeting with me. I hope we can make these feedback sessions a regular thing."

Travis sat up straighter. "Of course. I'd like that."

Sitting back in his chair, Son tapped a pen on his notes. He wanted to start things off on a positive foot since some of his observations would be a little tough to handle. "Are you getting settled in ok?"

Travis nodded. "Dottie has been super hospitable, and everyone in town is welcoming."

"Good. I've been trying not to crowd you, but is there anything you need from me? Tips? Lesson reviews? Prayer?" Son was warming up to the points in his notes.

"I feel like I have things pretty well handled, but I appreciate the offer." Travis casually sipped from a mug of coffee he'd brought in with him.

Son paused at his answer. He'd noticed a slight hiccup or

two, but perhaps the young man's dismissal of help was simply over-confidence or lack of experience. It took knowing people on a personal level to really see how they were reacting to you, and Travis hadn't had that time yet. He could learn. But Son wanted to give him a firm push in the right direction.

It was time to bring this home. "Good. How are you finding your time with the kids?"

"The kids have been amazing! So well-behaved and receptive. I thought after a summer without a leader they'd act out or push back, but so far, it's been a dream." The younger man's face lit up with excitement. Son tried not to grimace at his choice of words; the teens had been with him all summer and it was hard not to feel a bit territorial.

He took a breath, glancing at his notes. "Your lessons are impressive." Impressive for a seminary-level audience; the youth group just stared at him with their eyes glazed over while he talked. "Quite in-depth." He leaned forward and rested his elbows on the desk. "It would be nice to see you linger a bit more on the basics."

Travis cocked his head. "These kids have grown up in the church. Shouldn't they be past the basics by now?"

"Most of them are familiar." Son nodded his head. "But I think you'll agree that we all need regular reminding of the miracle of the Gospel. Especially at this… impressionable… stage."

Slowly, Travis nodded, his eyes squinched. "I see your point. What do you suggest?"

This was what Son had been looking for: receptiveness to his advice. "Take time to fully answer their questions. Show them how much their vulnerability means by honoring their prayer requests." What Son didn't say was how aggravating it was to watch week after week as Travis offered some general summary of the kids' requests instead of taking each one up in prayer. The group had already noticed this tendency and raised fewer and fewer hands each week.

"I can do that." Travis gripped his mug, eyeing Son. "Anything else?"

Son sat back. "Sometimes, it's better to skip a lesson point or two so you can spend time understanding what's going on with them." He bobbed his head as he echoed his dad. "Some of these kids are in really tough home situations." The first week he'd been with them, Son had given him a heads-up on who might need a little more encouragement. "They need to see you care more than they need a perfect three-point lesson. And knowing their challenges will help you shape future lessons."

With a frown, Travis looked down at his hands. "So, simpler lessons and more fellowship is what I'm hearing?"

Pleased, Son agreed, "That's basically the idea. I think you'll find the right balance in time."

Travis sucked in a breath. "All right. I can do that." He smiled thinly at Son. "Lots to consider."

"Excellent. Anything else you want to talk about?" Son didn't want to bulldoze Travis. He should be able to offer feedback of his own.

But the younger man shook his head. "Nope. All good here." He wrinkled his brow in thought. With a nod of thanks, he said his goodbyes and left, and Son leaned back in his chair, satisfied.

* * *

Vada smiled as she listened to Mahalia swoon over the movie's lead. For the first time in days, she seemed relaxed and happy. A big change from her stormy silence.

Sipping at her iced coffee, Vada nodded along. "I'm glad you enjoyed it. Thought it would do us both a little good to get out."

Mahalia's smile stretched wide and bright. "I love the movies!"

"Good. Maybe we could make this a regular thing?" Vada loved the idea of getting Mahalia to come out of her shell more, and she would stoop to a little bribery to make it happen.

"That would be awesome!" With a wiggle, Mahalia added, "We could go next week!" A thought flitted across her face like a cloud across the sun, and she sighed.

Vada took the pause as an opening. "So, how was your first week of school? You haven't told me much about it."

The change was instantaneous and complete. Mahalia scowled and huffed. "I told you it was fine. Why do you keep on asking?" The words flew out angry and biting.

Vada struggled to backtrack, aggravated with her miscalculation. "If you don't want to talk about it, that's fine. But I'm family and I'll always be around if you do."

The house broke into view through the trees as Mahalia shouted, "Maybe this family not leaving me alone is my whole freakin' problem!"

Quietly, Vada answered, "Ok." What had she said to cause such an outburst? She hadn't seen Mahalia this upset since the last time her mother had visited.

As she parked the truck, Mahalia flew into the house, the slam of the door ringing in the silence. Vada stared after her at a complete loss.

Chapter 27

A s the stars twinkled outside, Son sat next to the
window and watched what was happening in the
small classroom. Several weeks had passed, and Vada
was still a complete no-show in church that morning. His
shoulders slumped at the thought of her avoiding him. He
was exhausted from preaching, and the scene unfolding before
him wasn't helping his already dour mood.

Travis sat on a stool, lecturing animatedly on the hypostatic
union of Christ. Around him, teenagers slouched in metal
chairs and yawned loudly. Son didn't blame them; even he
wanted to roll his eyes. Obviously, Travis had taken his advice
and tossed it straight out the window. Along with Son's
patience.

He would speak to the young minister after class and make
his expectations clear as crystal.

Giving up on his lecture, Travis shifted irritatedly on his
stool. His eyes scanned the room, taking in the slack faces
and vacant expressions. He cleared his throat and abruptly

announced, "All right, let's pray then we'll be dismissed. Any requests?"

Son perked up as a few tentative hands rose around the room. Perhaps Travis had listened to something Son had said.

Most kids requested prayer for upcoming tests, the big home game next Friday, or something "unspoken." Only Mahalia broke the pattern.

She mumbled, "For my mom." Son tensed, hoping Travis would remember their discussion from weeks ago about the kids with difficult situations at home—and that Mahalia was one of them.

On his stool at the front of the room, Travis perked up. "Of course. Anything specific?"

A sour knot formed in Son's stomach as Mahalia glanced around the silent room. Carmel reached over and squeezed her hand. "She wants me to come live with her again. And I don't want to go. But I feel bad about it."

Surely, the Wilsons wouldn't let that happen? He hadn't met Tilda, Vada's aunt, personally, but he'd heard the stories of her addiction, the places the Wilsons had pulled her from. Mahalia was better off in a stable, loving household.

Around the room, a few kids muttered sympathetic words. They all knew her story, and several of them lived with grandparents or older siblings for the same reason.

Preston shook his head, eyes squinched in understanding. "Parents." He uttered the word like it was a curse, and Travis' eyes snapped to him.

"Well, the Bible says a thing or two about that doesn't it?" Son shook his head warningly as Travis zeroed back in on Mahalia. "What do the Ten Commandments say?"

Mahalia sunk lower in her chair, and Son stood from his

seat, trying to grab Travis' attention. But the younger man only glanced at him before asking again. "What do they say?"

"Honor your father and mother," Mahalia whispered, head hung.

"That's right." Travis nodded emphatically at her answer, the tips of his ears reddening. "And it's the only commandment with a promise attached to it, which shows us how important it is. The consequences of this sin..."

Tears slipped down Mahalia's cheeks, and Son clenched his hands. Shaming a young, vulnerable girl was not the way to "linger in the moment." As Travis pontificated on duty to their parents, Son placed a protective hand on Mahalia's shoulder.

She startled and looked up at him, relief flooding her face. Straining to keep his voice from shaking, Son spoke over Travis. "I think it's time we wrapped up. I'll close us out in prayer."

Travis frowned at the interruption but waved a hand for Son to continue. Like he would have waited for his permission. Quickly, Son asked the group to bow their heads and led them through a prayer, specifying each need they had voiced.

As he said "Amen," he looked up and caught Travis' irritated stare. With a sniffle, Mahalia swiped at her face, unmoving as students flooded out the door and to their parents' waiting cars.

Son didn't see Vada's truck. "You have a ride?"

She swiped at her face again. "I was going to spend the night at Carmel's."

"Do you still want to do that?" he asked softly. Without hesitation, she shook her head "no."

"I want to go home."

He patted her shoulder. "All right, let Carmel's mother know then I'll take you."

As Mahalia slipped out the door, he pinned Travis with a stern look. "That could have been handled much better."

"I was just following your advice!" He held up his hands in protest, cheeks reddening.

Son pressed a fist to his lips, measuring his words. "That…" He gestured back at the empty room. "…was not what I meant." He shook his head as he saw Travis' chest rise with a retort. "Let's discuss this in the morning when we both have clearer heads."

"Agreed," Travis said the word coolly, then turned and began gathering his materials. Son left him there. Let him lock up the church by himself.

He found Mahalia leaning against his car in the parking lot. She slid into the passenger seat wordlessly, and he pulled out of the lot and onto the highway, toward Vada.

He had just decided the girl had enough pressure on her for one night and he wouldn't press her when she spoke. "I'm sorry you had to do that. End class that way because of me." She stared out the window, chin lowered. A minute passed while he fumed over her silent tears. Why was she apologizing?

"Mahalia, I just want you to know, you've done nothing for me to be upset over." He took a breath. "I didn't end the class because of you. I ended it because he was wrong."

That got her attention. She looked at him, eyes wide with surprise. "So, you don't agree with him?"

He shook his head. "No. I don't."

"But it's in the Bible." Mahalia rubbed at her arms.

"Yes, it is. It says to honor our father and mother. But it doesn't say how does it?" He thought for a moment. "Your mother…" He hesitated. "…She isn't in a great place. Not a place to be a good parent to you. Honoring her would be to keep her from making the mistake of neglecting you again."

Mahalia nodded and sighed. "That's what I told her. Sort of."

Son saw the sadness in her eyes. "That's not all you told her, was it?"

"No." She sniffed. "I told her I didn't want to see her again until she was clean."

"That must have taken a lot of strength for you to say." He stared at the road slipping past them. No child should have to say that to their parent. "When have you seen her?" With the Wilsons having full custody, he knew Tilda had rules, of the legal sort, regarding her visitations and contact with her daughter.

"She's been coming to see me at school. During lunch. They let her in since she's my mother."

Son's mind spun. If the Wilsons knew about this, they'd have a fit. "Well, what she says isn't true. She can't take you. Not without your aunt and uncle agreeing, and they won't."

Mahalia bit her lip. "She tried to sign me out one time. Told me we'd go get ice cream. Like I was five years old. It didn't feel right, so I said no."

They were pulling up the driveway. A spotlight flipped on the porch, spilling light over the hood of his car. A second later, the front door cracked then Vada stepped out, waiting for them with her arms crossed over her chest. He hadn't told her they were coming, which was an oversight now that he thought about it.

Mahalia threw herself out of the car and into her cousin's arms as soon as he was in park. Vada looked at him alarmed.

Even with the barely contained panic on her face, she was still the most beautiful woman he'd ever seen.

"She's not hurt. Just upset." He patted Mahalia's shoulder, feeling out of place now that she was home. "Why don't we go inside and talk about it?"

Reluctantly, Vada waved him inside, and he followed unable to take his eyes off her back.

* * *

Vada had just settled in for the night with a steaming cup of tea and a plan to binge the next season of her favorite Netflix show when lights cut across the wall from the drive. Someone was pulling up to the house.

With her parents away again, and Mahalia spending the night at Carmel's, she had the evening to herself. But if Willow and Ruffin had decided she needed another batch of consolation cookies...

She would always take cookies. Hurrying out to the porch, she realized that instead of Ruffin's sturdy work truck or Willow's van Son's tiny sedan was bouncing over the gravel. Confounded, she stood watching and wondering what had brought him all the way out here on a Sunday night.

Dread curled in her stomach at the thought of seeing his dark eyes and wide smile again.

Mahalia burst from the car and flung her arms around Vada like she hadn't since she was six years old. An alarm flared through her as she looked up to see Son stepping out of the car with a grimace. Every line on his face read reluctance.

Vaguely, she heard his reassurances that Mahalia was all right, torn between her concern for her cousin and the racing of her heart at the sight of Son. Silently she led them into the house.

"Sit." She pulled out a chair at the kitchen table for Mahalia and gently pushed her into it. She slid in beside her, smoothing a hand across her back. "Tell me what happened." Son leaned in the doorway behind them, offering them space and a supportive presence at once.

Through her tears, Mahalia choked out how her mother had been sneaking visits with her at school and her youth group revelation. "She's demanding that I come live with her—and her new boyfriend. And I want to believe she's clean; she looks good." Mahalia swiped at her face. "But something doesn't feel right. I just can't believe her no matter how much she promises."

So that's why Carmel and Preston had been hovering around her at pickup for the last couple of weeks. They knew what was going on.

While she was sympathetic to her Aunt Tilda's illness, putting her daughter through this kind of distress without talking to her family first was way over the line. Anger heated Vada's face, but she clenched her teeth as she listened. "Mahalia, your mother is seriously ill. The last time we convinced her to go to rehab she left against medical advice. And I have no idea what state she is in now. That's why you're with us."

"She keeps saying that she should just take me, but I told her no." Mahalia leaned her head against Vada's shoulder. "I just don't know what to do!"

Vada's body shook as she realized how close her aunt had come to doing something she could never recover from. And the damage it would inflict on Mahalia. Kidnapping was a felony, and she doubted they'd be able to find her aunt as easily this time if she did spirit Mahalia away.

"Sweetheart, you don't have to go with her just because she asks." Vada rubbed Mahalia's arms. "And I think your gut is right. If everything was truly good with your mom, she would have come to Uncle Waymond and Aunt Sacia first. Not snuck visits in your cafeteria." She shook her head as she chose her words carefully. "You know we have full custody of you. As long as you don't get in a car with her, she can't take you."

Exhaling, she leaned back a bit to look at Mahalia's face. "I can tell the school not to let her in, if that would make you feel better."

"It's not that I don't want to see my mom…" Mahalia stared at the table. "I just…" She trailed off, biting her lip.

"I'll make sure you only see her when you want to," Vada reassured her. "I'll call first thing in the morning." And she would email the principal and administrative assistant tonight. She wouldn't leave her cousin's safety in an overworked secretary's memo.

Tucking Mahalia under her arm, she led her upstairs, glancing back at Son where he stood in the doorway watching him, hands shoved in his pockets. As she tucked her cousin into bed, she wondered if he'd still be downstairs when she returned. She couldn't decide if she hoped he stayed or not.

Suddenly, the idea of watching a show by herself seemed frivolous and lonely after tonight's shock.

When she returned to the kitchen, she found Son sitting at the table, a cup clasped in his hands and a fresh pot of earl grey set before him. The tightness in her chest eased at the sight of him. Thankful, she accepted the cup he handed her, and they sat in silence for a few minutes, relishing the fragrant brew.

Son sat next to Vada, watching her fingers clench and unclench on the cup's handle. After each sip, she pressed her lips together in a furious white line. He couldn't imagine the distress she was going through.

"I'm sorry." He reached forward and took her hand, gently prying her fingers loose from the cup.

Coming out of her reverie, she stared at him. "I'm not mad at you. This situation… My aunt knows better!" she spat.

"Like you said. She's deeply ill. Her sense of what's right is all skewed right now. She can only think of what would make her feel better in the moment and can't see what it does to others."

Vada sighed and closed her eyes. "I know. But I hate seeing Mahalia…"

He rubbed a thumb across the back of her hand. "I'm sorry I didn't realize what was going on sooner. I would have done more, not let it go so far." He spoke softly as he studied the side of Vada's face.

She laughed as she glanced at him, the sound low and bitter. "Are you talking about Mahalia or us?" Her eyes pinched at the corners, looking infinitely sad before she looked away.

"Why can't it be both?" He'd never longed for anyone the way he longed to scoop Vada into his lap and comfort her now. He pulled back and clenched his hands at the thought. He shouldn't go there, couldn't go there. It would hurt too much when they were inevitably pulled apart by their roles again.

Vada had been right. They would never work.

A tear slid down her cheek as she inhaled, holding her breath, and he wondered if she missed him as much as he missed her.

"I knew something was up with Mahalia—but I was just so busy with all my new students. I failed my family."

His heart ached as he watched Vada weep. Unable to stop himself, he pulled her into her chest, clasping his arms around her. "You're being too hard on yourself. Mahalia is safe." He closed his eyes as he felt her fingers wind into his shirt. "You are the most amazing person I know—running your own business, taking care of a teenager. You impress me."

Vada sniffled against his chest. "I do?"

He kissed the top of her head. "Yes." Reluctantly, he let go of her and stood. If he stayed any longer, he knew he would say what was really on his heart. That he was deeply and irrevocably in love with her. And it was tearing him apart.

Clearing his voice, he said, "I should go. You've got a lot to take care of, and I should get out of your way." Vada stared up at him, eyes wide with all that was unsaid between them, before she stood and walked him silently to the door.

Just as he stepped over the threshold, she grabbed his arm. He let her draw him to her as she went up on her tiptoes. Her scent, of shea butter and sugar, washed over him as she brushed her lips against his. A whisper tickled his ear, "Goodbye."

As he murmured goodbye back, his heart twisting in his chest, she was already turning, disappearing into the house. Leaving him alone in the dark.

Chapter 28

Son sat behind his desk gathering his thoughts and waiting for Travis to arrive. After last night's events and how coldly they had parted, he didn't know what the younger man's attitude was going to be.

He heard the swish of shoes on the carpet, then Travis appeared in the doorway. "You wanted to see me?" His words fell stiffly, and his face was closed off and wary.

Son waved to the chairs in front of his desk. As Travis settled into the squeaky leather, Son stood, rounded the desk, and settled into the chair beside him. He twisted the seat to face a surprised Travis.

"This is a better setup to talk openly. Don't you agree?" Son leaned an elbow against the chair arm.

Travis nodded, eyes narrowed. "Much." He snapped his mouth shut and sat staring at Son.

So, he would not make this easy. "Why don't we start with what you think of last night?"

"I was trying…" Travis shifted in his seat. "…to follow your advice. And you completely humiliated me!"

Son nodded, weighing his words, as the irony of Travis' perspective sank in. "I only stood up because I thought it necessary."

"Things were going fine," Travis groused. "The girl was clearly convicted by what I said."

A lick of anger flared up in Son. "The girl? You've been with this group for several weeks now. Can you even tell me her name? Her situation with her mother?" At Travis' confused look, Son prompted him, "We spoke about this, at length, your first week here. Surely, you remember something."

"Her situation is irrelevant to what's in the Bible." Travis slouched in his chair, looking more like one of the teenagers he taught than a leader.

"The Bible is about her situation. And mine. And yours. It is wholly relevant." Son paused. "I appreciate you were trying to follow my advice, but we don't teach at the expense of someone's heart."

"I wasn't..."

Son held up a hand. "You made her cry. You shamed her." A flash of guilt finally crossed Travis' face. "Truth spoken without kindness or understanding—without nuance—turns into a weapon we bludgeon our own congregation with." He shook his head. "I don't know about you but that's not the preacher I want to be."

Travis exhaled. "I wasn't trying to... bludgeon her." He raised an eyebrow at the word. "But I've never received that kind of disrespect before. I couldn't let it pass."

"We're not here to demand respect. We're here to serve. Respect is just a side effect, something we're given if our hearts are in the right place."

Clasping his hands, Travis looked up at him, uncertainty in his eyes. He opened his mouth and then closed it. Son waited for him to speak, confident they were on the edge of understanding each other.

Finally, Travis lifted his hands, palms up. "This has been so much harder than I expected. I don't know if I'm in the right place."

Son sat forward, leaning his elbows on his knees, eager to help. "You just need time to learn and adjust. I can..."

"No. No, that's not what I meant." Travis ran his hands through his hair. "I think I made a mistake. I don't think I'm in the right place."

Tilting his head, Son studied him. Was this just first job nerves or was Travis revealing something more? Slowly, he said, "First appointments are always hard. But we shouldn't give up because of that."

"I'm not giving up—I still want to be a minister. I just..." He waved his hands. "Can I be honest?"

"Please," Son invited him, trying to set the young man at ease.

All in a rush, Travis said, "I heard that Pastor Riser was looking for a new youth minister. And I jumped at the chance without thinking. I've heard so many good things about working with him. I never really considered if youth was where I was supposed to be."

Understanding crested over Son, along with disappointment. "Pastor Riser is my father. In Atlanta. And he is incredible to work with. That's why you applied?" So, Travis didn't have a burning passion for youth; he should have trusted his first instinct during their interview.

Travis nodded, mouth working. "I should have realized, but

now I'm here…" He looked down at his lap.

"You don't have to stay." Son didn't know what possessed him to say that. He needed a youth minister. Desperately. And now he was going to send away the only one who'd shown interest? But he kept speaking, "If you feel this isn't right for you, we haven't reached the end of your trial period yet. You don't have to sign a contract."

"And you'd be ok with that?" The hope that lit up Travis' eyes was almost painful to Son. How had he been so wrong?

"I think everyone should go where they're called. If you don't believe that's here, then…" He brushed at some invisible lint on his knee. "No harm, no foul."

Travis sank back in his chair. "That's a relief."

"Indeed." Son rubbed his hands together and wondered just what he'd done.

A few minutes later, Travis practically floated from the room. Son could see the relief reflected in his relaxed shoulders. They'd discussed his resignation, agreeing he'd work out his remaining two weeks. And he'd readily agreed to apologize privately to Mahalia. Now, Son sat back behind his desk, fingers steepled in front of his mouth, procrastinating the termination paperwork.

Lou Ellen slipped into the room, her ever-present coffee mug in her hand. "Well, that was certainly not what I expected." She took a sip. "I was looking forward to some righteous indignation from you. Fist pounding. Bible-thumping. The whole nine." Her lips pulled down in an exaggerated frown even as her eyes crinkled. "Quite disappointing."

He rubbed at his eyes. "You're not the only one disappointed." He spoke through his hands. "What am I supposed to do without a youth pastor, Lou Ellen?"

"You should just do it," she chirruped. As he glanced at her, he realized she was joking trying to lighten the mood. "You've already got an entire summer's worth of experience. Quite qualified. If you ask me. Which you are."

He shook his head, amused. "Don't you have a bulletin to print? Notes to type? Gossip to send down the prayer chain?"

She laughed and flounced out of the room, her words lingering behind her. What if he did? Pastor the youth group? Despite his years of practice, he still felt like a fraud in the pulpit. But with the kids, he felt free. Settled. At home.

But being a youth pastor was a huge switch. Not to mention much lower pay. And he'd probably have to give up the parsonage. And he could just imagine what his dad would say about walking away from the family legacy. It was a crazy idea to give up a lead pastor position.

And yet, it nagged at him. The idea nagged him all afternoon as he filled out paperwork, talked to congregants with varying troubles, and negotiated with the deacons to buy a new lawnmower. And as he sat in his office after all his meetings later that evening, he knew it wouldn't let him go.

He picked up the phone. It was time to have a long conversation with his dad.

* * *

Vada sat in a corner of the ladies' parlor, listening to the hum of voices around her. The Women In Ministry meeting was wrapping up, and around her, the ladies had broken into different groups to discuss their varying projects. The list made Vada's head swim.

Choosing a new Sunday school curriculum for the elementary.

246

Organizing the Fall Festival.

Raising money for the youth group's winter mission trip.

Voting on a new group president.

The new president asking them to remember the ongoing capital funds campaign for a new air conditioner. And a new roof. And fixing the front walk.

Announcing the sign-up for new Bible Study groups.

A dizzying array of community service programs.

The list kept going. Even as Vada struggled to take it all in, excitement tingled down into her fingertips. So, this was the heart of the church. Son may decide what to preach on Sunday, but the women turned the church into a genuine community.

No wonder Leora had encouraged her to join. As if thinking her was enough to conjure her up, Leora sailed over and clasped her arm.

"What did you think?" She waved a hand grandly at the room.

Vada laughed. "Y'all do so much. Very impressive."

"We don't do it alone, honey. Everyone in the church pitches in."

Vada nodded, understanding. These ladies might organize their efforts, but every member of the church contributed somehow or other. An organizer with nothing to organize was an empty position.

The sudden desire to be part of all this activity shocked Vada. She'd never thought of herself as a leader before. But here she was, surrounded by people who thought her gifted enough to join them.

Emma Jean, Vada's old high-school principal, sidled up to them. "So, I heard you were thinking about joining us." The two older ladies looked at Vada expectantly.

Vada's smile widened. She couldn't imagine a better effort to join. "I'd be honored."

Chapter 29

ater that week, Son looked out over the congregation as they settled into their seats with whispers and furtive glances at him. Travis had slunk out of the room after the first old lady had grasped his arm and given him an earful. News of Travis' leaving, and what had preceded it, had spread faster than the usual gossip.

Son glanced at Lou Ellen where she sat next to her parents, and she gave him a reassuring nod. Her mother tracked the exchange with a raised eyebrow. As she leaned over to whisper to her daughter, Lou Ellen just smiled and shook her head at her. Gratitude blossomed in his heart for such a loyal friend.

As the organist wound down, Son slowly stepped toward the pulpit, eyes scanning for the only face that mattered to him today. Her spot next to her parents was empty, and Willow shrugged discreetly at him. Still, his eyes traveled the room, but no side door opened, no eye roll from a pair of gorgeous dark eyes that stopped his heart. Vada wasn't coming today just as she hadn't come for the last several weeks.

Laying his notes on the pulpit, he shuffled the pages into an orderly stack. The room fell silent, watchful. He could feel the eyes on him as he tried to settle his nerves. Finally, he looked up, the first words of his sermon on his lips.

Under all those eyes peering at him, he fell silent. Suddenly, his sermon seemed misplaced. His announcement couldn't wait.

Son set the pages to the side and folded his hands, calm washing over him. "I had a lesson prepared. But I feel now isn't quite the right time for it. So would it be ok with you if I just spoke from the heart today?"

A ripple of curiosity spread through the crowd. Neighbors glanced at each other, surprise lighting their faces. He clenched his hands together.

"Oh, go on, honey!" Mayor Patty called. A nervous chuckle broke from Son, and the congregation echoed his exhale in a gust of breath.

"Thank you." He cleared his throat. "This week, something happened with one of our teens, as I'm sure you've heard."

Heads nodded around the room, along with darted glances of sympathy toward Mahalia. He held up his hands.

"I'm not going to rehash what happened. But the incident made me realize how important our families—those we're born into and those we choose—how important they are." He steeled himself. "As much as I preach following God's commands, I've left out the heart of the matter. There are more important things in this life than blindly following the rules and checking all the 'right' boxes. Our homes, our families, our relationships with each other—they should be what drives our obedience. To walk in love and truth. Isn't that the heart of the Gospel after all? God bringing man back into a right relationship with himself. Following this greatest of examples, we should come into a right relationship with each other and ourselves."

A whisper of agreement floated through the air.

His chest warmed as he looked out at the rapt crowd. "It's so easy to preach rules. It's so easy to tell you what to do, instead of living a quiet, Godly life as an example. I can't boil down life, with all its challenges and triumphs, into a simple how-to manual."

He straightened. "So, today, I'm going to start living what I've been preaching. Because if we're blind to the pain of the people who are most important to us, no checklist, no rule-following will ever make up for that. We have missed the heart of the Gospel."

"I wanted to thank you today, for choosing me to lead you. All my life I have striven to be a minister, spurred on by my father's amazing example. I followed the path I thought made sense." He took a second to look around the room, meeting each person's eye. "But I never considered what I was really called to do. After this past week, I know what that role is now—and it's not to follow my dad as a lead pastor."

He gestured with his hand toward them. "Many of you have already heard of Travis' upcoming departure. Please join me in wishing him well as he searches for his place." A scattering of confused applause sounded while Son waited for them to quiet again. "And now, I hope you will celebrate with me in the discovery of my role. I am called to work with our youth, to be there with guidance when our children need it and a helping hand when they don't. Today, I tender my resignation as your lead pastor. And I hope you'll consider me for your youth minister." Son smiled, as a weight lifted from his shoulders.

Murmurs echoed through the room. Finally, Clay called out, his voice gruff, "And what are we going to do for a pastor?"

Son grinned at him. "I already have an excellent candidate for you to consider."

A few minutes later, Son stepped out into the sunshine, the vote successfully cast to hire his father as their new lead pastor. And to shift his role officially to youth minister.

But one voice hadn't echoed out with the others. And Son realized now more than ever that she was the only vote that mattered to him. Already sweating through his suit, he jogged to his car and revved down the highway to Vada's.

* * *

Vada had lain on the couch that morning as her parents ushered Mahalia out the door and into the truck for church. She hadn't missed their skeptical glances at her as she curled up with a blanket and some Tylenol, willing the pounding in her head to go away.

Vada was never sick. And she certainly didn't get migraines.

But it seemed life was just full of doozies for her lately. Gritting her teeth against the dizziness that washed over her as she stood, she worked her way down the back steps and to the barn, swallowing against rising nausea as her head pounded in sync with her heartbeat.

Migraine or not, the stalls had to be mucked today.

Of course, what she hadn't told her concerned parents was that the migraine had bloomed as she'd stood in the shower that morning, panicking over facing Son and the dozens of sympathetic faces at church. She'd have to rip that Band-Aid off at some point, but not today. Not when she felt like this.

However self-inflicted her suffering might be.

Weeks had passed, and still, the thought of looking at Son behind the pulpit ached, her gaping heart crying out for his missing piece. It was too much, too raw, to look at him, knowing she couldn't have him.

Gingerly, she prodded at a pile of fragrant hay with her shovel as she considered the mess in the barn. Benny had been on schedule at the fire station the last couple of days, leaving her shorthanded.

Now, her reticence to ask her parents for help was coming back to bite her. She grimaced as she flung the pile into a waiting wheelbarrow.

Just as she began shoveling out the stalls, feeling sweaty and rung out, the sound of gravel crunching in the drive drug her attention away from her task. It was much too early for her family to be back yet.

Curious, she stepped outside and squinted through the blindingly bright sun as her head throbbed in protest.

Son's car pulled to a stop a few feet away. Her heart leaped as he got out of the car, flinging a suit jacket into the front seat, and strode past her into the barn. Her breath hitched as he grabbed a pitchfork and began flinging fresh hay into one of the newly cleaned stalls.

"What are you doing?" She gasped as her words rang through her head painfully.

He looked at her, his eyes bright and meaningful. "Showing up." Silently, he went back to work.

Her heart clenched at the sight of his broad back rippling underneath his shirt. What was he doing here—in his dress clothes no less? How could he be so foolish?

Just seeing him, sweat stains ringing his shirt, she was more convinced than ever that there was no future for them. He deserved a proper lady, not a cowgirl with mucky boots. Not someone who made him mucky too.

"You're going to ruin your shoes," she protested.

"I can replace shoes," he answered smoothly as he kept pitching straw.

Lost for what to do, Vada slowly picked up her shovel and went back into the stall she'd been cleaning. If he wanted to ruin his nice clothes, that was up to him.

Still, as they worked through the afternoon, the huff of his breath beside her, she had to admit to herself that she adored having him here. Next to him, her migraine eased from a roar to a whisper. She would soak up every minute of him working alongside her, even if her head screamed that this could only end badly.

When her parents returned, they looked at the two of them with raised eyebrows but walked on into the house without saying anything. Mahalia grinned and flashed her a big thumbs up, disappearing after them.

After finishing up, Vada walked Son back to his car. They had worked in silence all afternoon, but now she felt a growing urge to say something.

Before she could utter an ill-conceived speech about the hopelessness of their situation, Son spoke first. "See you tomorrow."

He got in his car and drove away as she stared after him, wondering. If he was going to all these lengths to just be near her, could she be wrong?

With enough hard work, could they make this last?

Shaking her head, she turned back toward the house only to run flat into a panting Mahalia who positively vibrated with excitement. "Did you hear?" Her cousin had clearly been quivering with this news all afternoon.

"Hear what?" Vada's migraine roared back to life. With a cozy couch nap calling to her, she didn't have the patience to play a guessing game.

"Son's no longer pastor—he's now the youth minister!"

The declaration shot through Vada like the bolt of an arrow. Son was no longer pastor. Her mind spun, trying to piece together the implications. She shook her head. Whatever the result, he was still a minister, and his time and attention would be dedicated to the church. He needed a wife who could support him in that, making their position still impossible.

With an incredulous laugh, Vada took Mahalia's hand, and they walked back to the house. Despite her stern lecture to herself, for the first time in weeks, her chest swelled with hope.

She would see Son tomorrow.

* * *

Vada gently threw a blanket over the gelding's back as she whispered soothing words into his ear. The horse startled slightly but did not buck or bolt. That was substantial progress from the day before. She had been out in the training ring with the young horse all morning, and still no sign of Son.

Disappointment fought against hope in her stomach as she glanced again at the drive. Usually, he would have been here for a couple of hours already. Each morning this week he had surprised her by showing up and getting to work on whatever needed doing. Even Benny expected him.

But as the drive remained empty, she begrudgingly admitted

to herself that he wasn't coming. Why should he with how reserved she'd been all week? She'd given him no sign of relenting. Of course, he'd given up.

Her heart berated her with a solid kick to her ribcage. A weird part of her had held her back from thawing towards him, as if determined to prove they would inevitably fail. Now, she could see that she'd enforced a self-fulfilling strategy.

If only she hadn't been so stubborn, she wouldn't have driven him away. He'd be beside her now.

Disappointment rolled through her, dark and heavy. As she released the gelding into the pasture to enjoy the rolling meadow, she faced the facts. This situation with Son was all her fault.

If she hadn't gotten scared and pulled back on the camping trip, and if she hadn't held him at arm's length all week, they would be together now. And she wouldn't be breaking her own heart by stupidly hoping that he would show up, despite her frosty exterior.

Vada stomped moodily into the house and filled a glass of cold water at the sink. As she sipped, she stared down the driveway, willing his car to appear in the distance.

"He'll come."

Vada spun to see her mom leaning against the doorframe to the living room, arms crossed smugly over her stomach.

"Sure doesn't look like it." Vada slammed the glass down and trudged out onto the porch, her mother trailing.

Nothing but small, fluffy clouds dotted the horizon. Vada turned away, unable to bear the waiting, not knowing if he would appear or not.

"Honey," her mother began. Vada glanced at her sharply. She didn't want any more of her parents' not-so-low-key encouragement. But her mother kept on speaking. "After all these years… everything you've been through… you deserve happiness. I hate seeing you hold yourself back from it." Vada's eyes smarted as she turned, not wanting her mother to see the impact her words had. "You love him. Why won't you let him love you?"

Vada rubbed at a knot forming behind her shoulder blade. "Because he's in love with the idea me. Not who I really am. No man—no preacher—wants a stubborn woman splattered in mud and horse sweat. Not when he can have lace and pearls instead."

Over the last few days, the idea of him as youth minister had settled inside her. She could no longer deny that if he—if they—were determined, they would find a way. Nothing would stand in their way, not even their jobs.

That is if she hadn't driven him off. Again.

The rcv of an engine echoed in the distance. Vada stared as a beaten-up pickup truck bounced down the drive, dodging the washed-out spots. Mud splashed up the sides from last night's rain. As the truck parked beside the barn and Son popped out with a wave, her mother snorted.

"Looks like he knows well enough who you are."

In disbelief, Vada followed Son into the barn. Grabbing the handle of the shovel he'd just picked up, she forced him to stop and meet her gaze. "Where is your car?"

Steadily, he looked into her eyes. "Didn't make much sense for farm life. I traded it."

She released the shovel and sniffed as she brushed at her cheeks. Son smirked at her, and she slapped his arm. "It's the hay dust, silly man."

Son had hurried up the Wilson's drive, carefully shifting the gears in the truck. He was unused to driving a manual. And despite the sales agent's painstaking lesson yesterday, Son felt timid behind the wheel.

He'd stared at the house up ahead, where he could just make out Vada standing on the porch. As he'd pulled up to the barn, he hoped he wasn't too late for the day's chores. With the time he'd spent out here this week, he'd had to work on his sermon this morning. His father wasn't due to start for another couple of weeks, and he was far behind.

Now, Vada stood before him, all the things he wanted to say to her clogging his throat as she sniffed. Hope beat furiously in his chest. All week they'd worked side-by-side, Vada never once acknowledging his presence—but also not suggesting he should leave. She had to know what he was doing at the church. She had to see how hard he was trying to prove that he loved her. All of her, barn included.

Now she was looking at him with those enormous eyes of hers, the same desire he felt reflected in her face. But just as quickly as the tender emotion had flashed across her features, she turned away.

When she turned back, her brow wrinkled in what he was sure was supposed to be anger but looked more like a mingling of hope and confusion. "How long are you going to keep this up?" She waved her arms at the barn, voice raised.

Gently, he answered, "As long as it takes." She sucked in a breath to retort, and he rushed to say more. "I will be here until you see I love you and believe in you. And then I'll be here beside you every day until the end of time."

Her eyes glimmered as she whispered, "I can't be a preacher's wife. I don't look or act like one. I've always got muck on me somewhere, even when I try to clean up. I'm not quiet or proper."

Taking her calloused hands, he pressed a kiss into each smudged palm. "Why do you think I want a quiet wife when I've been waiting my whole life for you?" She sagged toward him. Seeing the longing on her face, he drew her into his arms and kissed her, trying to show her what he felt for her with every fiber of his body. Against his chest, she froze, and for one panicked second, he thought he'd misread her.

Then her hands slid up to clasp around his neck and she was kissing him back like she would never stop. He drank in her lips, her cheeks, the curve of her neck, her legs wrapping around his waist as he pressed her back against the stall door. His hands cupped her thighs, the heat of her body sinking into his hands through the worn blue jeans. He was completely drunk with her kisses as she sighed against his lips.

Behind them, a cough echoed. Awkwardly, he dropped Vada's legs as he slid an arm around her waist. She swayed next to him as they turned to face Mahalia, who stared at them with a wide grin. "Do I need to give you two a little privacy?" she teased.

"Mahalia!" Vada reprimanded, and Mahalia held her hands up as she turned to leave.

"Carry on!" she called over her shoulder.

Son watched as Vada worked against the smile creeping across her lips. Then she pressed her face into his chest and howled with laughter. He wrapped his other arm around her as they held each other up, snorting with laughter until tears ran down their cheeks.

As their laughter quieted, he whispered, "I love you," against her hair. His heart soared as he finally held the woman he loved against his heart.

Vada beamed up at him. "I love you too."

Son had never heard sweeter words as he covered her lips with his.

Chapter 30

❦

Vada took a deep, shuddering breath as she stared ahead at the closed doors. For weeks, each day had crawled by, but now that the wedding was here, everything had flown by. Hair, makeup, and pictures blurred by her as she imagined this moment.

Anticipation curled through her, and she fidgeted with her dress, a fitted, white linen A-line with a scoop neck and the most gorgeous lace cap sleeves she'd ever seen. The skirt bustled around her, full and fluttery. Her mother had outdone herself sewing it.

Beside her, her dad shot her a smile. "You're beautiful." He patted her hand, wrapped around his arm, as he whispered, "I am so proud of you." His usually stoic gaze filled with tears, and Vada's eyes misted in response.

"Stop it, you old softie," she scolded gently. She fanned at her face, willing the tears to dissipate. "You're going to ruin my makeup."

"You don't need makeup. You've always been my beautiful,

kind-hearted daughter." He cleared his throat.

Before she could reply, a blast of joyful organ music echoed around them, and the doors cracked open. A rush of people stood to their feet, faces turned expectantly to her. Vada blushed and smiled shyly as their movement wafted out the scent of hundreds of perfumes and colognes on a cool breeze—Leora's gift of a new A/C for the church having been installed just in time.

All of Midnight Bluff had shown up for this wedding bearing casseroles and presents.

The faint scent of all the casseroles in the fellowship hall hit Vada's nose, and she thought eagerly of the amazing spread. They had decided on a simple ceremony followed by an old-fashioned potluck reception.

All of that would come in just a few moments. But now, her eyes skimmed the crowd, nodding at each of her friends, and chuckling at her openly weeping mother. At the top of the steps, Mahalia bounced eagerly on the balls of her feet in her soft lavender dress, grinning at Vada. Pastor Riser, in his long robes, pressed a hand to his heart.

And to the right… Vada's breath hitched as she locked eyes with Son, his face glowing as he drank in her appearance. Her jangling nerves disappeared as the room melted away.

He was the only person who mattered now. Eagerly, she stepped forward into her perfect forever.

* * *

Son swayed with the horse's easy gait, tilting his head back to enjoy the cool, morning breeze. Each hoof impacted the sand beneath them with a soft *plop*. Beside him, Vada smiled into the rising sun, contentment on every line of her face.

He had been astonished when Clay had gifted them with an all-expenses paid honeymoon to Kiawah—complete with sunrise horseback rides along the beach. As they crested a dune above the beach, the ocean whispered against the sand, welcoming a new day.

Their first full day as husband and wife. Overwhelmed with the awe and gratitude of the moment, Son reached over and grasped Vada's hand. She smiled as he slid his thumb over the simple gold band on her ring finger. He'd wanted to order her something more elaborate, that spoke to the beauty he saw in her. But she'd assured him over and over that simplicity was more her style.

"Besides," she'd teased, "Simple is more fitting of a minister's wife." He had just laughed and let her have her way.

Now, plovers peeped on the beach around them while gulls cried overhead, riding the strong, ocean breeze. As the first rays of sunlight broke over the horizon, gilding her face, he knew she had been right. Simple, unadorned beauty was best.

He tugged her toward him, leaning to kiss her as the horses shifted beneath them. As his lips met hers, tenderly at first then hungrily, he swelled knowing that Vada—stubborn, talented, incredible Vada—would always be the greatest blessing of his life.

* * *

Several weeks later, Vada stood at the door of Son's new office watching him work. She smiled. The smaller space suited him better, stuffed homily with books and pictures and large, plush chairs. Two enormous windows let in copious amounts of golden light, keeping the room from feeling stuffed. As he scrawled notes across a page, Bibles and commentaries stacked around him, she snuck up behind him and wrapped her arms around his neck.

He chuckled as she kissed his cheek. "Your camp counselor is here."

He turned toward her with a grin, and she slipped onto his lap, nestling into his arms. She pressed her lips to his, savoring the taste of his tongue, sweet and earthy with the coffee he'd been drinking. One small thing she'd converted him to enjoy. He groaned against her lips.

Huskily, he protested, "I have work to do." His hands ran up her back as he looked at her with unveiled desire.

She tapped his notes. "You can finish this later." Standing, she took his hand and tugged him toward the door. He followed her willingly. As they ran giggling down the hall, Pastor Riser glanced up at their passing with a fond shake of his head.

Lou Ellen called after them, "Have fun, you two!"

As they dashed for Vada's truck, Son asked, "Where are we going?"

She grinned at him. "On an adventure."

How To Leave A Review

Love this book? Don't forget to leave a review!

Every review matters— and it matters *a lot!*

Head over to Goodreads, BookBub, or wherever you purchased this book to leave a review for *High Horse: Midnight Bluff Book Four*.

Thank you so much for your support.

Bonus Reads

Want to immerse yourself in the world of Midnight Bluff?

You are in luck! I've paired each of the Midnight Bluff books with its own companion short story, so you can get one more peak into our hero's lives!

Claim your free stories today!

Claim your free short stories here:
https://susanfarris.me/free-reads/

Acknowledgments

Writing a book seems like a solitary effort but a host of unseen people stand behind it.

So, thank you, dear reader, for your interesting questions, gentle prodding to keep going, and for your devotion to my work, I don't know how to express how grateful I am to have you behind me. Your encouragement has often been the push I need to keep going when I hit a snag (like I did many times with this book.)

To my beta readers, Dawn, Abbie, Kim, Brenda, Andrea, and Josh, who ask the best questions and push me to do better with every new work, thank you. I couldn't do it without you.

And to Pete, for always taking care of me, even when life surprises us with a rocky point and we both need all the midnight ice cream. I can't tell you how blessed I am to have you as my partner in all things.

About the Author

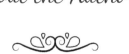

Sweet stories with a Southern twang.

Susan Farris is a Mississippi author and poet with a passion for local stories and local voices. She holds a deep belief that a cup of tea solves many of life's problems. Many of her favorite local places appear in her books— along with her favorite foods!

When she's not wrangling words on the page, she loves to garden, go on long walks with her husband, or snuggle up with her three cats and two dogs.

You can follow her on Instagram and TikTok (@authorsusan-farris) as well as on Goodreads and BookBub.

CPSIA information can be obtained
at www.ICGtesting.com
Printed in the USA
LVHW021932111022
730461LV00003B/350